Then Arthur said, "Riderch, the chief of the bards who are with me, should not be silent before you, and I would beg him to entertain us. It was the custom of kings in days past to hear a story every night between Samhain and Beltain. It would please us to hear a tale from him."

Riderch came out from among the bards and said, "Head of the Island, what manner of tale would it please you to hear?"

And Arthur replied, "Tell us a tale of our people, of the land we love and defend; a story of Britain. . . ."

Bantam Spectra Books
Ask your bookseller for the titles you have missed.

THE
HIGH
KINGS

BY
JOY CHANT

MAPS BY DAVID LARKIN

BANTAM BOOKS
TORONTO • NEW YORK • LONDON • SYDNEY • AUCKLAND

THE HIGH KINGS

Bantam Hardcover edition / November 1983
2nd printing . . . December 1984
Bantam rack-size edition / November 1985

Maps by David Larkin

Library of Congress Cataloging in Publication Data

Chant, Joy.
The high kings.

1. Celts—Great Britain—Fiction.   2. Great Britain—
History—To 449—Fiction.   3. Mythology, Celtic—
Fiction. I. Title.
PR6053.H3465H5   1983   823′.914   83-90655
ISBN 0-553-24306-3

Published simultaneously in the United States and Canada

PRINTED IN THE UNITED STATES OF AMERICA

.O   0 9 8 7 6 5 4 3 2 1

CONTENTS

HE colossal figure of Arthur has tended to obscure all the other heroes of Britain both before and after his time; but there were indeed other heroes, and it cannot be doubted that the Celts of Britain had a verbal "literature" of history and legend as rich as that of their neighbours in Ireland.

Arthur was the defender of a nation with a heritage which included centuries of Celtic life, as well as the period within the Roman Empire that created Roman Britain. The long and predominantly happy association with Rome seems not to have seriously weakened the native heritage, for Roman characters and Roman stories simply became part of the tradition, while great Romans were "adopted" as ancestors. It is significant that in the last days of Roman Britain many Celtic princes asserted their Roman citizenship by giving their sons classic, even old-fashioned, Roman names; like Cato. It is a great mistake to think of Britain as "shaking off the Roman yoke." It was, in fact, the long agony of the Anglo-Saxon invasions subsequent to the departure of the Romans, which had such a devastating effect on British culture.

The Roman legions were withdrawn over a long period, beginning about 380 A.D.—although of course no one then knew that this was the end; they thought it only a temporary measure and were prepared for years for the army's return to protect the Island. Meanwhile, the British maintained their government and defended themselves in the face of increasing barbarian pressure with a success which was the admiration of other provinces. However, in the 440's Saxon troops originally brought into the Island as mercenaries mutinied, and the devastation caused by this marked the beginning of the end of Roman Britain.

Though that mutiny was put down, it was at terrible cost; and once part of her coast was held by what had now become the acknowledged enemy, the Island was vulnerable to further invasion. The wealth of the country was a temptation to the Saxons (to the Celts, all the various Germanic nations were Saxons) who were being driven from their homelands by hunger. They came to reinforce their fellows in ever greater numbers; soon raiding turned to settling, and England had its beginning. Nevertheless, the Britons fought back hard. Arthur was the last and the greatest of their leaders, imposing his authority and uniting Britain's defences so effectively that peace and good government survived for a generation after his time.

But this long struggle turned the Island of Britain, up to that time a cultural and linguistic unity, into the separate nations which survive today. The relatively brief period, in historical terms, was a communal nightmare to the British, a shock so profound that it changed the very language spoken by the Britons in little more than a century. British, a language comparable to Latin, lost its syntax and structure, even changed its sound, to become Welsh, in barely three generations. Men and women who had learned British at their mothers' knees might have heard their grandchildren speaking a different tongue. It was as if the language of Dickens and Mark Twain were to be unintelligible to us.

During such a cultural trauma it was inevitable that much of the centuries-old verbal tradition should be lost; and that the great name of Arthur, who held back the darkness for a generation, should dominate the national memory and hide the fame of his predecessors. For this was a watershed in the history of Europe, and it is hard to exaggerate the magnitude of the changes the people of that time faced. One letter writer, looking for a comparison, could find nothing less than Noah's Flood to express the terror of the experience.

It was indeed the end of a world; the end of the urban sophisticated world of more than a thousand years of growth, centered on the Mediterranean.

Hindsight can see a new world being born, but the people of that time had no such comfort. They saw only the destruction of law, learning, Christianity; civilisation collapsing into incoherence, and nothing ahead but the night. The poets of Arthur's time and soon after were living in a permanent state of emergency, and they were obsessed with the present in a way no Celtic bards had been before or were again.

Something, however, did survive. A few stories complete, many others as hints and fragments, and probably much in the form of superstition that was never recorded—the Celts were traditionally reluctant to write their literature down, preferring to rely on their highly trained memories. The first and highly popular attempt to restate the past was Geoffrey of Monmouth's *History of the Kings of Britain;* not history in any sense, though entertaining reading. Even in Geoffrey, however, there are enough traces of Celtic culture to make it seem possible that he had some contact with the remains of the tradition—no doubt much survived in his time that never reached ours. His "old Welsh book" may have been neither a pretence nor a mysterious lost manuscript, but the ancestral race history handed down in the memories of men of his time and before.

This book is an attempt to interpret that long gone past—the era which ended with the age of Arthur—for a modern audience. The form of the stories is conjectural; the aim has been to remove the medieval gloss from those which have survived, and to reconstruct others from the fragments which remain (aided by analogy with other Celtic stories and deduction from the traditions of the literature) and to retell them in the way in which they might have been told in the last days of Britain.

Whether my guesses come anywhere near the truth is impossible to know, but I hope that the stories are entertaining in themselves. None were chosen for inclusion that belonged only to one of the realms of a divided Britain; these are the stories of the Island of the Mighty. I also hope that readers will find in the book some idea of the civilisation that once was Britain, and of the people and events of the years which shattered that civilisation.

It is superfluous to say that this is not a work of scholarship, but I have depended heavily on such works, and would here like to acknowledge my debt to two in particular: John Morris' *The Age of Arthur*, and Rachel Bromwich's edition of the Welsh Triads, *Trioedd Ynys Prydein*.

JOY CHANT

HE classic ideal "Nothing in Excess" would not have made much sense to the Celts. If they had written a guiding principle across the center of the world, it might perhaps have been "No Holding Back!" Their contemporaries were generally agreed upon their character; they were energetic, talkative, sociable, creative, and intelligent; also proud, warlike, unstable, and vain. If it were ever possible to define a whole people so simply, it might be true to say that the keynote of their character was extravagance.

They lived with an energy and impetuosity which dazzled and often appalled foreigners. Restraint and moderation were not virtues which they prized greatly; the prudence they admired in their leaders was not so much caution as the astuteness of men not easily to be outwitted. Although the British Celts came to identify themselves closely with the Romans, they never completely assimilated the soberer qualities of their Latin conquerors. It was the ideal of Rome they loved; significantly, her *greatness*.

The much renowned Celtic imagination was capable of surrounding the whole of life, and of investing even mundane everyday matters with an intense glamour. It was this which bound them in such close sympathy with the natural world about them, and at the same time made the supernatural seem so close; which charged every aspect of nature with divinity and made the gods familiar if unpredictable neighbours, members of the most powerful of all clans who yet occasionally sought human help. The Celts were enthusiasts, wholehearted in all they did, in thought, in feeling, in action; in bad as well as good. Among them no quality was so prized as generosity; nor any so scorned as meanness: to call someone "niggardly" was to plumb the depth of insult.

Asceticism was no part of their culture; yet when Christianity entered their lives and it became important in the life of the Church, those who adopted it did so with typical energy, and became extremely ascetic. Few saints were so unworldly as the Celtic saints; they indulged in self-denial, as in all else, to glorious excess.

The high Celtic civilisation in Britain flourished from roughly 500 B.C. to 500 A.D., but their imagination pushed their history farther back, so that these stories cover a time from about 1200 B.C. Geographically the stories belong to Britain; no legends from the sister civilisation of Ireland are included. The heroes they celebrate are the early Britons, who became the Roman Britons, who became the Welsh, Scots, Cornish, and also Bretons.

Celtic culture once dominated Europe. There were big fair Celts like the Gauls, and smaller darker Celts more like the modern Welsh, but they shared a common way of life. Two facts about them should be understood from the beginning, for they provide the key to much in their life which may seem strange to us. The first important point about them is that theirs was a tribal society; the second, their tremendous veneration for words and their power.

Their tribalism both united them closely within their "clans" and made it difficult for them to achieve a wider unity as a nation. Every member of a kin-group was responsible for every other member, to the extent of being answerable for his crimes. The most famous and dramatic manifestation of such societies is the blood-feud, but it had more subtle expressions. For example, personal self-esteem as we would understand it mattered comparatively little; it was prestige, the respect of the group, which was all-important. This need for social approval had many results, being the strongest possible deterrent from crime (whatever was gained by the crime, shame came with it; and public shame was little better than death), a spur to excellence in craftsmanship, and to display of any kind. To be "well spoken of"—the phrase is significant—was a vital matter, and of course it was most vital to the aristocracy, the warrior caste whose business was the defence and enrichment of the tribe: for them, the quest for glory was the whole of life.

These close bonds and mutual responsibilities also heightened emotional ties, and encouraged the expression of feeling; their loves and loyalties were as total as their enmities and angers, and as freely displayed—the theatrical instinct has never been lacking among the Celts, and it is notable that the arts in which they excelled above all, music, song, story-telling, were all *performing* arts. Not that their strong feelings were necessarily violent: their poetry in particular displays a passionate tenderness, with merry songs to children, gently affectionate observations of animals, and a lyrical response to beauty—a blackbird's whistle, a white thorn flowering in a dark wood, swans calling across a lake at evening.

And probably few qualities would endear them more to a modern mind than their capacity for humour, especially self-mockery. Their emotions were constantly fed and reinforced by their social structure. Their society drew them together for decision-making and all important concerns, and this communal life made them an intensely sociable people, who loved company and conversation above all other pleasures.

At the same time this tribal interdependence made for a society wherein each individual had value, where, for example, women were equal to men, and children had legal rights rather than being at the disposal of their parents. Rulers were usually elected from among an eligible group rather than succeeding by right, and their authority was far from absolute; a King was subject to law, and his people could pass judgment on him.

Law was part of the province of their most highly respected caste, the men of learning, known to us collectively as the bards. There was no written culture, and the bard with his highly trained memory in which was stored their history, their custom, their law, as well as the songs and stories that were their delight, was a figure of almost mystical power. The enormous gusto of the Celts' outer lives, their physical force and energy, their reckless gaiety, was balanced by the high value they set on the life of the mind. This gives the lie to any notion of the Celts as the stereotyped barbarian, incapable of restraint or discipline; in intellectual vigour they are comparable only to the Athenians.

Their reverence for learned men and especially for men skilled with words, indeed for wit and eloquence in all men—what that modern Celt Dylan Thomas called "the beautiful gift of the gab"—is still legendary, and it penetrated every level of their lives from the merely playful "blarney" to the sacramental. Honest speech was imperative, and so great was the power of words that they believed misuse could bring physical destruction: there are tales of Kings' houses which fell down because a false judgment was given in them. The word was, must be, absolute.

The "Celtic twilight" of the nineteenth century romantics was always a myth. Even at its most magical, their literature is vivid, precise, of brilliant clarity, a vision of a world acutely observed and recreated with the force of reality. The world was a blaze of wonder to them; they were drunk with the excitement of life; and their vision of paradise was of that life made eternal, freed only of winter and age. Any hour—the freshness of dawn, the blaze of noon, the riotous splendour of sunset, even the glitter of night—any time of day would be more appropriate to them than the dim twilight. Welcome, then, to the Celtic daylight.

BRITAIN

The Picts

Manau
Votadini

THE WALL

ALBANY

Brigants

Votadini

Coritani

LOGRIS

CAMBRIA

Dubuni

Iceni

North Folk
Saxons
South Folk

Trinovantes

Catuvellauni

Belgae

Cornovii

CORNWALL

Saxons (oesc)
Saxons (aelle)

DUMNONIA

Invasions by the Picts

THE SAXON SHORE

N ARTHUR'S time the British language had begun its breakdown, and personal names were changing their forms like other words. For both Roman and British names the process was roughly that endings disappeared, vowels were lightened, and consonants softened; later, certain sound combinations were modified to make them easier on the tongue and ear—this is the "mutation" which is so famous a feature of Welsh. Thus over the years Tacitus became Tegid; Gaius, Cei; Cunobelinos, Cynfelin; Ambrosius, Emrys; and in one dialect, Artorius, Idris. All these examples are from Welsh, but there were other tongues descended from British, in which Dubris became Dover; Tamesis, Thames; Cornovia, Kernow; Dumnonia, Devon; and Isca, Exe, or Usk, or Ouse. Guinivere is an Anglicisation of Welsh Gwenhwyfar; but the same name came through Cornish to reach us as Jennifer.

Very few of these names were recorded in their transitional form, and the only one to become well-known in that form was, of course, Arthur. For use in this book, both the original forms and the Welsh were misleading, and without the advantage of ease, so I resorted to conjecture once more wherever certainty was impossible. I tried to follow the name through the usual pattern of phonetic change (one of these, not easily guessed, is that V became GU) and to "freeze" it at a point which would not give, I hope, too false an impression.

However, for the names of the realms of Britain used within the stories themselves I chose familiarity at the expense of accuracy. "Albany" is not too far out, for Alban was one of the early names of the Island, and "Logris" is a reasonable version of the name for the rich lowland realm— England is still Lloegr to the Welsh. But "Cornwall" is an English word—the land of the Cornovian Welsh or "foreigners"; and there is no warrant at all for Cambria. The remnants of the British called themselves "combroges," "fellow countrymen," and the names Cymru and Cumber(land) both derive from this—they mean only "the land of our people." Cambria is the medieval Latin form of Cymru. In Arthur's time, what is now Wales was known only by the names of its tribal realms, chiefly Demetia (Dyfed) in the south, and Venedotia (Gwynedd) in the North; while Cornwall was Dumnonia or Cornovia. In the stories, Cornwall refers to the whole southwestern peninsula of Britain, and not only to its tip.

TORY-TELLING and poetry were at the very heart of Celtic life. Hearing stories was not only enjoyment, it was an important ritual, and the art of the bard was magical as well as literary and dramatic. Many, probably at one time all, stories were held to have specific powers of blessing and protection; they were in the old and literal sense spells. There were rules as to their treatment—it was taboo to write them down, for one thing, and many could only be told by darkness and in winter—hence the Kings who hear a story "every night between Samhain and Beltain," that is, from November to April. An example of a rule and a specific power combined is the duty of the King's household bard to recite to his warband before battle the song called "The Monarchy of Britain."

Story-telling was probably the older art; many of the earliest poems occur in prose stories at the moments of high emotion. Later the two arts separated, and in Britain the poet came to outrank the story-teller. The length and complexity of these stories in their original form is staggering; most are, in fact, story cycles, with each part taking about six hours in the telling—and this telling would of course include a good deal of "acting" by the teller.

The feat of memory represented by a good story-teller's repertoire is almost inconceivable to the modern mind, nor do we find it easy to understand the stamina of the hearers. The fact is, of course, that though they were illiterate, the Celts were members of the most verbally alive culture there has ever been, and had skills of ear and mind lost to literate people. They were not only good listeners in the ordinary sense, they were also a very sophisticated audience, quick to catch hints and allusions, alive to patterns, sensitive to the words as well as to the matter of the story.

Consequently in Celtic societies the bard was, as indeed his modern equivalent still is, much more than simply an entertainer; nor was he speaking to a minority. He was the keeper of the soul of the people, a "poet-priest."

Partly this was because their society was tribal, and the bard was the custodian of the ritual which is so important in communal life, and of the history and genealogy which defined their identity. Some of these duties in early times were shared with the druids and the third class of learned men, for whom we have no name— perhaps "jurists." These were the men of learning, whose rank in Celtic society is often compared to that of Brahmins in India.

Bards were highly trained—an accurate memory was one of the most vital needs, as well as creative skill; the traditions had to be handed on intact and perfect.

Within the order of bards there was a strict hierarchy with clearly defined functions and privileges for the various ranks. The lowest rank was the "buffoon," contemptible but still a bard and so to some extent privileged, and the highest was very high indeed: the Chief Bard was the equal of a King, and in medieval Wales the foremost bard of a court, the "Head of Song," ranked next to the King's heir. In some ways the bards provided a counter to the royal power, an assertion of the traditional rights of the tribe as opposed to its leaders. It was almost impossible for a King or anyone else to defy a bard or refuse his request.

The coming of Christianity only increased the magical power of the bard, by removing his sharers in it, the druid and the "ovate." The eulogy to the ruler, so important in later poetry and easily misunderstood by us as flattery, was in part magic; the conjuring of the desired qualities in the man. These powerful poets were not simply paid to flatter— the King had to deserve their praise, and nothing was more vital to him.

The importance of the eulogy is made plainer

by the dread of its opposite, satire. To put a bad
name on someone meant to mock him, not to curse
him. Satire was so feared that the threat of it would
force any action, however suicidal, and the actual
use of it could kill. This again is a feature of a tribal
and of a verbal society, where men, and especially
leaders, lived by the esteem of their fellows, and
to be spoken ill of was social death, which could indeed become actual death, the latter often prefer-
able. In the Celtic context, the value of a man's word,
his honour, and his life, were all equal.

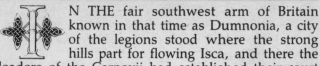I N THE fair southwest arm of Britain known in that time as Dumnonia, a city of the legions stood where the strong hills part for flowing Isca, and there the leaders of the Cornovii had established their court when they came south from their lands about the Severn to govern a new realm and to drive the Irish from the coasts of deep-valed Dumnonia as they had driven them from the highlands of their old territory. That lovely fertile land had not suffered in the uprising of the heathen Saxons; there fields were tilled, taxes and rents were paid, and there was maintenance for warriors and pasturage for their horses.

The present stronghold of the Cornovii in Isca Dumnoniorum, the ancient royal dun, was not so stately and splendid as the great mansions of their former home, though it was furnished with the wealth they had brought with them; but in those days of Britain's danger it was more fitting for a ruler to live in a fortress than in a villa.

Upon a day in the year of Our Lord 482, a generation after the Saxon uprising and two generations since the Cornovii had come south, Gerontius, Prince of Dumnonia, rode out to greet a guest and brought him with high honour to his court; and that guest was the Emperor Arthur. He did not come for courtesy, nor to dispense justice, nor for maintenance of his people, for few of his household came with him. But all of his warband rode at his back, and that of Gerontius was gathered also; it was for war they came together. The conflict that lay before them was bitter, for their enemy was neither Irish nor Saxon, but a man of their own speech.

Cerdic, ruler of the Belgae, unwilling to accept Arthur as overlord, had rebelled against his young authority and made alliance with the Saxons. It was a harsh blow, and the more grievous since the Belgae held the southern coast of Britain, which they had now opened to more barbarian invaders. Within two days Arthur and Gerontius would lead their host against Cerdic and his allies, to force back the invaders and, if it might be, to win back even the westernmost of the forts of the Saxon shore.

That night the Prince feasted the Emperor, and though they did not sit in the noble room of a villa and the fine things about them were treasures of the past, no longer to be obtained in Britain, yet the men and women gathered there spoke a pure Latin as freely as they spoke the British tongue, and they were a noble company. Arthur's bards were with him, and the chief of his officers, and Gai, the friend of his boyhood; while with his host were the nobles of Dumnonia, and the Bishop of Isca Dumnoniorum. Gerontius, though no older than the Emperor, had a wife at his side, and his small son Cato leaned on his knee. Also beside him was his kinswoman Gueneva, of a loveliness to beggar a bard of his words. Arthur looked long at her, thinking equally of her beauty and of the value of a strong tie with the great Cornovii: but always she avoided his eyes.

The wine was poured into goblets of glass, and Dumnonia's Head of Song sang for the company, and when he had done so the Emperor thanked him, praising his skill with well-chosen words, and giving him a gift fitting to his high station.

Then Arthur said, "Riderch, the chief of the bards who are with me, should not be silent before you, and I would beg him to entertain us. Yet it is not easy to sing where Cunomorus has sung before, and let us not follow sweet with sweet. It was the custom of Kings in days past to hear a story every night between Samhain and Beltain. It would please us all to hear a tale from Riderch, if he has one at command."

Riderch came out from among the bards, and said, "Head of the Island, I have many such. What manner of tale would it please you to hear?"

And Arthur replied, "Tell us a tale of our people, of the land we love and defend; a story of Britain."

Riderch sat by the hearth and put his harp on his knee, and he looked into the flames. He felt the eyes of all the company upon him, the Bishop and lovely Gueneva, the old man to whom he deferred— Merdyn, who had been bard to Arthur's uncle, Ambrosius—Gerontius, their host this night, laughing as he raised the glinting cup, and finally, the mighty young man whom he served. And beneath their pride and gaiety, beneath the courage and courtly dignity, Riderch felt a sadness, a yearning. They were Britons, they were Romans, they were a Christian and cultured people: but the Saxon revolt lay between them and their past. Through war and upheaval memory had not been handed on intact, and those who had fled to Armorica across the narrow seas had taken many records with them. The days of their grandfathers were grown shadowy to them, while between them and the morning of their people stretched the glorious afternoon of Rome.

They had fought hard to defend their land; Ambrosius, High King before Arthur, had halted the invaders, and now his mantle had fallen upon Arthur who had begun to force the barbarians back; yet not all things can be defended with the sword. Riderch felt their sense of loss for all they could not hold, for the heritage slipping like water from them. It was his part to staunch that flow, to summon a past for them out of the fragments of memory.

So he gazed silently into the fire, calling the shadows into life; and he deliberated upon which story was fittest to tell to hearten them, and to honour the King, the Prince of Dumnonia, and the Cornovii: until he touched his strings and began:

"Listen now, and hear the story that is called *The Winning of Britain*."

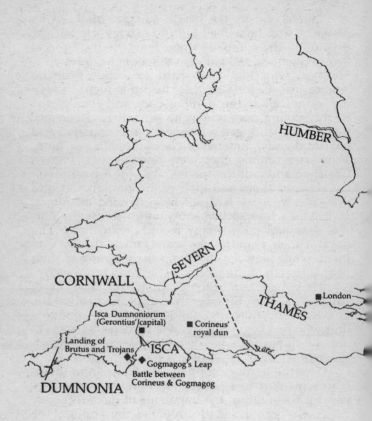

HUMBER

SEVERN

CORNWALL

THAMES

■ London

Isca Dumnoniorum
(Gerontius' capital)
■

■ Corineus'
royal dun

Landing of
Brutus and Trojans
◆   ◆ ISCA

Gogmagog's Leap
Battle between
Corineus & Gogmagog

DUMNONIA

ENEAS White Shield was born of a goddess. His descendant, Brutus of Troy, was the first High King of this Island, and the founder of our land. And this was the manner of it:

When noble Hector died and great Troy fell, alone of the Dardanian princes Aeneas White Shield escaped alive, bearing his son in his arms and his old father on his back. He seized one of the ships on the shore, and with such of the Trojans as had also escaped the swords of the Greeks he set sail. The smoke of burning Troy went up behind them, and the reek of it followed them while they wept for royal Priam and his people.

After many journeys they came to the shores of Italy, where the people received them kindly and gave them lands to dwell in. There the Trojans prospered, and Aeneas was their King; from that people descend the race of Romans.

The baby boy Aeneas had carried from Troy was named Ascanius, and when, in his turn, he became King in his father's place he too had a son, the grandson of Aeneas, and this boy was named Silvius.

When Silvius was grown to manhood and had won renown he chose a wife of noble birth, and in time she conceived a child. Silvius rejoiced, and went to a woman who had the long sight.

"There is to be born a son of Dardanus, a Prince of Troy, and heir to Aeneas White Shield," he said. "Foretell concerning him: what is to be his Fate?"

"An ill Fate and a good Fate," she replied, "but ill for you. This boy will kill his father and his mother, and he will wander in exile; but he will not live without kindred, and he will be a great ruler in the fairest of lands."

"Before the Gods," said Silvius, "this is a rough son they are sending me!" For that word, when the boy was born, they called him Brutus.

And it happened as it was foretold; for his mother died at his birth, and when he was grown to manhood, by mischance he killed his father while they were out hunting together. In bitter grief Brutus carried the body home, and all the Trojans lamented over the dead Silvius and the tragedy that had come to Brutus. Then old Ascanius, his grandfather, overwhelmed with sorrow, bade him go out from his father's people into exile, putting a ban on him, that he should never set foot in his homeland again.

So Brutus took his weapons and the things that were his, and mounting into his chariot he departed full of sadness. Nor did anyone attend him, not harper, nor shield-bearer, nor charioteer.

For long his heart was heavy and he wandered, not heeding his way. But he was young, and valiant, and he came of a noble line. So on a day he said to himself, "I have tasted the bitter of my Fate, but there was sweet foretold also. Am I not to find kinsmen, and to be a King in a fair land? It is time to take courage." So he lifted up his heart, he bathed and adorned himself, appearing again like a man of prowess and one of royal blood. With the splendour that was on him, and the gleam of his burnished weapons, and the fiery eyes of his shining horses, the glittering brightness of him was like the sun upon a waterfall. Thus he drove until he came into the lands of the long-haired Greeks.

There he passed through the lands of a King called Pandrasus. Here Brutus saw many people so fair and noble of bearing that he marvelled at them, and more he marvelled that they laboured at base tasks, and some were even in chains. Brutus greeted them courteously and receiving a like response could not forebear to exclaim, "Never have I seen a sight so strange as this—that men of good blood should do such work, and wear such ornaments. Fitter for your necks a golden torc than these you wear!"

"Alas!" they answered him, "for the misfortunes of our fathers we bear this Fate. We are in bondage to King Pandrasus and his Greeks, for our ancestors were brought captive from Troy."

When Brutus heard this he was angry. "Before the Gods! It is not fitting that the descendants of my ancestor Dardanus should suffer this shame!" Then he made himself known to them, and if they had welcomed him courteously before, they welcomed him joyously now. Soon they esteemed him above all others for his generosity, his valor, and his wisdom; and when he told them of Trojans who lived free, his tales fired their hearts.

"Lead us to freedom," they said, "and you shall be first among us, and your descendants shall rule our descendants." So Brutus considered how to bring this about.

Pandrasus had a half brother called Assaracus, and there was war between them, because Assaracus was the son of a Trojan woman and Pandrasus sought to take his inheritance from him. Assaracus had few warriors, and his half brother gave him no rest, raiding his cattle when he went to defend his strongholds, and attacking the strongholds when Assaracus tried to protect his cattle.

Brutus went to Assaracus and said, "Why should you suffer this wrong, only because you are the son of your mother? It is time to turn to your mother's people, whom Pandrasus holds in bondage. Let us make alliance."

"That is good counsel," said Assaracus.

So they took oaths together and, with their women and children, all the Trojans gathered to Assaracus and he gave them weapons. Soon they were a great army, and Brutus was the foremost in valour and skill and the acknowledged leader of them all. Pandrasus led his warriors against them, and the hosts fell to fighting. The battle between them lasted a day and a day and the night between. The noise of it was heard a day's journey away, and ravens gathered out of all Greece and its islands to hang above it. The Greeks were skillful warriors and fierce as wolves, but the Trojans came forth as a dragon from its lair, savage with long hunger, and they had the victory. Where there were ten Greeks that came there, nine did not go away except they were carried, and the Trojans cut off the heads of the slain.

Pandrasus was taken captive. In bitter mockery he said to Brutus, "Is it my head you require, or will ransom content you?"

"I will take counsel concerning that." Brutus replied without rancor for he was not a man to gloat in victory. He called an assembly of the people, and they advised, "Let us not divide these lands with Assaracus, nor stay in this place where we were slaves. Ask for ships and gold, and let us seek our own lands as your ancestor Aeneas did."

Brutus was of one mind with his people and he sent for the Greek heralds. When they came, with them came Imogen, daughter to Pandrasus, to plead for her father's life. She was a maiden bright as the morning when the sun and the dew come together. A spear was not more straight than she, nor the blackbird's wing darker than the braids of her hair, and where she walked the flowers were not bruised. Brutus was straight away filled with love of her.

She knelt before him, but he raised her up. "Do not do so," he said gently, "for where I have honour you shall have it also."

And she answered, trembling, "It does not befit the daughter to be honoured where the father is shamed."

Then he took her two slender hands between his, and smiled. "Lady," he said, "this love becomes you even more than pride. Fear not, your father shall live."

Then he asked for ships and gold of Pandrasus, and also that he should have Imogen for his wife, and Pandrasus granted it. That very same day they held a great marriage feast, and that night the lovers slept together. Thus Imogen, a Greek, and Brutus, Trojan descendant of a goddess, became the ancestors of all the Kings and Queens of the Island of the Mighty.

The time came when the Trojans must sail away, and Imogen wept to leave her homeland, stretching her white arms to the shore. Brutus held her close. "The grief you feel, I have known also," he said, "it is bitter to part from kindred and friends. Dear one, I shall be your healing, as you have been mine." Thus he comforted her, and presently she smiled again.

After they had sailed a while they came to an island. It was very fair, with all fruits in abundance, and in the midst of it a lake, but there were no people dwelling there. The Trojans rested about the lake, and as they did so a woman of surpassing beauty came up out of the water. They were amazed, but she greeted them kindly and bade them take their ease and their pleasure, for no delight was unlawful there. So they stayed, joyfully passing the time with feasting and games, with music and love-makings and with much lively talk for they were a people who delighted in conversation, elegant or boisterous or thoughtful according to the mood that was on them.

The goddess from the lake spoke to Brutus apart and said, "What would you ask of me, son of Aeneas?"

"I would ask counsel, Lady. What is the best place for us to go to find a home?"

"That is easy to tell you," she said, "you must go out of the Middle Sea, beyond the Pillars of Hercules. Deep in the western ocean there is an island, fairest of lands, well-watered and most abundant in its gifts. There is the place given to you." When she had spoken she returned to the lake, and Brutus led his people again into their ships.

They sailed west toward the Pillars that divide the Middle Sea from the Ocean. Many times they landed on the coasts of Africa and did deeds of valour; and they sailed close by the Sirens, whose singing draws sailors to death. But the harpers of the Trojans sang more sweetly still, so that the Sirens fell silent, while Brutus and his people sailed safely by. Then they passed the Pillars of Hercules and sailed up the coast that borders the Western Sea. There they landed in Iberia, where they met another nation of Trojans. These were descended from Antenor and his companions, and were led now by a man called Corineus. Though young he was wise, and though prudent in counsel he was a man of great courage and audacity. He enquired of Brutus whence he and his people came, and who were their ancestors.

Brutus told him, "My people were captive in Greece until we overcame Pandrasus, and they are descended from Helenus son of Priam and others who were taken into bondage; but I am the son of Silvius, son of Ascanius, son of Aeneas White Shield, and I was born in Italy."

Corineus remarked, "Indeed. I have been in that land, and dwelt among the giants of Etruria."

Brutus raised his eyebrows for he had heard of the savagery of these creatures. With some irony he remarked, "It is to be hoped they gave you good entertainment."

"Oh, they did!" Corineus was grinning under his fair moustaches. "They wrestled with me, and when I departed there was not one left alive."

"Before the Gods, they found you an ungentle guest!" Brutus exclaimed.

With perfect seriousness, Corineus replied, "Not so; I did not send them desolate to the darkness, but gave them company, for I drove them there two or three at a time!"

The two men eyed one another for a breath and then burst into laughter. So they were merry together and there came a fast friendship between Brutus and Corineus. Corineus, a man ebullient and of high humour, did much to relieve the seriousness natural to Brutus, while himself developing a deep respect for the courage and responsibility of the Trojan leader. When the time came to depart, Brutus said to his new companion, "Come with us to the land we seek and you shall have your own kingdom there."

Corineus responded instantly, saying, "That is well indeed," and accordingly he and his people sailed with the company of Brutus. Corineus was second only to Brutus among the Trojans, and not Brutus himself was so mighty in battle. In all the wars they fought in Gaul he bore the foremost part, for none could stand against the warrior who had driven giants to hell by two and by three.

Long they sailed, and they passed through many hardships but they were not daunted. The prows of their ships were to the open sea, and on a day there could be seen land ahead of them. Brutus called his helmsman to him, and bade him look and tell what he could see. For the property of this man was that he was so keen of sight he could count the feathers of a bird a day's journey away, and look into her nest to see the color of her eggs, and tell which egg was barren.

Now he stood on the prow of the ship and shaded his eyes. "I see a land more fair than any I ever saw," he reported. "Its hills are clothed with trees, and I see shining rivers between broad meadows, and high places where the wind blows. Beautiful is the rippling of the grass on those high places, and the running of the deer there. Very beautiful are the mountains with the light upon them, and the flowering valleys, beautiful the white waves upon the shore. Surely there is no music like the music of those waves."

"That is our land!" cried Brutus, exulting. "There shall we dwell, we and our children, until the sky with its showers of stars falls, or the earth bursts, or the seas rise to swallow us!" A great roar burst from the company and all turned their faces to the new land, watching eagerly.

They came to the shore in the south of the Island, near the place that is now called Totnes, and they set forth to see what kind of land it was. They found it full of every good thing, with rich soil, abundant game, and rivers that teemed with fish. Truly no land was ever so fitted for men to dwell in. Three great rivers there are, Thames and Severn and Humber, reaching out like three arms, and three great islands close to the shore, Man and Anglesey and Wight. Between Wight and Severn Brutus made a rampart, and all that lay to the west of that he gave to Corineus for his kingdom. It is called Cornovia, that is Cornwall, after him, and one of the Three Coronets of Britain is worn there.

Brutus built for himself a city on the Thames, greatest of the rivers, and he called the city New Troy, that is Trinovantum: but after it was called London, and there the Crown of the Island is worn. Until that time the name of the Island was Albion, but Brutus gave it his own name, and it was called Britain; and the Trojans after that called themselves Britons.

There were no men living in the Island, but there were giants. These giants were born of the earth, and they were horrible in aspect and fearful in strength. Other powers they had; they could bring a darkness about them, or they could blight the standing corn, sour the milk and shrivel the fruit. They contended with the Britons for the Island, and because of their strength they were not easy to overcome, nor was it easy for men to face them, because of the fearful ugliness of them. Nevertheless Brutus led his warbands against them, and in many fights they slew giants.

But Corineus fought in another way. Wherever he heard of a giant he went to seek him out, and with merriment and mockery he called on that giant to wrestle with him. Alone and unarmed he strove with them, and not one giant escaped alive from him. Soon the giants fled from the fear of him, and those the Britons had not slain (they were few) hid themselves in caves in the mountains.

Yet the chief of the giants still lived, and his heart burned in him with hatred for the Britons, and especially for Corineus. His name was Gogmagog, and he was the eldest of the giants. There were two protections on him; the first was a property he had, that while there was earth under his feet he could neither weary nor weaken because he was first-born of the earth; the second was a Fate on him, that his death could not come by any mortal. He gathered twenty other giants to him, and they resolved to fall upon the Britons.

When Brutus and Corineus and all their people gathered together to hold a festival at the place where they had landed, Gogmagog and his giants stole upon them. All the food and drink that was there Gogmagog destroyed by his magic, and after this he brought a storm, and with the storm the giants rushed upon the Britons. Then there was a terrible battle. Many Britons were slain that day, but in the end no giant was left alive save Gogmagog. The warriors wished to kill him, but Corineus prevented them. "Bad luck on the man who takes his death from me!" he said; and he challenged Gogmagog to wrestle with him. Gogmagog was glad and took the challenge; for he had no fear of the giant-killer because of the protections that were on him.

In an open place by the river they came together to fight, and all the Britons gathered to see the battle and to urge on the Champion of Britain with shouting. Indeed there was such a clamour raised that day that the whole Island rang with it, and the remnant of the giants in the mountains crept deeper into their caves, hearing the name of Corineus.

Never had the Champion fought such a wrestling match. If he bore Gogmagog to the earth the giant only rose stronger, and if he fastened on his throat he could not choke him, and though the morning passed as they fought no weariness came on the giant. The sun passed noon, and still they fought, and Corineus' strength began to grow less. Gogmagog seized him in such a grip that some of his ribs were broken, and his blood ran down. At that Gogmagog laughed. "Your blood on the earth is a good sight to me!" he roared. "The less strength will be yours, the more mine. No mortal can overcome Gogmagog!"

Then Corineus knew why he could not defeat the monster, and a great rage filled him. "Yet no giant can overcome Corineus!" he cried. "And if I cannot slay you I know one who can!"

Thus saying he rushed upon Gogmagog, and despite his wounds and the pain he seized the giant and raised him above his head. Then Gogmagog could not touch the earth, and straightaway his strength began to ebb. Though he roared and struggled Corineus hoisted him high in the air and ran with him from the wrestling ground. Nine miles he ran with that monstrous burden, and Gogmagog did not make it easy for him. But for all the giant could do Corineus bore him up until he stood upon the edge of a great cliff. From that cliff he hurled his enemy far out to sea, and the waves closed over him. Not even earthborn Gogmagog was so mighty as the immortal sea. He sank, and was drowned; and so perished the greatest giant of the Island of the Mighty.

And from that day Corineus fought with giants no more.

HE giants were the first of the Plagues of Britain," said Riderch, "and not the least. Yet by reason of the valour of the people and the leadership they had, this Plague was overcome, and the Island freed of it.

"And now, in this time of the greatest Plague that has come upon us, let God be praised who in the hour that He has sent us a new Gogmagog for our testing, has sent us also a new Brutus, a new Corineus."

The notes of his harp died away, and the lamps flickered over the listeners. Small Cato slept in his mother's lap, and Arthur's hound at his feet. Gerontius thanked and praised the bard, and gave him the goblet from which he himself had drunk; a princely gift. Presently the Bishop gave the blessing, and taking leave of one another they went to their beds to prepare for the morning: Arthur and Gai and Gueneva and Gerontius, for whom already the gates of Heaven stood open.

ARRIAGE was usually lifelong and to one partner, but there were other forms. One interesting custom was the "temporary marriage." The laws list ten kinds of marriage, of which only three were permanent. Full marriages were marked by "bride-gifts," by the "maiden-fee" paid to a virgin bride or to her kinswomen, and by the woman's removal from her parents' home to that of her husband. In a temporary marriage no gifts were given, and a husband would live among his wife's kindred. These partnerships were open, legal, and honourable, but they were not intended to be binding, and could be dissolved at will, without pretext, leaving both free to marry again.

Often the husband would be a visiting stranger, from another kingdom or another world. Princesses whose children would be heirs to a kingdom often took such husbands. The children of these unions were not illegitimate (though bastardy never mattered much in Celtic societies, where illegitimate children inherited on the same terms as legitimate) but some of the heroes who are known as sons of their mothers, like Fergus MacRoich, may have been the offspring of temporary marriages.

The custom seems to have been especially common in royal houses, where marriage was likely to be for political advantage. Many of the famous examples involve reigning Queens: the British Queen Cartimandua discarded a husband whose political ambitions conflicted with her own for a more reliable ally, and the legendary Maeve of Connacht changed consorts so often that it was said of her that "she never had a King but there was another in his shadow."

British women enjoyed a status unusual in any time, remarkable in theirs. They were the equals of men not only in their private lives but in government and the conduct of war.

"Women-warriors" are common in the legends

of Britain and Ireland, and the divine patrons of battle were women—though when they took human form it was often, appropriately, as "hags," that is, sterile women. The custom of women going into battle appalled the Romans. "A whole troop of foreigners," wrote one, "would not be able to withstand a single Gaul if he called his wife to his assistance." In Britain they learned from Boudicca the treatment a Celtic Queen expected.

Some peoples were always ruled by Queens, and the ruling house in North Wales inherited through the female line until the ninth century A.D. Perhaps all Celtic tribes began by tracing descent through their mothers, for there are many things which suggest it. The gods, for example, have a mother but no father; and the close relationship between a man and his sister's son looks like the relic of a time when men were not "related" to their own children.

Stories show one interesting result of this importance of women; many Celtic tales portray a figure who was not to reappear in literature for a very long time, the man defined in relation to a woman. In most warrior aristocracies, the amorous exploits of heroes are smoking-room stories, meant to impress men by their number and audacity; love has little part in them. Some of these the Celts had, but they had also the heroes, like Naoise and Diarmiad, who were remarkable above all for their beauty and tenderness, and whose merit was in their devotion and fidelity as lovers. Lancelot is their natural son.

Even Roman women, by no means downtrodden, were impressed by the freedom and authority of their British sisters, although they might be scandalised by their free association with men. One great lady, jesting with a British noble woman about her sexual freedom, was rebuked with splendid hauteur: the British way was better than the Roman, she was told, for "we consort openly with the best men, you in secret with the worst."

N THE FLAT lands that were hardly kept from the sea, the sky was all. The dull red which streaked it was reflected in the metal of shields and harness, on the blades of swords streaked themselves with a different red, and in the open eyes of men. Sometimes a man not yet dead stirred and groaned, but most of the host lay quiet now. From the great drainage ditches mist was swelling, turning the evening from rose to grey, dimming the distance, pearling yellow hair with dew. As the light failed birds rose from the battlefield crying angrily and fled to their roosts, but the other scavengers, dogs and men, remained. Slowly the summer night moved in from the sea, advancing against the defiant west, bringing darkness at last to the men who had found sleep with light in their eyes.

Within the great fortress of Lindum not far away, the victorious army held its triumph. To rewin this vital stronghold they had forced their way through Saxon-held lands, and the battle had turned back a host from territories so long lost to the barbarians, that there they divided themselves into North Folk and South Folk. This had been no crashing cavalry strike, but a great campaign on which the survival of Britain had hung: and Arthur had led them to victory. No more could new waves of invading Saxons seek to unite with the successors of Octha in the north, for Lindum was Roman once again, casting a mighty shadow far about her, holding fast a wedge between north and south clear to the Saxon shore.

The Britons had good cause to rejoice; and good cause had Arthur for the healths he drank to them as he stood before his officers in the chief room of the Commander's quarters, and for the pride that fired him. The room had been cleaned of much of the effect of long neglect; window glass reflected the lamplight, mosaic and bronze reminded of Roman grandeur, though the central fire burned on a raised British hearth and the couchless guests sat on rugs upon the floor. The Emperor, like many others, wore a bright tunic over his cavalryman's breeches, and not his toga; but the mantle falling from his shoulders was the true imperial purple. He indeed had more than his victory to rejoice in, for in Dumnonia beautiful Gueneva waited for him to claim her.

The food was gone and the wine went round; Riderch had sung his song of praise to the warriors, and the feast grew merry. Gai sat at Arthur's left hand, and on his right sat a newer comrade, Bedvir, come from Armorica at the head of a troop to serve the Emperor of Britain; only the first, it was to be hoped, of the returning exiles. When Arthur stood again to pledge his companions, improvising a poem of his own as he did so that brought applause and laughter from them, it was dark-eyed Bedvir who called out, "Peace! Great Caesar, show mercy! Arthur, Chief Dragon of the Island you are, but of the Three Vile Bards of Britain, by God, you are the vilest!"

Amid the cheers and merriment Arthur laughed, raised his cup to his people and drained it in their honour. Stepping back to his place he said, "Truly, I usurp the place of Dumnoric. Where is my household bard, to entertain my warband?"

From the place his rank gave him rose a man in a gay chequered tunic. "King and Emperor, I am ready. Shall I sing, or tell a tale?"

"A song!" cried some, but more, "No, a tale; we have heard fine singing tonight."

"So be it," said Dumnoric. "Will my lord choose a tale or shall I?"

Then from the warm place beside the hearth an old voice spoke. "Arthur, give this choice to me; a gift for Ambrosius' sake."

Respect for him who spoke so rarely quietened the company, and Arthur responded, courtly and grave. "You could have made a harder request and won it, for I am thrice bound to grant your asking: since I cannot refuse a bard, nor would refuse anything asked in the name of Ambrosius, nor anything asked by Merdyn. Name the tale we shall hear."

Merdyn turned his head, more white than grey, to Dumnoric and said, "Then tell us of *The Two Queens of Locrin*."

The silence deepened suddenly, and Dumnoric paused and ceased to smile. Arthur looked keenly at the old bard, who stared back at him, while the company watched them both. For though this was a British court and their Emperor their comrade, yet a court was a court, and an Emperor an Emperor.

Gai's colour rose to his copper hair and he said angrily, "That is a poor tale for the victor of Lindum to hear, and worse for a bridegroom!" Bedvir looked curiously at him, for he had not been among them three years before when Gerontius died, when the marriage with Gueneva was first suggested and Merdyn spoke his mind.

But now Arthur laughed, put his arm about Gai's shoulder, and said, "Schoolfellow, are you forgetting the teaching we had of Saint Illtud, and turning to superstition? What harm can lie in a tale? It is a good tale, and that makes it fit for any man, be he victor or bridegroom. Come, let us hear it."

So the company eased, and old Merdyn turned back to the fire; and Dumnoric took his harp and began the tale of *The Two Queens of Locrin*.

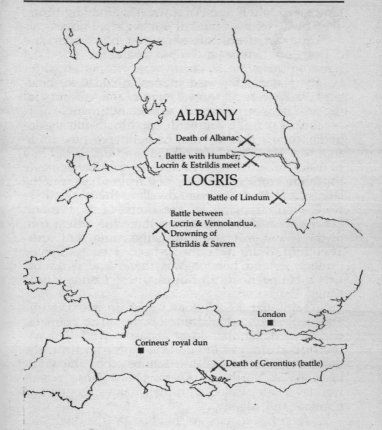

ALBANY

Death of Albanac ✕

Battle with Humber;
Locrin & Estrildis meet ✕

LOGRIS

Battle of Lindum ✕

Battle between
✕ Locrin & Vennolandua,
Drowning of
Estrildis & Savren

London ■

Corineus' royal dun
■

✕ Death of Gerontius (battle)

BRUTUS of Troy was the first High King of the Island of the Mighty. Imogen, his Queen, bore him three sons, Locrin and Kamber and Albanac, and the Island did not hold their match. Locrin was without equal for beauty, Kamber for wisdom, and Albanac for boldness. They were all three generous and valiant, and the love between them ran strong and joyful.

In his old age Brutus decided to divide the inheritance among them and he pondered how to do so justly. He called bold Albanac and instructed him to make three divisions of the Island. Albanac made the lands north of Humber one realm; that was the largest, but few men were dwelling there and there were desolate places in the north of it. West of Severn he made another, and there the wisest men of the Island were wont to gather, and the bards. The third realm was the richest; Thames flowed through it, and London was there, and it lay between Humber and Cornwall where Corineus was King.

"Now that is well done," said Brutus. Then he added, jovially, summoning Locrin, "The youngest has divided, let the eldest choose." And that has been the custom of Britain ever since. Locrin chose the mid-part of the Island, Kamber took the West, leaving the North for Albanac; and those realms were ever after called with their names, Logris and Cambria and Albany.

When his years were fulfilled Brutus died, and the Britons mourned him and made him a rich grave. Locrin was High King after him and wore the Crown of London. Still he loved most to be with his brothers, and he did not go wooing: until the people though they loved him began to say, "Is the High King a youth or a man? A King without children is but half a King." Then the elders of Britain came to Locrin and said, "Lord, it would be well for you to choose a wife."

The thought did not displease Locrin. Indeed he

had been thinking about it himself. He said, "It would be well, but there are many fair and well born maidens in Britain. How should I choose?"

The elders asked, "Is there no lady whom you love?"

Their handsome young King grinned, "No, for all alike delight me! Come, advise me. If there is one more worthy than the rest, tell me."

They answered, "Corineus, King of Cornwall, has a daughter. None could be more fitting for the place at your side."

"Is she fair?" Locrin returned.

"Indeed she is!"

"Then I will see the maiden." Thus Locrin agreed to journey into Cornwall.

There, in high summer, he was the guest of great Corineus, and a feast was made for him. The daughter of Corineus came into the feast; she was beautiful and proud, and her name was Vennolandua. The red berry of the rowan was not more glorious than her hair, nor its blossom whiter than her skin. Her brows were black and fine, and the glance of her eyes bright as the glance of a falcon on a cliff. Her dress was of green silk, gold-embroidered, and she wore a gold torc about her neck, with fair gold bracelets red-enameled on her white arms. The bards when they sang praise to her need sing no more than truth.

She bore mead to Locrin in a cup of fine workmanship, and when she looked on him and saw his beauty which had no like in Britain her heart grew warm. Locrin saw her tall stately figure and her bearing like a Queen and he could find no fault with her. It was clear she would make a fit partner for the High King and accordingly he asked that she should be his wife.

In those days it was the custom to perform a thing in the same half of the year in which it was planned, lest ill luck follow; so that those betrothed in summer-half were married before Samhain. Accordingly, a day was appointed on which Locrin and Vennolandua should sleep together, when the trees change to russet and gold, and she would then depart with him to his home. Meanwhile Locrin returned to his own kingdom.

But before the time was come that he should fetch Vennolandua from her father's house a grief befell Britain. A foreign people came to the Island, landing in Albany. Under their chieftain, Humber, they began to ravage the land to the North.

In fury, Albanac said to his elders, "This land was given to my father, Brutus, and to his kinsmen, and to no others. Let us drive those strangers out!"

But the elders of his people argued, "Lord, the men of Albany are few. It would be well to summon your brothers with their warbands."

Albanac roared at them, "And shall I always be sheltering behind my brothers' shields? Before the Gods, I will not do it. I desire this deed and this praise for myself!" For Albanac was the youngest of the three.

Accordingly he gathered his warriors about him, and they mounted in their chariots and went out against Humber. Then there was trampling and hacking, thrusting of spears and denting of shield-bosses, and the noise of groans and cries. Wherever the fight was thickest Albanac was there, running out on the yoke-pole of his chariot to hurl his spears, shouting and exhorting his warband. Fierce was the onslaught; but by reason of the great numbers of the invaders the men of Albany were overcome, and young Albanac was slain.

When Locrin and Kamber heard of it they came together, and great was their grief. Lamenting him they cried out, "Alas for the hair that was yellow and curling as the flower of the broom, there is dust and blood upon it! Alas for the cheek where no beard had grown, it was red as the foxglove, now it is pale! Alas for our brother, the shining hawk of battle, the handsome merry youth; there is neither speech nor laughter in him now, and the eagle feasts on his flesh!"

Then they resolved to be avenged for Albanac and to drive out the invader. They called their warriors to them, a great host, and their speed into the north was such that the turves cut by the hooves of their horses hung over them so thickly, it would be thought a flock of birds was there.

Word of it came to Corineus and straightaway he called for Vennolandua and said to her, "It is a bad portent, daughter, but it is necessary to name another time when you may become the wife of Locrin even though I fear that time may be beyond Samhain and the year's turning, in winter-half."

But she said only, "It is not fitting to talk of weddings when there is fighting to be done."

Humber brought his army into Logris, and at the border Locrin and Kamber met him and fell upon him. The face of the sun was hidden with the dust that went up from the battle, and the din of it was louder than a fierce storm in winter when the sea contends with the rock. The men of Britain had the victory, and the invaders fled them. Though Humber escaped from the battle, in his flight he fell into the river and was drowned, and many of his people with him; and for that it bears his name. Then the Britons cut off the heads of their enemies and made heaps of them.

The ships of their enemies were near that place, and they seized them and all that was in them, and divided the spoil. Locrin had gold and treasure for his portion, and there were also young women in the ships, captives of the invaders. Among them was a woman of such beauty that when Locrin beheld her it seemed to him there could be none so lovely and perfect among the women of the world. She was as white as the swan, as the snow of a single night, as a lily on a lake. The yellow of her hair was more pale than the petal of the primrose, and her eyes were the sky of spring. Her bearing was all gentleness and grace, and when she stood before Locrin she wept so that her tears like pearls fell through her slim fingers. The heart of Locrin melted in him; he chose her for his own, and that very night he lay with her. She had been the concubine of Humber before; she was a woman of Germany, and her name was Estrildis.

From that time Locrin was continually in the company of the slim shining girl, and his love for her grew until it was past measure. He was not content that she should be his mistress, but he desired to make her the Queen at his side.

When this was known the men about him were uneasy and displeased. "It is fitting," they said, "that the High King should have a beautiful woman to sleep with him, but this woman is a foreigner and a slave, and she is not worthy to be Queen of the Island of the Mighty."

They went to Kamber to ask him to persuade his brother not to marry her. Kamber the Wise came to Locrin to reason with him. "Though the woman is fair as the first light of morning, yet she is not fit to be your wedded companion," he said. "It would be better for you to marry the daughter of Corineus."

"It is not clear to *me* that it would be better to lose the company of the girl I love so dearly."

"Yet there is a reason," said Kamber.

"Tell it to me."

"You will fulfill your oath in doing so."

"That is a heavy reason," said Locrin, "but not so heavy as would be the parting from Estrildis."

"I have another reason. Your marriage with Vennolandua would bind Cornwall to Logris."

"Cornwall is a rich realm," said Locrin, "but a richer treasure is my lovely gentle girl."

"I have another reason."

Locrin sighed. "Very well, tell it to me," he said.

"It is no better to insult Corineus than to insult

a god. Terrible will his anger be if you put this slight on his daughter."

"That is a fierce reason," said Locrin, and he fell silent. Then he said, "To please the people and to avoid strife I will marry Vennolandua. But I will not send Estrildis from me."

His brother embraced him, and relieved that he had won Locrin to his view, Kamber said, "In this you must do as seems good to you. But as for the marriage it is far better for you to decide as you have than for the people to appoint a man to judge you."

"Indeed," exclaimed Locrin, "that would have shamed me."

Then Locrin returned to London, and he called magicians and bade them make a hiding place for Estrildis. They hollowed out a great cave under the city, and the air of it they made sweet, and there were fruit trees and springs of water in it, nor was it dark. In that cavern Locrin hid Estrildis, and she dwelt there.

When all was safe, he went to the house of Corineus with the bride-gifts and the maiden-fee for Vennolandua, and he fetched her to his own house. She had heard word of Estrildis, and when she came to London she kept jealous watch. But she found no trace of her rival, nor any rumour, for none knew of the secret cavern, but all thought that Locrin had sent the girl from him. Then Vennolandua was content, and believing that the heart of Locrin had returned to her, loved him as much for his imagined faithfulness as she already did for his great beauty. But Locrin continually went in secret to the cavern under London.

In time Vennolandua bore a son and they called him Maddan. When he was grown to boyhood he was sent to be fostered with Corineus.

Estrildis also bore a child, a fair daughter, and her name was Savren. In all the years that passed Locrin never ceased to visit his mistress, and his love for her was undiminished.

There came a time when age was heavy on great
Corineus, and he died. All the Britons mourned
him, the slayer of Gogmagog, the Champion of Britain, and they buried him richly. Great was the grief
of Vennolandua for her father, and Locrin mourned
without feigning; nevertheless a fear was gone from
him. The longing to make Estrildis his Queen was
still in him, and now the dread of that mighty man
no longer restrained him.

Accordingly, when the funeral of Corineus was
past and the mourning over, he summoned the chief
men of the kingdom and told them that he proposed
to put Vennolandua away and make another his
wife. And this time he would not listen to counsel.

When this word came to the Queen she bade
her women bring her mirror, saying, "Has my cheek
grown hollow, or my eye dull?"

"Lady, it is not so," they answered her, looking
to see her weep. But a terrible anger filled her. She
rose up, and she robed and adorned herself, and
went to Locrin.

When she stood before him she said, "What is
this that you will do? When you asked me of my
father Corineus it was not said this was to be a
temporary marriage. Were there no bride-gifts at our
wedding? Did I not leave my father's house to dwell
in yours?" Her great eyes flashed as she spoke and
she flung her words like spears. "Have I brought
you no alliance? Are the men of Cornwall without
mettle, or their chariots few? Do the warriors I maintain, feasting them on meat and wine, not carry their
spears at your command? Have I contrived against
you, or betrayed your honour?"

The High King looked at her, and saw her tall
and majestic, with an eagle's glance; and he thought
of Estrildis of the soft speech, and was silent.

Then the Queen stamped her foot upon the
ground and demanded, "Answer me, *husband*! I am
the lady of most renown in Britain, and so I was

when you married me. Will you now set me aside for one who is a slave?"

For a space, Locrin did not speak, but fingered the carving of his chair. At last he raised his eyes and said heavily, "Lady, I choose to do so." And that was all the answer he made her.

Then fire came into her eye, she shook out her burning hair and the blaze of her anger burst from her. "Is it in your mind that because Corineus is dead the blood of Cornwall is grown tame?" she cried; "by mountain and by sea, *you will find it is not so!*"

With that, she whirled and strode from the room, her garments fluttering in the wind of her raging departure. Immediately she gave orders to gather all that was hers together, and working deep into the night she put all her affairs in order. Then summoning the warriors she maintained, with their chariots and charioteers, and leaving nothing that was hers in London, she set out straightaway and returned to her own realm.

Locrin said to himself, "Maddan is young, and he is my son also, and there is no other man of her house." And he had no fear of her anger. Then he fetched Estrildis from her hiding place and set her by his side, making her wife and Queen of Britain, and his daughter Savren also he raised to honour. So there was great joy among the three of them that they were all together in the sight of men and the light of day.

When Vennolandua came to Cornwall and to her own house, her kinswomen came out to meet her, lamenting the shame that had been put upon her. But she was the daughter of Corineus, and her mettle was not less than his.

"This is no time for weeping," she said. She sent for her son Maddan, and embraced him. He was a goodly boy, though far from manhood, and Corineus had trained him well in arms. Vennolandua told him, "My curse is upon Locrin, that he should put this slight upon one of the blood of Brutus and Corineus, upon a gold-torqued Prince of Britain!"

But her son answered her stoutly, "The shame that is put on me is bad, but worse by far is the shame on you and on my foster father Corineus. If he lived you would not lack a champion." Then he hesitated, looking up at her. "But now I am troubled for it is ill for a son to fight against his father."

She embraced him again and quietly she said, "I shall not ask it of you, my son."

Then she went about Cornwall and ordered the craftsmen to make weapons and chariots. All Cornwall filled with the clangour of the forges and their fires burned by day and by night. From the horsefields she chose horses for the chariots, and the four finest she chose for herself.

She summoned the master of all the smiths and bade him make weapons for her, helmet and shield, long spears and short spears and the barbed spear and sword. Fit for the Lady of Battles he made them; Govannon himself could have wrought no better. They were inlaid with gold and white bronze and fine enamelling; the short spears flew to their target as if they had sight, and the long spears had each a ball of gold on the butt of them.

Then Vennolandua called a muster of the men of Cornwall, and they gathered to the royal dun. There she made a feast for them, setting fresh pork before them and filling their cups with mead; for a year meat and drink did not fail them, nor the singing of bards.

At the end of a year she armed herself and appeared before them, and called upon them to avenge the insult to her and to the house of Corineus. They rose with a great shout and took up their weapons. Nor did they scorn to follow a woman to battle, for she was the daughter of Corineus and the battle-rage was upon her so that she appeared like one of the goddesses who delight in battle and in offerings of slain men. Until that time it had not been customary with the women of Britain to go to war, but it was the custom after.

She mounted into her chariot, and her son Maddan was standing by. He spoke formally to the Queen, "I wish success to your venture, swiftness to your wheels, sharpness to your weapons, and the protection of seven shields about you!" But then, moving closer, he murmured, "Oh, my mother, it is hard to take leave of you. I wish I did not have to stay here!"

"Not so," smiled Vennolandua, "for it is time that you were a shield-bearer." At that he mounted joyfully beside her. Then the men of Cornwall went forth, and their warrior Queen led them.

They entered Logris, and began to ravage the land. Wherever they went they burned and despoiled, driving off cattle and leaving ruin in their wake. The bards that were with them continually sang praises to Vennolandua while mocking and satirising Locrin so that his name had no honour in the land.

Men came to the High King to tell him of it. "Lord, make haste and go forth against the Queen of Cornwall, for she is laying waste the land and your people are in fear of her; also the bards make satires upon you."

"Alas," Locrin grieved, "how can I do this thing? How can you ask this of me? The woman has lain at my side and her son is my son."

"Nevertheless, Lord," they insisted, "if you do not, the country will be utterly destroyed." And at last Locrin called his warband about him and summoned his chief men to bring their warbands. Then he went forth against the army of Cornwall.

Locrin sent out men on swift horses to find where the army of the Queen might be, and they found her and came into her presence. They said to her, "What is the cause that you bring armed men into Logris and make war upon the King of Britain?"

Vennolandua answered harshly, "Tell that crooked-tongued oath-breaker who brings dishonour

to the name of Brutus that I come seeking a bull of
mine that has gone astray!"

They returned to the High King with all speed.
"It is not hard to find the Queen," they reported,
"for where she is there is smoke rising."

Between the Stour and the Severn the two hosts
met. The spears of the men of Cornwall were thick
as barley, and the sound of the hooves and of the
wheels of their chariots upon the earth was like the
roar of the landslide when a hill falls into the valley.
Not less was the army of Logris, and the day grew
dark with the dust of battle.

In the midst of the field Vennolandua and Locrin
met together. Locrin cried out, "Lady, you do wrong
to bring spears against me, for the Coronet of Cornwall is subject to the Crown of London!"

"Do you bleat to *me* of wrongs?" she raged.
"What of the wrong done to me and to my son?"
Then she shook her spears and challenged in a great
voice so that all might know of it: "Hear me!" Her
call went out over the host. "I am Queen of the
Island of the Mighty, and bitter to me is the sight of
my people dying, since the quarrel is between the
High King and myself only. Let none fight but only
him and me."

Locrin's heart was sick and heavy. He said only,
"It is better so."

Then the carynx was blown and the two hosts
drew apart. The Queen and the High King dismounted from their chariots, and when Locrin saw
that Maddan was his mother's shield-bearer tears
burst from his eyes. He said to Vennolandua, "Let
me embrace my son before we fight."

"You must ask him for that," she said.

"He had better not ask me," said Maddan. "The
back of my hand would be my answer!" Then he
turned his face from his parents and wept.

Now a dread stillness fell on the hosts and there
were no cries of challenge, or insult, or encourage-
ment. In the dusty space between the two watching

hosts the King and Queen fought in bitter silence. Locrin was valiant and a man of prowess, but the battle-fury was on Vennolandua so that her frenzy overcame him and he was overthrown, and she slew him.

When the spirit was out of him she cut off his head and held it up before her face and lamented, "Alas for the head that had no equal for beauty, and for the lips that I have kissed! My mouth knew no kisses but yours, my husband, and I remember the weight of your breast on mine. My grief that your death should come by me; if it were not for the wrong you did me it would not have been so. Mine is the mouth that last shall touch yours," and she kissed him once full on his blood-dabbled lips. That was all the keening she made for him.

Then Vennolandua took the head and tied it by the hair to the timbers of her chariot. Maddan wept to look upon the face of his father, but he said to his mother, "The blow was well struck. Now we are avenged for the shame put upon us."

"Not so," Vennolandua replied, "for there is more." She commanded that Estrildis be brought before her.

When Estrildis came and Vennolandua looked for the first time upon that gold and white beauty, a great anger filled her. "Before the Gods," she cried, "was it for such a weak, pale thing that Locrin cast me aside? My curse on him, the insult was worse than I knew!" She glared at Estrildis. "Woman, do you see the head of him that was my husband?" But Estrildis hid her eyes, weeping bitterly, for she had indeed seen the head of Locrin, her beloved. "Weep on," said Vennolandua, "water is fitting for you; by water you came to us, by water you shall go."

Then she sent for Savren, and the girl was brought before her. She was a maiden even lovelier than her mother. She was more fair than stars over the sea, or than the star of morning: and all the host fell silent as they looked on her, for she seemed not

like a mortal girl but like one from the Earthly
Paradise.

Seeing her youth and her innocence, there was
not a man there but would have had mercy on her.
But Vennolandua saw in the unearthly beauty of the
girl an aching echo of the man she had honoured
and loved so deeply; and she remembered the wrong
done to her son. She commanded that mother and
daughter should both be drowned in the great river
that was near at hand. Then Estrildis fell down before her and begged for mercy for her daughter.
"Spare the child," she entreated, making the only
plea she knew might sway the Queen, "for she is of
the blood of Brutus. She is your son's sister!"

"She is my son's supplanter," said Vennolandua.
She regarded the woman a long moment. "I will not
spare her, but for her birth she shall have this honour,
that the river shall be called with her name." Then
she commanded her warriors to cast woman and girl
into the river and it was done.

So Estrildis died, glad of it because of the death
of her love. But the people of the Living Land beneath the water had pity on Savren; they took her
with them to that happy place where there is no
guilt and the young men never grow old, so that she
did not perish but lived like one of them. She became the guardian of the river; and still she dwells
in bliss under the glassy waters of Severn that bears
her name.

Then Vennolandua sat in the chair of Locrin,
and ruled as High Queen until her son was a man,
when she returned to Cornwall. There have been
other Queens ruling over the Island of the Mighty,
illustrious women: but the first woman to be exalted
with the Crown of London was Vennolandua the
warrior Queen.

HE company applauded Dumnoric, and Arthur led them. "A worthy Empress!" he said: then turning to Gai went on, "Well, friend, interpret this ill-omened story for me. Should Kings of Britain learn from it to avoid Cornovian ladies?"

It was Bedvir who responded. "It would be better if they learned from it to be true to Cornovian ladies, and to avoid yellow-haired women of German race."

The officers laughed, and Gai smiled. Arthur said, "That is easy for me; I am no Vortigern."

"Who could think it? Well, Caesar, let us wish you a bride as noble and courageous as Vennolandua, as lovely and gentle as Estrildis."

The other men shouted their approval. Gai said, "If you had seen Gueneva, Bedvir, you would know that as for beauty, there is no need of wishing."

"True!" cried Arthur; "and as for my faith, who having seen her could look elsewhere? Come, friends, it grows late, and we have laboured today. I'll to bed and dream of weddings."

Merdyn by the fire seemed to sleep, and sat unmoving as the room emptied. Left alone he sighed and murmured to the flames, "Your uncle Ambrosius never married: well he understood that jealous Queens harm their rivals. You pledged your faith twelve years ago, Arthur, when you took your weapons. Britain is your bride."

ELTIC religion remains very much a mystery. Not only did the taboo on writing mean that little evidence has survived, but on this subject the Celts were even reluctant to speak openly—hence the oath "I swear by the gods my people swear by," which avoided naming them. Roman writers described their religion in terms of Roman gods, so their accounts are often misleading. However, it seems plain that the Celts had a nature religion, a belief in the holiness of the physical world; and that to this was joined a worship of the creative intelligence manifested in human beings. We cannot even be really certain that it is right to talk about a universal "Celtic religion," though it is a fair guess that they shared some beliefs. A few of these survive as superstitions—the supernatural atmosphere of May Day and Hallowe'en, for example, were once even more significant as Beltain and Samhain.

Their gods were often local, and connected with something very specific, a place maybe or a craft. Certain natural features were always holy— rivers especially, many of which, like the Seine and the Boyne, still bear the names of their Celtic goddesses; but also mountain tops, lakes, islands. On the whole these were governed by goddesses, while the gods of learning and skill were usually male. Some animals, above all the pig, were sacred, also some trees, chiefly the oak, the apple, the hazel. Some gods appear to have been universal— for example, the Great Queen, who is the Welsh Rhiannon, the Irish Brigid. But we should not think of her as anything so simple as a "mother goddess"—it is dangerous to apply such terms to a pantheon where the patrons of war were female, and even older than the Great Queen was the Good God, who was the embodiment of eternal energy and fertility, the possessor of an inexhaustible cauldron. Gods in Britain and Ireland were called the Children of Don or the Children of Danann; but of this mother of the gods

we have no more than the name. One tantalising
glimpse into this old faith hints that Merlin may once
have been a god, maybe the creator or guardian
of Britain: for the oldest name known for the Island
was "The Precinct of Merlin."

But we know very little for certain, and since
our picture of the gods is largely drawn from stories in which they appear, we naturally see them as
personalities; the people who worshipped them
may not, in fact, have had such a clear image of them.
In most of these stories the gods appear as the people of the happy Otherworld: the Land of Summer,
the Underworld, the Land of Youth. There fortunate mortals may be invited, although trespass is
punished. The sea-god lived on beautiful islands,
or maybe under the waves— Lyonesse and other
drowned lands may be a memory of this realm.
His islands do not seem to have been the same as
the Islands of the Earthly Paradise, the places
where the happy dead made merry beneath the holy
apple trees—one name for such an island was The
Place of Apples, which is what Avalon means. This
ancient belief that the souls of the dead crossed
the sea survives in the British superstition that death
can only come with the ebbing tide, which will bear
the spirit away. All these islands were in the west.
The Isle of Man, the Scillies, Ireland, still have a
mystic aura to the mainland British, and in Brittany
it was thought that the souls of the dead went to
Britain.

One thing is sure: the Celts had no belief in the
omnipotence of the gods. One divine tribe might
be overthrown by another, as some had been; and
there are poems which represent the pagan gods
as having wrestled with Christ and lost.

HE old residence of the Vice-Prefect in London was decaying and comfortless; when Arthur brought his court to the city his officers and officials had their quarters there, but he and the Queen were guests of the Bishop.

Though it was but spring and not all the buds on the apple tree had turned to blossom, the day was warm as May. Ladies had discarded their shawls and men their cloaks, and even the children splashing in the water where Tamessa's tide had spread onto the lawn did so without rebuke. Ankle-deep in water, the Bishop's two small sons leaned on the fence and watched the river, while their mother, a baby trampling her lap, watched them.

Under a tree the King and Queen sat with a chessboard between them. Arthur leaned frowning over the game, but Gueneva sat upright and calm, her eyes moving mischievously from the board to her husband. A great wolfhound wandered up to Arthur, pushing his head against him; its shoulder struck the table, the board tilted, the pieces slid and scattered.

Arthur exclaimed in annoyance, and Gueneva laughed. "I swear you have trained him to do it!" she said. "Whenever I am winning, Horse comes and knocks the board away."

"He feels my distress." Arthur rubbed the dog's head. "Praise God, the Saxons do not defeat me so often." He rose, shaking out the folds of his toga. Formally dressed and well barbered, today he was all Roman, save for the golden neck-ring he wore, the torc of a Celtic Prince. "I wish I had time for revenge, sweet warrior, but Patric and Maglos will be waiting for me at the Residence." He touched her shoulder in farewell, and moved towards the gate, the Bishop rising to accompany him, the other men following. Not looking after him, Gueneva collected the chess pieces and returned them to their box, then turned to her hostess. The Bishop's wife, not much her elder, had become a close friend. "Well,

Antonia?'' She clapped her hands and held them out to the baby. "How shall we amuse ourselves?"

"Is that a call for me?" The household bard rose from a bench against the wall. "Noble ladies, shall I entertain you with stories?"

Whatever the noble ladies might have answered, the children shouted eagerly. While the other women gathered about the Queen, Dumnoric asked, "What shall I tell?"

Antonia said laughing, "Since my husband is not here, let it be one of the old heathen tales."

"A good idea; and since *my* husband is not here, let it tell of a King who is not a warrior, and have no battles in it."

"You mock him; there is no such tale."

"Indeed there is," said Dumnoric, "and if you will hear it, I shall tell of *Bladud, the Blemished Prince.*"

LADUD, A PRINCE of Britain, kept swine for the space of seven years, and this was the way of it:

Bladud was the son of Rud Hudibras, who had no other son.

He was well made in his person and handsome of face, eloquent and witty in his speech, and of all the Princes of Britain in his time he was most loved by the people of the Island, even though he was not famed for judgment or for war.

He was a cunning magician, and he desired always to increase his knowledge. He cared more for that than for hunting or feasting, more than for the singing of poets or the company of friends or than his arm about a girl. The practice of magic was more to him than the golden torc he wore. He went about the Island and sought out the wisest magicians, and learned of them all they could teach, until there was none in Britain to equal him in skill or power.

Yet his desire was not satisfied, and since his knowledge could not be increased among men he resolved to go into the Land of Promise; for there the child of seven years is as wise as the wisest of men.

Yet it is not easy to find a way into that land, except by the guidance of one of the people of it. Therefore, though Bladud searched diligently for three years, he could not find such a way. Then it chanced that as he was travelling in the west part of the Island, night overtook him and he had no shelter. His charioteer saw a swineherd's hut at the edge of an oak wood. "Lord," he said, "let us seek lodging here." They went down to the hut, and it was empty, save for musty straw upon the earth floor, and some stale bread in a basket. The charioteer unharnessed the horses, then he lit a fire and made a bed for Bladud upon the straw. They made a meal of the stale bread, and laid down to rest.

But Bladud could get no sleep, because of the dampness of the floor, the smoke of the fire, and the smell of the hut and the straw. Also when he lay down vermin crept out of the straw and bit him, so that he could get no peace for their pricking and itching. He said to himself, "It is not fitting that the blood of Brutus should be food for these. I will make a bed elsewhere." He rose and went out of the hut. The night was fresh and mild. A mist lay about the stream by the hut, and he thought to go beyond it before he found a place to rest, so he took a brand from the fire. At the foot of a round hill he built two fires and lay down between them; then covering himself with his cloak he slept.

That night was the night of Beltain. Within a short time he was awakened by light and the sound of music. Putting his head out from under his cloak he saw that there was a door in the hillside, and the light and the music came from this door. Through the door came fifty birds with gold chains about their necks, singing more sweetly than any birds he had ever heard: and when they alighted on the ground they became fifty young women of surpassing beauty. Then out of the door came fifty stags, and when they came where the women were they were transformed into fifty handsome young men. The young men and women began to make merry together, and Bladud watched from beneath his cloak.

When the wind of morning blew, the company ceased their sport. The women took on the form of birds again, and returned into the hill. Then Bladud rose swiftly, putting a charm of concealment upon himself; and when the young men became stags and ran towards the door, he cast his arms about the neck of the foremost stag and ran beside it into the hill. But though that stag had been first, all the others outran it, so that it entered into the hill last of all. Bladud loosed its neck and went away from them, and the spell he had made hid him from their eyes. When the stags became men they laughed at the one Bladud had held, asking if the sport had wearied him. "No," he answered, "but when I began to run suddenly I felt a weight upon me; if Death who clings to mortals had fastened upon me the weight could not have been greater."

They went towards a fair hall that was not far off, and Bladud followed them; and he saw that the land about him surpassed all other lands for beauty, as did the hall outshine all the kings' houses he had seen. He went into the hall behind the young men and women, and stood beside a pillar of the house. In the midst of his people sat the King of that place. His hair and his eyes were dark and his skin was white; he was the comeliest person in that fair company.

Bladud thought to remain concealed, but when he took his place the King rose and cried out, "There is a dead man among us!" Then Bladud found his protection of invisibility taken from him, and he was brought before the King.

The King demanded of him who he was, and Bladud replied, "I come of blood that would not shame you in a guest, and I claim of you the hospitality you should have of me if our places were changed: the best of meat and drink and a fair woman to serve you, harpers to sing your praise, the best place by the fire, and clean linen on your bed."

"Here is a bold asker!" said the King. "Why did you come here? For those who come unasked find their lodging in Oeth and Anoeth."

"I came here," said Bladud, "because I thought it fitter lodging for a man of noble blood than the swineherd's hut."

"What reason can you show why you should not be confined in the narrow chambers of Oeth and Anoeth?"

"I swear by the gods my people swear by, that I wish no harm to your people or ill luck upon your country, and that all my taking would leave you no poorer, since all I desire is to learn some of your knowledge."

At that the King laughed. "It would be past your strength or cunning to harm anything that is in this land," he said. "As for our knowledge, we do not part with it lightly. Yet I had thought it beyond the wit of any mortal to find a way here, unless it was Bladud, son of Rud Hudibras of Britain."

Bladud said, "I am that man."

"Then," said the King, "the nobleness of your blood and the impudence of your speech shall save you from the Castle of Bone. Instead for your punishment you shall tend our pigs, though you find a swinecherd's hut unfit lodging for you."

Then Bladud was taken away and bound to the service of the people of the Living Land. And in the morning his charioteer woke and found him gone, and though he searched he could find no trace of him, except two fires burned to ash. So with a heavy heart he returned to London with his news, and the High King and all the people of Britain mourned.

Bladud kept the Swine of the Smith, that provide the food of the Ever Young. The property of those magic pigs is this, that so often as they are killed and eaten they are alive again the next day, and it is eating the flesh of those pigs that preserves the people of that land from age and death.

At first there was a watch set on Bladud so that he might not escape, and at the year's turning when the ways stand open they set an enchantment of sleep upon him for a night and a day. But Bladud had no desire to leave that place, for he was where he had wished to be, though he deplored his poor state; and when they saw that, they ceased their vigilance over him.

For seven years Bladud watched over those swine, and he never so much as smelled the fragrance of their cooking, but in the evening servants of the King's steward would come and drive away as many animals as were needed for the night's feasting, and in the morning they would drive them back to the herd. All the while Bladud watched and listened to learn the arts of that people, and for all his low condition he grew in knowledge and power, until his opinion of himself was that there had been no such magician in Britain since the days of Math the Old.

At the end of seven years he was herding his pigs by a stream one day, when he saw a hunt beyond the stream, and a pack of dogs, brindled above and white below, coursing a stag; and the stag was white as salt, with scarlet ears. The hounds were at the heels of the stag, and he ran down into the ford and across the stream: and the dogs did not follow him, but ran baying up and down the farther bank seeking his scent. They did not see the stag, and Bladud knew by that that the ford was one of the crossing places to the lands of men.

Presently the hunters came up and called the dogs away; and seeing them Bladud felt himself strangely moved. He looked upon the weaving of their garments, the ornament of their horses and weapons, the warrior patterns on their arms; he heard the sound of their speech, and he remembered all the ways of his people. Then a great longing seized him, so that tears burst from his eyes, and he lay on the ground and wept for the Island of the Mighty and the people of it. From that hour he lost his delight in the Living Land, and his desire was to be among men of his own speech again.

Therefore he determined to return to his own people, and he would not ask leave but he would go in secret, for he thought that the arts he had learned would keep him safe. Accordingly at Samhain when the ways stand open he set out for the ford of the stag; and as he went he drove nine young pigs of the herd before him, for it seemed to him a desirable thing that the people of Britain should eat of such meat.

However, the young pigs raised such a squealing and an outcry that the people of that country were aware of him, and the King pursued him, and

all the arts that Bladud had learned did not avail to
conceal him from the King. First he turned himself
into a fish and the nine pigs into nine scales upon
his back: but the King pursued him in the form of an
otter. Then he took the likeness of a squirrel and put
the pigs as nine seeds into a pine cone: but the King
pursued him in the form of a marten. After that he
took the likeness of a heron, and the pigs became
nine feathers on his neck: but the King pursued him
in the form of a hawk. Last he put on the shape of a
wolf, and carried the pigs as burrs in his coat: but
the King overtook him in his own form, and shook
his staff over them, so that they stood before him in
their own shape, Bladud and the nine pigs.

Then the King said, "Here is an unfaithful
swineherd."

"Not so, Fair One, son of the Bright One," said
Bladud. "I have given you good service. All the time
these pigs have been in my care you have suffered
no loss of them, whether by straying, by wolf, or by
eagle. Not so much as the hair of a pigling has been
lost, but as for the good I have had of them, I have
not so much as laid my finger on the skin of one
when it was smoking, and after licked my finger. No
hire have I had of you; therefore it seemed good to
me to take a small part of the increase of the herd for
my hire, and I did this so that I should not be
dishonoured by an insult nor you shamed for miserli-
ness."

"That was ill spoken!" said the King. "A sore
trial would these pigs be if ever they entered your
land; your dead would be more than your living
before they were slain. Hire of another kind shall
you have of me!" Then he struck Bladud with his
staff so that the man fell senseless; and when he
came to himself he was in the land of Britain, and of
the magic pigs there was no sign.

But the blow he had of the King of the Underworld had blighted his form, so that he had lost all
beauty and seemliness. The hair of his head fell and

his teeth were loosened, while his flesh was become livid, and he had the appearance of a dead man. When he understood this he grieved bitterly. "I foresee a cold homecoming," he said. "This is not a form to win praise from poets nor acclaim from noble companions, nor smiles from the bright-eyed ladies."

He gathered leaves and laid them together, then by enchantment made a garment of them that covered him from the crown of his head to his heels, and then he made his way to London. He would not be parted from his garment nor uncover his face until he came into the presence of the King, and he put such awe on all whom he met that none hindered his passage. But when he came to the door of the High King's hall he was stopped, for the porters were unwilling to admit a man with neither face nor name to the King.

Bladud said, "I am a man who can tell the King of marvels; and also I have tidings of his son Bladud."

When Rud Hudibras was told of this, he called the stranger to him and said, "What news have you of my son Bladud?"

Bladud answered, "He stands here," and uncovered himself.

When Rud Hudibras saw the dreadful appearance of his son the High King wept, and all the nobles of Britain, and Bladud wept also. In a while meat and drink was brought to him, and he ate, and told his story; and after that he deliberated with his father and the Council what would be best for him to do.

He could not take his former place among the gold-torqued Princes, for a blemished man cannot be a King, nor was Bladud willing to go much among men in his blighted shape. Accordingly a house was made for him where he dwelt alone with servants to tend him, and a message was sent out bidding all the doctors of the Island to try what their skill would do. But the most skillful doctors of Britain could not

take the leprosy from him, nor did all the arts he
had learned avail to cure him. So Bladud dwelt alone,
taking part in no sport or society, and for years he
kept that ghastly appearance, so that men did not
willingly come into his presence, nor was there any
woman who would lie with him.

One day when the blemished prince sat alone in
his house, his servants came and said, "A man has
come who desires speech with you; but he is a base
man, neither craftsman nor singer, so we would not
admit him without knowing your will."

"This is a marvel!" said Bladud. "Make him
welcome, for I am eager to see a man who is eager to
see me." The man came in, and he was a churl
without beauty or bearing, and a bitch of no breed
was at his side. Nevertheless he seemed fair and
gracious to Bladud, because he came willingly into
his presence and showed neither fear nor disgust at
the sight of him. He greeted the churl courteously,
and asked where was his home and what brought
him to that place.

"I am a man of Cornwall," he answered, "and I
made this journey to see you, because I have good
news for you."

"For good news I should be grateful," said
Bladud; but he was puzzled at the man.

"See my bitch that I have brought to show you,"
said the man. "Is she not a fine bitch?"

Bladud looked at the cur and was perplexed for
a courteous answer; for though she was strong, bright-
eyed and white-toothed, there was not a good point
to her. She was lopeared, crook-legged, long-jawed,
swaybacked, rough-coated, and her tail was as knotted as a worm-cast. He said at last, "Indeed she
cannot have her match in the Island."

The man was pleased by that answer, and he
said, "Lord, you would not have said so had you seen
her a month ago. Then she was a sorry sight. Lame
of two of her legs, dull of eye, and so eaten with the
mange there was not a thumb's breadth of hair on

her anywhere; and she had been so from a pup. That was my bitch, and now she is as you see her. Since she has been cured, why not you?"

"This man is not a flatterer," said Bladud to himself. "In all the comparisons the bards were wont to make for me, they never compared me to a mangy bitch." Yet he was touched that the man should make a journey to offer him comfort. He said, "Friend, I rejoice in your good fortune and I thank you for your consolation. But this affliction was given me by one of the Mighty Ones, and no art of medicine or magic has sufficed to cure it."

"You have not yet heard how her cure came; will you hear it?"

"Tell me of it."

"I was walking on a hill called Badon, and my dog behind me, when a hare ran across our path. My dog chased her, though she was slow-footed, and she would not come back to me. She followed the hare, and I pursued her, and I found her in a great pool of mud, and it was hot to the touch. She was altogether covered in the mud, not a hair of her but was loaded with it. When she came out of it she drank at a spring by the pool. Then I cleaned the mud off her; and when it was washed off, I saw her as you see her now. So if the pool healed my bitch, why not you?"

At that, hope leapt in Bladud and he cried, "Take me to this place! For if the pool cleanses me in the same way, you will be a rich man that moment, and your bitch shall have a collar of rubies."

That same day Bladud set off with the man into the southwest of the Island, until they came to the place, and found the pool of steaming mud. Then Bladud cast off his shrouding, and went down into the hollow. He covered himself entirely with the mud, even to his hair and his eyelids, and it caked upon his leprous skin; then he washed himself clean of it in the outflow of a spring, and the spring was hot. And when he rose up he was clean and whole, and as comely a man as he had ever been.

Bladud exulted, and then he wept for gladness; and he robed himself in the good garments he had brought with him, and put his golden torc about his unblemished neck. After that he drank of another spring there, that was cold; and the taste of it was unlike the taste of any water he had drunk before. When he had drunk he perceived a woman sitting on a rock by the springs. She wore a white cloak over a scarlet tunic, and the nine braids of her shining hair were fastened to her head by nine golden combs. The whiteness of her brow and neck and arms was like the whiteness of a cloud with the sun shining through it. Tall and beautiful as she was, Bladud knew she could not be a mortal woman.

"Son of Hudibras," she said, "does that form please you more than the one which the Fair One gave you?"

"Great Lady, it does," he said. "It seems to me I have you to thank for my healing. That gift is too great to equal, but if there is any bidding you would set upon me, do so."

The goddess said to him, "Build me a shrine at this place in which an undying fire burns; also appoint priestesses of noble blood to tend the springs. If this is done I shall be a source of healing to the people of Britain for as long as the name of Sul is remembered." When she had spoken she vanished, and Bladud was left alone.

He returned swiftly to London and showed himself to his father, and the rejoicing of Rud Hudibras and the nobles and people of Britain was very great at his restoration. The churl was a rich man to the end of his life, and his bitch had a collar of gold and rubies. Bladud caused the shrine to be built near Badon as the goddess had commanded him, and there were priestesses of noble blood tending the healing springs and the perpetual fire. The name that place now bears is Aquae Sulis, the waters of Sul, and they are famed for giving health.

From that time there was no blemish on Bladud, and his place among the Princes was his again: and when his father died he became High King after him. But through all his life he never ceased from the search for knowledge or the practice of magic, and in his time there were many magicians among the people of Britain.

It was his magic at last that brought his death upon him, for there came a time when he determined to fly. So great was his skill that he was able to do so. He made himself wings, and fastened them to his arms, and by force of magic he rose into the air. He soared above London, and all the people of the city exclaimed in wonder at him; and Bladud beat his wings and turned in the sky above them, swooping down and mounting up again. But this deed of his displeased the Bright One, the Rider in the Sun. So as Bladud flew above the Temple of the Sun in London, suddenly the Bright One put out his long hand and struck him. Then his power was taken from him, and he fell upon the roof of the temple, so that his body burst in pieces, and he died.

he children made shuddering sounds of satisfaction, and some of the boys began to flap their arms, leaping up and down then falling on their backs with horrible cries. Gueneva said laughing, "Shame on you, Dumnoric, to ambush us with a bloody ending after all! Were there no Kings of Britain who died in their beds of old age?"

"Indeed there were." Solemnly, he began on a list. He was quickly interrupted.

"Well, but where are the stories?"

"Stories? But they died in their beds of old age! Is that a way to win fame?"

Most of them laughed, but Gueneva shivered. Then she brought back her smile, saying, "You tease me. There have been Kings who died famous and old."

"True, but they fought battles before that. You asked for a tale with no battles."

"I do not mind the end, but why were there no women in it?" said Antonia. "Tell us another, Dumnoric, and let it contain noble ladies."

"And let the King die old, in his bed," added Gueneva.

"Mercy! But you must have battles, then. You cannot deny me a battle."

"One, then. We will allow you one battle."

Dumnoric cocked his head and looked at the sky, musing, as he stroked soft music from his harp. "You wish to hear of noble women and a King who grew old. That will not be hard for me, though you think it hard. It seems to me that you are asking for the tale of *Leir and His Daughters*."

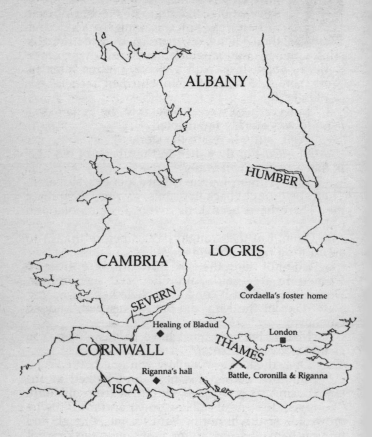

ALBANY

HUMBER

CAMBRIA

LOGRIS

SEVERN

♦ Cordaella's foster home

♦ Healing of Bladud

London

CORNWALL

THAMES

✕

♦ Riganna's hall

Battle, Coronilla & Riganna

ISCA

LEIR WAS THE SON of Bladud, and wore the crown of London after him. He used no magic, but he was a mighty King, and in his time Britain grew very wealthy. His court was of marvelous splendour, and there noble people sat upon silver couches and brocade cushions. Daily Leir feasted three hundred men of his warband; the least of the men in that hall drank from a cup of gold, and delicate balls of gold swung glinting from every braid of hair on each woman. Each night between Samhain and Beltain Leir heard a different story told before him, and no bard told a story twice, and each bard was of the first degree of bards.

Leir had no brothers to divide the inheritance with him, so for sixty years he ruled alone over the Island of the Mighty: and by reason of his wealth and his preeminence among the men of Britain he grew very proud. He had no sons, but when his hair was grey three daughters were born to him. Goronil and Riganna were the names of the elder two, and he loved them well; but his love for Cordaella the youngest was so great that he cared nothing for all the sweetness of the world beside.

When he was eighty years old he determined to make the division of the Island between them: but he was not willing that Cordaella should receive no more than her sisters. Therefore he resolved to put them to the test of declaring their love for him before the assembly of the noble people of Britain. This he did to please his pride, but also so that he should find a pretext for giving Cordaella most; he did not doubt that the love she bore him would make her more eloquent than her sisters.

Accordingly he made a great feast, and if the gatherings that had been held in that hall before were splendid, three times as splendid was this gathering. Treasure of gold and bronze glittered in the firelight, nor was there any lack of fine raiment among the nobles and bards and craftsmen assembled about

the hoary-headed, handsome King. In the middle of
the feast Leir called on his daughters to declare before the people how they loved him; "For," he said,
"she who loves most, most does she deserve."

First Goronil rose, a dark-haired majestic woman,
and she said, "To speak my love, that is not a hard
thing, for my heart is so full it spills out at my lips. I
count it honour to tell before this assembly how by
summer and winter, in waking or sleeping, my con-
stant thought is of the love I bear my father."

Turning, she addressed him directly and earnestly. "The swallow who returns each summer to
her nest is not more faithful than is my heart to you,
and as the salmon seeks the place of its spawning so
does my love return to you, my father. Sweeter than
the light of the sun or the air of morning is the
thought of you to me, and you are dearer to me than
the life of my soul."

"Now that is well spoken, and well shall it be
rewarded," said Leir approvingly; and he alloted
Albany to Goronil, and called her its Queen.

Then yellow-haired Riganna spoke: soft and tender was her voice, but more tender the look she bent
on her father. "Though I delight in the sight of the
noble people of Britain, more delight have I in looking on my father. Though fair are the green woods
and the bright hillsides, and sweet it is to behold
them, it is more sweet to behold my father. I would
sooner be at his side than sharing the sport of the
gaily dressed maidens. I would sooner hear him
speak, than to listen to harps and the singing of
bards, though Belgabred himself sang among them.
Two sisters I have, and I love them well, but I love
my father more. Though dear to me is the sweet-
heart who comes wooing, dearer than all the wooers
of the world are you to me, my father."

"That is kindly said, and kindness shall it have,"
said Leir, and he gave Riganna Cornwall for her
portion. But Logris and Cambria he kept for Cordaella;
and his elder daughters took note of that.

Then Leir bade Cordaella speak, but she, seeing his folly and understanding his purpose, for shame would have avoided it. She sat upon her silver couch and said lightly, "If coronets are to be given for golden words, my father, you must bestow them upon the bards; for I have no such skill."

Yet Leir would not be satisfied but insisted that she speak. "For," he said, "eloquence is fitting to those of noble blood."

Then the slim auburn-haired girl stood forth and spoke: "It is fitting to give honour to noble men. Also it is natural for parents and children to love each other. You are my father, and a most kind father have you been to me; and as is fitting, so I love you."

Now Leir's anger began to kindle. He said sternly, "By the Three Rivers of Britain, that is coldly spoken! I looked for bounty from my daughter, but it is the speech of a niggard I hear from her!"

Cordaella's pride was not less than his, and at this insult she grew angry and turned on him. "Am I your daughter, and do you ask me to perform the antics of a buffoon before you? My heart is not so light that I can make this kitten's play with it. We do not hear fine speech here, but the bawling of market women; a disgrace would it be to me, to have such a skill! Falsehood in a King's house brings destruction upon it. This is unworthy of you, my father, and shame and not honour will it bring you! But if what I have spoken is not pleasing to you, then I will say this: by as much as you have, so much are you dear to me, and I love you to the measure of your wealth. For Kings, you will learn, are worth what they have to bestow!"

When he heard that a great rage possessed Leir. His face became swollen and dark, the locks of his hair rose away from his head, his eyes bulged out of their sockets, and he trembled all over. He would have struck Cordaella, but the bards ran between them to prevent that dishonour.

Then the King cried out, "My reproach upon your mother, you are no daughter of mine! The blood of Brutus is not in you, and that golden torc is shamed by the neck that wears it. Cast out the foul unnatural hag, and let no one make her way pleasant, but let curses and pelting be her farewell! No inheritance shall she have of me except the violent death that I shall give her if ever I look upon her again. If any man would have her for his wife, let him know this: her dowry is my curse, and the man who takes her to his hearth, him will I account my enemy!"

All in the room were still. In the silence only the King's harsh breathing could be heard. Father and daughter stood a long moment in challenge, eye to eye, pride to pride, anger to anger. Then Cordaella moved. She said no word but tore the golden torc from about her neck and hurled it down. As it rang on the floor, she swept out of her father's hall, and she took nothing with her but the clothes she wore.

When she had been gone a while Leir's frenzy abated, and he wept. Now he cried out, "Alas for the sorrow that is come upon me! No daughter was ever so dear to her father as was that girl to me, and for her sake I would have wronged her sisters! May the hard-hearted wretch have the Fate that she deserves!"

Cordaella's foster parents had not been at the feast, because of a bond that was upon all of their house, that on certain days in every year they should not leave it; and the feast had been held on such a day. When Cordaella left her father's court she considered what to do and determined to go to her foster home though there was no way of going but by walking, and she would be some days upon the road. She lived on food left for her by kindly villagers while never catching a glimpse of any of them because of the curse on her.

But the news of the bitter wrong that had been done to her travelled faster than she, and her foster father, Maglocun, set out to seek her, and so did his sons. He found her quickly enough, seeing her from a long way off walking proud and weary. When they were come together he saw that she was dusty, with the shoes worn from her feet and his anger with Leir grew even as he held her tenderly. He took her into his chariot, scolding gently, "Child, you are not shod for the road. Is it fitting for the daughter of a High King to go about in this way?"

She answered, "I am not the daughter of the High King, but a woman without a home. Take me under your roof again, for if there is no place for me at your hearth there is none in Britain."

He shook his head. "My dear, a blessing is on the roof that shelters you. Where you were nurtured, there is your home."

Then he took Cordaella home where her foster mother embraced and clucked and fussed over her, exclaiming, "How is this? My little one all dirty and tired: come now, you need fresh clothes and a dry, clean bed and warm wine to hearten you. . . ."

But she interrupted their warmhearted fussing, much as she longed for it, and said, "Yet the anger of the King may be roused against you for my sake."

"Yes, yes! I will take note of that," said Maglocun, but he seemed unimpressed. So they took her to their hearth, and that night she slept upon down under a brocade coverlet; but her presence in the house they kept secret.

On a day Maglocun said to her, "Daughter, I will seek a worthy man to be your husband."

"Alas!" said Cordaella, "that will not be easy."

"Nor will it be hard, my dear."

"But I fear it will indeed be hard, for I have no lands or cattle for my dowry. I will bring to my husband neither raiment nor jewels, neither household vessels nor store of linen, but only the enmity of my father and the curse he gave me. Since he who is my husband will have the High King for his enemy, what man of Britain will take me to his hearth?"

Her foster father smiled on her fondly and shook his head. "Yet though you think it will be hard to find a worthy man, it will not be hard," he said, and he embraced her.

Then the good man left his lands and cattle to the care of his sons and journeyed into Gaul. He journeyed all about that land, and was a guest in many houses; and wherever noble men were praised he heard one name praised above all others. That was a King called Agannipus, and he was commended for his wisdom and generosity, for his valour and beauty, above all the people of Gaul.

Cordaella's foster father went to his hall and was made welcome there. He saw Agannipus had not been praised beyond his deserving, for he was comely in his person, with hair brighter than red-gold, eloquent and courteous to his company. He sat Maglocun at his side and they conversed together all that evening, and the wit of Agannipus was as pleasing as his beauty.

Late in the evening, comfortable with good wine and courtesy, Maglocun said, "I marvel that so excellent and noble a man as yourself should have no wife."

"That is a grief to me," replied Agannipus, "but I have not found a maiden in Gaul to love."

"There is a maiden in Britain of whom I would speak to you. She is like the birch tree for height and slenderness and grace, and the sweetness of her aspect is like a summer morning. Her hair is bright as scoured bronze, her skin is like the foam of the wave. The locks of her hair curl like young fern fronds, and to see the small tresses of it on her white brow, that is the fairest sight I know. Yet better than her beauty is her dignity, the lightness of her touch and of her walk, and the sweetness of her voice. If a man has heard her speak, birdsong will not sound so melodious to him after that."

"It is a fair woman you describe," said Agannipus, "yet wisdom is as needful for a queen as beauty."

"Indeed she is wise. There is in the Island of the Mighty none more excellent in counsel than she is, nor is it easy to deceive her. She is just in judgment, nor is it easy to deceive her."

"It is good to be fair and wise, but better to be generous."

"That quality she has also. The cauldron of the Good God is not more bounteous than the lady of whom I speak."

Agannipus laughed and said, "It is a very paragon you describe—unless courage is lacking in her?"

"No, no! Not so. If she has a fault it is that her courage outweighs her prudence. She is valiant as befits a Queen, and it is not easy to overawe her. She can ride in a war-chariot and harness the horses to it; she can cast a spear and wield a sword, and she is not one who shrinks from the place where blades are dented and shields broken."

"By my head," said Agannipus, amused, "the woman of whom you speak has every excellent quality."

"She has! She has!" By now Maglocun was in full spate. "And she has another quality I have not told of, that there is no falsehood in her, none whatever. . . ."

"If that were not so, it would mar her excellence," said the king gravely but with a merry eye. Yet though he smiled, his heart stirred at Maglocun's words. "I would suppose that the noble men of Britain are vying together to have her for a wife?"

"They are not."

"Why should that be so?"

"It may be that she will bring no cattle to her husband, nor jewels, nor raiment, nor household vessels, nor store of linen."

"Are the men of Britain merchants? With such a woman, who would want a dowry? But perhaps she

is not well born and that is why they do not seek
her?"

"Indeed, she is of noble birth." Maglocun paused
and turned his cup; then he said quietly, "Her father
is the High King of Britain."

When Agannipus heard that, he was confounded
and did not speak. Then Cordaella's foster father
told all that had happened, and when the young
King heard how she had been unjustly disinherited,
he was angry at it. "By my head," he said, "wicked
shame it is that one of her rank should have been
treated so. And shame it would be to me if I did not
save so noble a lady. Tell me, how may I see her? If
you can bring me to her, do so!"

"I can do so and gladly I will," said Maglocun,
and rejoiced in his heart. So there was cordial agree-
ment between the two men and presently they set
forth together and crossed the Narrow Seas.

When they came to Britain they did not turn
aside to be any man's guest but went directly to
Cordaella's foster home. When she saw the Gaulish
King, and his splendour like gorse upon a hillside,
the colour of the foxglove came into her cheeks and
her heart grew warm. Agannipus looked upon her
glowing beauty and was instantly filled with love of
her, marvelling that such loveliness could be real. So
they two stood wordless, gazing one upon the other,
until the good wife came bustling in chattering of
this and that.

Then Agannipus moved to Cordaella. "By my
head," he said, "I did not hear you praised falsely."
He put out his hands, and she took them, and their
eyes held fast together. He said in a low voice, "I
swear by the gods my people swear by, now that I
have seen you, if you are not willing to be my wife
I shall have no other."

She answered him formally, "If you were to be
my husband, I would think a happy Fate and not a
sad one was mine."

Tentatively he reached up and cupped her face,

amazed and delighted that so fragile a proving was
held between his hands. Wordless, breath held, she
gazed at him with great shining eyes. And at last
they embraced. Maglocun and his wife exulted together at his success. So it was settled between them
that they should be married, and the feast was made
for them without delay, and after the feast they slept
together.

Then Agannipus returned with his bride to Gaul;
but he sent a message to Leir, and he said, "Agannipus of Gaul greets Leir of Britain: the heifer you
turned astray I have taken, and if I am your enemy
for this cattle-raid, then I am gladly your enemy."
When Leir received this message he was angry, but
he said nothing of it, nor did he seek to pursue
Agannipus; and it was not known to any but those
few where she was gone.

King Leir turned again to the rule of Britain, but
his joy in it was gone, and his kingship was less
skillful than it had been formerly. And this was so
although he had no more than half the Island to
govern, for Goronil ruled over Albany and Riganna
over Cornwall.

When his two daughters perceived how careless
of his governance the King had become they met
together and came to Leir. They greeted him lovingly; Goronil clasped his hands while Riganna hung
about his neck, and they said, "Dear father, do not
sorrow any longer for your unworthy daughter. We
grieve to see you take no more delight in song and
feasting and in noble company, nor in any of the
things that delighted you before this. Though we
have lost a sister, our grief does not overpower us
while we have you; alas, that our love is not a
comfort to you."

The heart of Leir was touched at that, and he
said, "It is not such grief I feel; but it is not an easy
thing to govern Britain, and that causes the weariness you see."

Then Goronil said, "For sixty years you have

been the roof over the people of Britain and the door
for their protection, and are all the years of your life
to be spent in such labour? We would be glad to take
this burden from you, so that you might spend your
time in pleasure and comfort."

"How might that be done?"

"Divide the realms you govern between us,"
urged Riganna, "and let us have the care of them."

"But that is a thing not known before, that the
High King of the Island should forego his place in
his life, unless force compelled him."

And they replied, "What High King before you
has ruled so long, or worn his crown in such venerable age?"

Leir considered on what they proposed, and
presently he said, "It would not be easy for me to
diminish the honour and the splendour of my life."

Goronil quickly protested, "It would not be necessary for you to do so. You would keep your warband
and your bards, and noble men would resort to
you, and your provision would not be less than
it is now." And they reasoned with him gently,
they beseeched him sweetly, they persuaded him
very lovingly; and Leir consented to do as they asked.

Then Leir gave Cambria to Riganna, and Logris
and the Crown of London he bestowed upon Goronil,
and after that he took no part in the rule of the
Island. He passed his time in hunting and watching
sports and in boardgames, in hearing the bards and
conversing with friends. And he found much pleasure with them so that the sadness of his heart was
lessened. The splendour of his state was not diminished, for every day he feasted three hundred men
of his warband.

At the end of a year Leir said to Goronil, "I will
take my bards and my warriors and my servants and
go into Cornwall to lodge a while with Riganna."

The Queen replied, "That is fitting, for it is right
that my sister should have your company, and Corn-

wall the honour of your presence, and other lands the maintenance of your household."

Riganna sent word that she would be glad of his coming; but she asked that Leir should bring not all of his warband but two hundred only, since her guest-halls were not spacious enough for so large a household as his.

Leir readily agreed to this. He went to Cornwall, and with his bards, his servants and warriors, the charioteers and the shield-bearers, they were a great host. He stayed a year with Riganna and then returned to London. But when he came back, the hundred men of his warband that he had left behind were not to be found, and for all his asking he could get no explanation of it.

"By my head," he remarked, "they did not diminish so fast when I led them in battle!"

Then Leir lived as formerly in Goronil's court, only that his warband was less great than was customary for a King. Goronil said secretly to some of her warriors, "It would not displease me if quarrels arose between you and my father's warriors," and soon there was much strife between the two warbands.

Goronil came to her father and said, "Alas, Lord, I am afraid for the peace of my house." And when her father asked the cause of her concern, she went on, "There is strife between the young warriors who serve the two of us; it is no pleasure to say it, but the young men of your band have sought quarrels with my warriors."

Leir was angry and said, "This came without my knowledge, and I will punish them for it."

"No, no! Do not do so," she said, "for they have not much deserved your anger. Consider, my father, that when young men are idle they are apt to quarrel; if you were leading them to battle it would not be so. I would not have them punished, if we can find a way to avoid strife."

"That is gently spoken," said Leir. "What would your counsel be?"

"Perhaps we should no longer maintain these young men in your warband. For young men desire the praise of their deeds and they will be ill content to follow one who by reason of his age will not lead them to battle; and the grandfathers of these men were warriors at your side. It would be better for you to keep about you only men who have won renown; and men who are older will be fitter for your conversation so that you will have more pleasure in their company."

Leir did not much like that, but he was persuaded by her. Also he was ashamed that disorder should come about because of his warband, for he put the cause on his great age. Yet though he was less mighty than in his youth, King Leir was not feeble, and he was a big man and well made.

After that a rivalry arose between the bards who served Leir and those who served the Queen's household. The bards of Goronil abused the Chief Bards of Leir and called them household bards and said they should leave being praise singers and sing only soothing songs in gentle voices; they mocked his household bards because of the small number of the warband there was to entertain, and the lack of noble women. The Chief Bard of Leir was no longer called Head of Song, and the foremost place he had enjoyed was taken by another. Leir protested at that; but Goronil answered that it was not for her to judge between bards, and that surely the Head of Song must be the foremost bard of those who praised the one who wore the Crown of the Island of the Mighty. The bards were less willing to serve Leir after that, for there was less honour in it, but many of them made their songs to Goronil, because she was Head of the Island.

From that time Leir found that the courtesy and honour given to him diminished, and Goronil began to reason with him to keep fewer attendants about him, and her speech was less gentle. But Leir refused to lessen the dignity of his household, and a quarrel arose between them because of it, so that Leir resolved to go to Riganna; for he expected more kindness from her.

He took his household and went to Cornwall, and it was a smaller host than had gone that way before; it was not easy to know the rank of him who led them. But the welcome he got from Riganna was less generous than he had hoped, for she asked that he should bring none of his servants into her house, and no more than half of his warband; she said it was not easy for her to maintain so many men, and also she was afraid to receive a hundred armed men into her house. "For," she said, "I have heard they were riotous at my sister's court."

The journey had been long, and King Leir felt old and weary; now this welcome chilled his heart and made it heavier than anger could do. He said bitterly, "When I was its King, Cornwall was not so poor nor so timid."

"Nevertheless," his daughter insisted, "unless you agree to this I cannot receive you into my house; and you shall be well enough attended by my own servants."

Leir thought of the long road, and of the fire and beds within; but he thought also of the shame of turning away those who followed him. He cried, "Is this the promise you gave me, that I should not be asked to diminish my dignity? I will return to Goronil, for though she is discourteous, she is neither coward nor niggard!" Riganna would never forgive him for that word. He turned angrily from her and went back the way he had come, with his household behind him, and he had no rest between his going and his return.

He told Goronil of Riganna's words, and Goronil said, "My sister speaks prudently. It would indeed be better for you to dismiss all your attendants and the men of your warband also."

"It is not at all clear to *me* that it would be better for me to do so."

"Nevertheless," Goronil said harshly, "it is clear to me!"

Then an ugly quarrel arose, and being full of weariness, the end of it was that Leir kept no servants to wait upon him, and no more than fifty warriors to honour him, and few bards. After a short while Goronil bade him dismiss even those fifty warriors for she said that she would not have warriors who did not serve her in her house, but only those she maintained herself.

"Also," she pointed out, "these warriors are few and old and no defence is to be had from them. And my father cannot be ill defended in my house. Nor is there honour in having such a warband but mockery rather."

"It was a better warband that I had at the beginning," Leir said, "also it is the right of a King to have a warband, and the number of it should be three hundred."

Then indeed Goronil looked coldly on him; the eye of the viper would be kinder than her eye. She said, "It is not the right of any man to lead warriors who cannot maintain them. What cattle and wealth have you, to make provision for them? Can you feast them on fresh pork and put wine in their cups? It is I who have maintained these men, and I will do so no longer."

Now Leir was reduced to pleading with her, but she would not relent; and at last he asked for one attendant only, for he said that a King should not be without a bard to entertain him. Goronil consented to maintain a bard for him, if he could find one who was willing to serve him. Leir was hard put to find such a bard; there was only one who was faithful to him, and that of the lowest rank of bards, for he was a buffoon.

After that the courtesy with which King Leir was treated diminished daily. When the pig was

carved at feasts the King's portion was not given to
him, and seldom was there wine in his cup, nor was
new raiment easy for him to obtain. His company
was not sought by noble men, and to be among
them was only to be bitterly reminded that he had
once been foremost among them. The only companionship he had was that of the buffoon. Yet though
the man was loyal and a good servant it was neither
fitting for a High King nor could the man serve to
divert Leir for long.

Then he began to observe what manner of ruler
Goronil was for the Island of the Mighty, and he
saw that she was the worst that could be found. She
was as false as she was harsh: a good judgment was
not to be had from her, nor was she wise in counsel
or generous in patronage; and when strife arose
between Kings who were subject to her, she delighted
to make it worse than it might have been.

Leir was sitting in his lodging with his buffoon,
his feet in the ashes, and he cried, "The state of
Britain is worse than my state, and shame on me
that gave the Island to such women! When my daughters were weak I cherished them; now I am weak
they despise me and cast me away from them. When
what is now theirs was mine, I shared it freely, they
lived in splendour, fine raiment was theirs; now that
what was mine is theirs, they give to me grudgingly.
If I did not beg I should have nothing! Sixty years I
was King of this Island; now I have no honour for it.
No bard sings of it. Three things are needful for
kingship: leadership in war, judgment, hospitality.
When I gave them away I did not know what I did.
When I had all these things my daughters were
loving to me. Now Goronil is a wolf, and Riganna a
kite. The children that they bear, may they devour
their mothers as they have devoured me, may they
make their old age bitter, and may they live long to
suffer it! When I was young, when I was a King, I
had pleasure in life; it would be better to have died
before this."

When he ended his lament he bowed his head on his hands and covered his knees with his breast. The good-hearted buffoon watched him in silence for a while, then he mused, "Though two cows are dry, why should not the third give milk?"

"What is your meaning?" Leir grunted.

"When you were a King you had three daughters; when you sent your youngest from you, you sent your luck with her."

"Alas, that is true. More," and the old man stabbed his buffoon in the chest with a gnarled finger, "it was truth she told me when she said that I should find a King was worth what he had to bestow."

Now the buffoon became a little bolder. "You have thrown away the wheat and kept the husk. If you knew where your youngest daughter was to be found, I would counsel you to go to her and seek your comfort there."

"Well, as to that, I know where she is to be found. But why should she be kinder to me than her sisters considering how I have wronged her? And if I do go to her and she will not maintain me, I shall be shamed before the noble people of Gaul."

"Then your state will be no worse than it is, and it is better to be shamed before the people of Gaul than before the people of Britain."

The King looked keenly at his companion. "In the days when I was High King of the Island of the Mighty, I would not have believed this, that I should take counsel of a buffoon!"

"Yet it is good counsel for all that," his man responded calmly, and he added, "those who have no horses must go by foot."

A sudden smile lit the tired visage of the old King, and the buffoon rejoiced to see it. His master said, "Lucky am I, that even Britain's buffoons possess such wisdom. . . ."

Yet for a while still shame kept him from seeking Cordaella. Only when the manner of Goronil to him had grown more contemptuous than he could bear did he feel that even death in a strange land would seem better than the slights he endured of her.

Then he left her court, and the buffoon went with him, and they crossed into Gaul; nor did any on the ship know him for his apparel was miserable and his attendance meager. They went through Gaul to the kingdom of Agannipus, but when they came near to his hall, King Leir was weak with weariness and his heart began to fail him. Therefore the buffoon found a lodging for him, and left him in it, and after that he went to the hall.

Since he was a bard he was not hindered and he came into Cordaella's presence where she sat with her ladies, and greeted her. She said at once, "By your speech you are a man of Britain."

He bowed. "Lady, I am; and that is why I desired speech with you."

"Tell me then, how is it with the Island of the Mighty and its noble people and my father, King Leir?"

The buffoon told her, "It is ill with the Island, and worse with its people. But worst of all for your father, King Leir."

Cordaella rose in dismay. "Why? What is amiss? What has befallen my father?"

Then the buffoon told her all the story, and it was hard for her to know which was greater, her anger with her sisters, her sorrow for her father, or her joy that he was come there. She went straightaway with the buffoon to where her father was, and when they met together she clasped him in her arms and wept, and Leir wept also. He said to her, "The wrong I did you is a shame to me; and the sorrow I have had, it is not worse than was fitting for my fault."

But she only said, "Let it be forgotten, and never spoken of again between us. Now," she went on, "you must remain here one more day, and I will

send you provision, for it will be better for your
dignity if you do not appear before Agannipus until
you are rested and may do so as a King." Seeing
how gently thoughtful she was both of his comfort
and his pride, Leir wept again, but for gladness; and
after his heart was light and he held up his head
proudly; all the bitterness and humiliation he had
suffered slipped from him like a discarded cloak.

Cordaella sent servants to him with rich garments and ornaments, and attendants to wait on
him properly; and when he was fitly clad, and his
hair like fine silver was dressed and there were royal
ornaments about him, the dignity and majesty of
King Leir were not less than they had ever been.
Then he went to the hall of Agannipus, and the
buffoon he took in the chariot at his side.

When he came to the court he was received
with courtesy and richly lodged and Agannipus welcomed him and sat him at his side. The portion that
was carved for Agannipus he gave to Leir. Seeing
this honour Leir said to him, "You welcome me
according to your excellence and not my own; for
the wrong that I did Cordaella, though she has for-
given it, it is hard for you to do so."

But Agannipus replied, "It is not so hard as you
think, for if it had not been for that wrong I would
not have had her for my wife."

"That is true," said Cordaella, "and it is a better
thing for me to be the wife of Agannipus than to be
Queen of Britain." So Leir was reconciled with them,
and forgot his grief. There was much merriment that
night: long they sat by the fire, discussing old times
and old joys, and the buffoon sat at Leir's feet.
Cordaella rejoiced to see how fast friendship grew
between her husband and her father.

In that house Leir's strength came back to him.
His spirit was rekindled and he remembered his
wrath against Goronil and Riganna. It seemed bad to
him that they should govern Britain so ill, and worse
that they should have what was Cordaella's. So he

said to Agannipus, "Though it is a better thing for
my daughter to be your wife than Queen of Britain,
it would be a better thing yet for her to rule over the
Island of the Mighty and to do that with you at her
side."

Agannipus replied, "How could that be?"

"An equal share of the Island is hers, according
to the law of the Britons; and it would be right for
her to claim that share, if she could do it with an
army. Also," and his face grew dark, "she is wor-
thier than Goronil to wear the Crown of London."

They took counsel with Cordaella, and Agannipus
asked her directly, "Is Britain cause enough for war
between you and your sisters?"

She answered, "I have the harm to Britain and
the wrongs to my father to avenge upon them; that
is cause enough. Let us lead an army against them.
But I shall not wear the Crown of London, for it is
the right of my father to do that in his life, though I
shall wear it after his days."

Then they summoned their warbands and raised
a great host of the people of Gaul and led it out.
King Leir went at the head of the host, and when he
was armed with his helmet and his three-bossed
shield and his great spears, he appeared so noble
and mighty that the young men contested together
to fight at his side. The great army crossed into
Britain and sent out challenges to the two Queens,
and the bards that were with them went about singing mockery upon Goronil and Riganna. When it
was known that King Leir had returned with Cordaella and a great host, the noble people of the
Island gathered to them, and among them was the
foster father of Cordaella. When they met together
there was great joy between them, and Agannipus
embraced him also; and Leir said to Maglocun, "You
shall be a greater man in Britain than you have been,
for the sake of the generosity you showed my
daughter."

Goronil and Riganna were dismayed, but they

summoned their warbands and the hosts they could
muster, and they came together to take counsel.
Riganna said, "It would have been better if our father had not been allowed to leave Britain."

But Goronil replied, "I will not bear the reproach for that, for it could not be foreseen that
Cordaella would succor him, seeing the slight he put
upon her. Nor is this a time for reproaches for it is
needful to do battle with them."

However, they saw that their host was sullen
and displeased, while the host of Leir was fierce and
high-spirited and eager for battle.

Riganna said, "It would be better for you to lead
the host, for you have the greater skill in battle.
Therefore I will send the men that are with me with
your host, but myself will remain here."

With a hard mouth Goronil replied, "No, my
sister. Though I shall lead the host, it will not be
better for you to remain behind. We will both go to
the battle. Therefore arm yourself and ride with your
chariot at the side of mine." After that they set out.

When the two hosts met together Riganna gave
her enemies no defiance, but Goronil rode out between the hosts and taunted them with bitter language, and called Leir mocking names; and when
she turned across before the host she turned the left
side of her chariot to them. At that insult Leir gave
the command. The carynxes blew and the two hosts
fell upon each other. Then there was hacking and
smiting; heads were broken and limbs hewn off,
there was neighing and trampling of horses, and the
bitter cries of men meeting violent death. There was
blood on the bright grass and the dust of the battle
made a darkness about them, and the kites that
waited above them were so many that no sun could
reach them, but they fought in shadow. The host of
Leir had the victory and Goronil and Riganna were
slain. After the battle they piled the heads of the
slain into two heaps, and it was a great number; and

upon the top of one heap was the head of Goronil, and the head of Riganna on the other.

After that King Leir wore the Crown of London again, and ruled over the Island of the Mighty, nor was it wearisome for him to do so, but he ruled with splendour and justice for ten years, and then he died. Cordaella buried him in a rich tomb; and after that she was Queen of the Island of the Mighty.

UMNORIC let the notes fade away, then looked merrily at the Queen and her hostess. "Was that King old enough? And were there enough noble ladies to content you?"

"Noble! I would not call them all that; but we will content ourselves with Cordaella."

"What happened to the buffoon?" asked one of the children. "Did he stay friends with the King, and did he live a long time?"

"Why, he lives still, and always as Leir's companion. He is part of the story, and people who are in stories do not die so long as the stories are told."

"Let my name be forgotten then," said Gueneva. "The way into a story is too hard for me."

"Those old warrior Queens!" said Antonià. "They made sure of being remembered. Who has forgotten Boudicca?"

"In Camalod she is remembered, sure enough," said the Queen. There was no laughter in her voice. After London, the court would go to Camalod, and that old often-sacked city always oppressed her. There were parts of it where ruins still covered unburied dead, and for her the ghosts Boudicca had made had not ceased to haunt the streets. She said with an effort, "Well, Arthur's name is sure enough of living, then. Will there be stories of him, Dumnoric?"

"Surely; if any are left to tell them, or to hear them. . . ."

For a bard, it was a tactless remark. But before the silence grew long, Antonia's little boys leapt to their feet and ran back into the water, shouting and pointing at the river. "Ships from Gaul! Ships from Gaul!"

The adults turned to see. Large vessels were coming up Tamessa, sails furled, moving backs of oars winking. The old port had begun to thrive again, since the truce with the Kentish Saxons had made the seaways safe. Antonia said, "I do believe they are right for once."

"Gaulish traders!" The brilliance came back to

Gueneva. "Cloth for summer dresses! Perfume and silk! Oh, how long do they take to unload? Where can we see what they bring, Antonia?" She stood up, sparkling with delight. "Come, we've plenty of occupation now!"

NOTHING is so symbolic of ancient Britain and its people as the druids: so it is galling to have to admit that we know very little about them. The descriptions of classical writers were coloured by their own philosophies and prejudices, and in the case of the Romans sometimes by propaganda. Some mentions survive in Irish stories, but these were recorded by Christian monks whose tolerance, though wide, was not limitless. So our reliable information is scanty.

Certainly druids were men of the learned class which included the bards, and were "men of art" who ranked as high as nobles. Almost as certainly they were priests, although we should not understand that word in a Christian sense. Caesar says that they officiated at the sacrifices, and that they were seers and judges in disputes: these two last are clearly confirmed by Irish stories. The word "drui" ("druid" is the plural) could be derived from the word for oak tree, or the word for knowledge, or both. Wise Men is the safest translation—and the Greeks compared them to the Persian Magi. The link with the oak agrees with the story that they held their rites and kept their schools in oak groves; we know that forest clearings were sacred places to the Celts, and druidlike wise men such as Merlin were associated with forests long after Roman times. Some authorities, however, point out that Irish druids (like Cathbad and Curoi) lived like other men, and suggest that the oak woods may have been a refuge from Roman persecution rather than always their haunts. But the widespread existence of placenames with "nemed"—sacred forest or grove—is against this; perhaps Ireland was merely short of such forests! In Gaul and Britain the Romans persecuted the druids to extermination, for they embodied that part of Celtic life which could not be accommodated by the Empire. Rome could come to terms with the warrior nobles, but not with the druids; an early example of dissident intellectuals.

Their learning was certainly prodigious, although the fabled twenty-year training may be an exaggeration. Some of it we know they imparted to outsiders, for the sons of nobles were taught by druids, but no doubt much was kept within their order. Like bards they were guardians of the law and of the history of their people, and had practical learning also—we are told of their medical skill, and they calculated the calendar; no easy task then. Greek writers identified druids with their legend of the virtuous Hyperboreans, and idealised them as the philosopher-rulers of their people; they even linked them with Pythagoras. This may have been because the Celtic belief in the immortality of the soul could only be understood by the classical world in terms of rebirth—they could not grasp the idea of a life continued in another world.

On the whole it seems that the Celts kept the secrets of their priests as successfully as they kept other secrets of their religion. Two things are certain. One is that druids held a very important place in Celtic society. The other is that they had nothing to do with Stonehenge. The idea that they built it is, in fact, less than three hundred years old. Perhaps the druids made use of these relics of a much older people, but it is likely that the stone circles were as much of a puzzle to them as they are to us.

Yet even shorn of his long white robe, his flowing beard, his golden diadem, the druid remains himself. For the Celts, a figure of power; and for us, of mystery.

A LONG LIFETIME had passed since the great general Coel the Old had commanded the Army of the North, but his fame lived. Old ways were returning faster there, in a region always governed by generals and not magistrates, among a people whose chief pride was in their valour and the prowess of their leaders. Coel's province had begun to break into smaller states, but the men who ruled them still called themselves his heirs. They called themselves Kings, too, in Arthur's day. That was not uncommon; rulers in Venedotia and Demetia had also begun to use such titles. But the foremost of the Princes of the North was the one man in Britain who could invest his title with the authority of the Dux Brittaniarum; the General of the Britons. In Eboracum there was a King who could challenge Arthur's supremacy.

Strife between rivals had too often weakened Britain, and the Emperor was not willing to risk that; but neither was he willing to forego his authority. So although the victory of Lindum made contact between the two rulers possible, neither made haste. Cautious courtesy marked their first exchanges, and when, three full years after Lindum, Arthur went north to meet the heir of Coel, the warmth of their greetings was matched by watchfulness.

In his letter the General had called himself Marcus, but he was March among his own people. A man some years older than Arthur, swarthy and curly (not all the legions stationed on the Wall had been British), he had the manner of a Roman commander—matter-of-fact, without dash—rather than that of a Celt. But Arthur could see that his lack of glamour did not affect his hold on his people's loyalty. He had not seen many leaders followed with such devotion. Moreover, when they left Eboracum to see more of the North, it was plain that March's authority was accepted by all the lesser rulers. Nor was it hard to see why; but Arthur did not intend to let his personal liking weigh too much with him.

March was not the man to save Britain from the
Saxons.

They had hunted together over the wintry sunlit
hills, ridden in company to the stud farms, together
appraised the young men in training. Now their
journey had taken them nearly as far as the Wall.
When it came within sight they drew rein to gaze. It
was a windy glittering day, and the view was clear
for miles. Arthur had not seen the Wall before, and
he looked at it in silence; as things usually do, it
looked smaller than imagination had made it, and
less tidy, patched with repairs and cluttered with
little settlements.

But its length, climbing up and down hills from
sea to sea, was more impressive than he had expected, and its symbolism took stronger hold on
him, so that scanning it he presently said softly,
"The Wall!"

"The end of the Empire," said March. "Not that
it's important as a boundary these days, with even
the Votadini reliable allies on the other side. Up here,
whenever we curse the old Overking for sending us
Octha the Saxon, we remember he took Cunedag
from us, and stop."

Arthur laughed: he was not used to hearing
Vortigern, the old King, called anything but the Great
Traitor. "Did that balance the scales?"

"Very nearly!"

"In Venedotia they'd be shocked to hear it. They
bless Cunedag's coming; no more Irish occupation
there."

"Set a thief to catch a thief; though it didn't
work with Octha." He turned his horse's head more
into the wind, and pointed east. "There're still a few
Saxon villages there, though they're mostly farther
south now. But that was where they stationed Octha
and his army; to strengthen the eastern end of the
Wall. The Picts had come round by sea more than
once." Arthur nodded. March's voice was without
bitterness, as it had been when he showed the watch-

towers of the coast, built against the Picts fifty years
before, left by the Saxons as ruins full of British
bones. No southerner spoke so of the barbarians,
but March's people had no memory of sacked towns
and despoiled countryside, no ruined churches and
villages to remind them of the price of defeat.

Arthur looked back at the Wall. "How good to
have lived in the days when all our enemies were on
the other side of it, eh?"

March laughed shortly. "Well, since Lindum we
have the wolves in a kennel. All praise to you for it!"

"Praise is precious from the General of the un-
conquered North!"

March answered with the glint of a smile, "Such
words are good to raise morale or to rouse emulation, or from bards at a feast; but you know as well
as I that we might have fared no better than you, if
our lands had been as well worth taking."

"Well: that is to imagine another world. It's true
I'd rather have these hills to fight in than our rich
open farmland."

"Remember too, we aren't as burdened with
shopkeepers, lawyers, clerks, to defend; here, almost every man is a soldier." His face was wried
against sun and wind; it was hard to read his
expression.

Arthur only nodded, answering quietly, "Yet
when we do not have such people to defend, the
Saxons will have won."

The night before their return to Eboracum they
rested at March's own house, and there he and
Arthur sat in equal honour at a feast more British
than Roman. The singing over, Arthur said to his
host, "My story-teller had thought to tell you a tale
praising Cunedag since the North gave him to us;
but I said, 'No.' "

The General laughed. "Oh, such men are better
in tales. Sending him south was certainly one of
Vortigern's better ideas."

"How mildly you speak of him! In the South I

hardly dare suggest to anyone that perhaps he did not intend harm from the beginning."

Plenty curse him here. But he wasn't the first to employ federate troops. Besides, who was afraid of the Saxons before the Mutiny?"

"My people remember the forties, and no wonder; but they forget how unwilling they were to pay the taxes that should have paid the troops."

"It's only men like us who can pity him. Not all men have to think like Kings."

Gai and Bedvir exchanged glances, though men who knew Arthur less well would not have noticed his tension. He answered smiling, "And let us hope, not all Kings have to think like Vortigern."

March smiled broadly. "God grant they do not! But come, we grow too solemn for a feast. These wild nights after Samhain, we should be hearing stories; and here is Venogad waiting to entertain us."

The story-teller came forward, and seeing the look they exchanged Riderch raised his brows and glanced at Arthur. There was prearrangement here. The hall was quietening, but between these two men utter silence lay, and the Emperor watched them narrowly.

March said, "Tune your strings, Venogad; and let us hear you tell of *The Mighty Brothers*."

OROBUDIC was the eighteenth heir of Brutus in direct line, but after him that line was broken. For in his old age his two sons warred together, and one slew the other; then in her grief and rage the mother of them both resolved to be revenged on him who slew his brother, and with her own hands she killed her son. At that Corobudic's heart burst with sorrow, and he died before an heir to him was named.

Then began an evil time for Britain, for there was no man whose right to wear the Crown of London was better than another right, but all those gold-torqued Princes contended together for the kingship, and the Island was filled with slaughter from sea and sea. But the greatest Prince and warrior of his time was Dunvallo Malamud of Cornwall, so that in the end he had the victory and was exalted with the Crown of London.

Dunvallo Malamud was a greater High King than any that had been since the time of Brutus: he is one of the Three Pillars of the Island of the Mighty. He called together all the men of law, and with their counsel he formed rules that should prevail throughout Britain, regulating the laws, customs, maxims and privileges of the people, and establishing just relations between all men, between tribe and tribe, between King and neighbouring King. Under the protection of these laws equity and justice could be obtained by all in the Island of Britain, and they endure to this day. Because of that he is called Dunvallo the Lawgiver.

By his noble wife Tonuvenna he was the father of two sons, and they were born at one birth. All the time that they were in the womb they strove together, and Tonuvenna said, "There is a storm in my body that will be a peril to many; crows will follow these two." When her time came she was not delivered quickly; she cried out, "Two rivals are here, and neither is willing for the other to go before him." When they were born, one came gripping the ankle of the other; and they were alike even to their fingernails, so that they could not be told apart. Their parents named one Belinos, and the other Brennios.

Those brothers grew into fair children, into merry and active boys, strong and comely and quick to learn. Their father delighted in them, but their mother watched them with both pride and foreboding; for she saw that the contest they had begun in the womb was not ended. When they were children at play neither would yield in anything to the other, and in the Boy's House, whether they were learning a warrior's skills or at sports with their companions, each strove always to outdo his brother, and could not. As they were matched in form and feature, so were they in wit and prowess. For strength and daring, each had no rival but his brother. While there was honour enough for both each gloried in his brother's victories as in his own, but though their contentions were in sport Tonuvenna shook her head and warned her husband, "If these two should court the same girl, there would be a rough wooing."

When the boyhood of Belinos and Brennios was past and the time came for them to receive their weapons, they came together to their mother to be armed. When the two noble youths stood before her, like twin stags in their beauty and pride, she laughed aloud for her joy in them, saying proudly, "Did ever a woman bring forth two such Princes?"

Then with her own hands she armed them, with helmet and shield and sword, with long spears and throwing spears and the barbed spear. The arms of Belinos were inlaid with white bronze, and those of Brennios with red enamel. Then Tonuvenna said, "For the sake of this day I put a bidding on you both; that neither shall come armed into the presence of the other unless I arm him with my own hands; for I am not willing that two such warriors

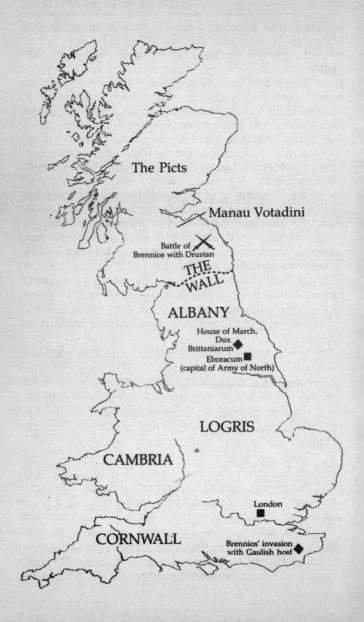

The Picts

Manau Votadini

Battle of
Brennios with Drustan

THE
WALL

ALBANY

House of March,
Dux
Brittaniarum

Eboracum
(capital of Army of North)

LOGRIS

CAMBRIA

London

CORNWALL

Brennios' invasion
with Gaulish host

shall be seen together and I not there to share the sight."

The mighty brothers grew into men of authority and renown, and there began to be things in which they were not equal. Belinos was a soberer man, and more famed for judgment, while Brennios was matchless in battle; but they were both proud, high-hearted men, valiant warriors and generous patrons, and both were loved and admired by all the people of the Island. Belinos chose a wife in his youth, but Brennios did not set his love on one woman more than another.

After long life and rule death came to Dunvallo Malamud; and it came as a sudden sickness, before he had made the division of the Island between his sons. He was laid in a rich tomb, and the Britons mourned him; few Kings had such mourning made over them as Dunvallo the Lawgiver. In their grief for their father Belinos and Brennios were united; but when the mourning was over came the day their mother had feared, for there were two Princes of equal renown, but only one could wear the Crown of London.

Each asserted his claim to be High King and would not yield to the other; and the people and the elders of Britain were equally divided between them, so that no choice could be made. At first the brothers were rivals without bitterness; then when they came into each other's presence they did not smile, and after that for a while they would not meet together at all; and when they sought each other again, whenever they spoke together there were insults and quarreling. At last the dispute grew so bitter that words could not contain it; they forgot the love that had formerly been between them, and began to make war on one another.

Then there was fighting in many parts of the Island, duels of champions and the battling of armies, until it seemed that the evil days Dunvallo had ended had returned with the contention of his sons.

Nor could they decide the matter in combat between themselves, because of the ban their mother had put on them.

Belinos came to Tonuvenna and asked her to arm him for battle against his brother; he urged her strongly, "Our champions divide the honours equally, and I defeat his as he defeats mine. Unless we strike at each other this matter will not be settled."

But she refused, crying, "I will not do it! I held him at my breast as often as you, and he drank as much of my milk."

Brennios came to make the same request, and she answered him, "Your brother filled as much of my womb as you, and I strove as hard to deliver him. I will not arm you."

Then the brothers came to her both at once, and asked her again to arm them. "Many men of Britain are dying to settle the quarrel between us," they said. "It would be better for us to meet in single combat."

Then Tonuvenna grew angry. "Though I sorrow for the men of Britain, shall I arm one of my sons to kill the other?" There was a great carved pillar by her door; she sat down by it and called her servants to bind her hands one on either side of the column. When they had done so she swore an oath, "By the Three Rivers of Britain, my hands shall not be unbound so long as there is war between my sons. Here I shall remain, in heat and cold alike, and the rain shall wash the dust from me; but one palm shall not know the other until there is peace between my sons!"

The Chief Bard in Britain at that time was called Teudoric. When he heard of this deed of the Queen he summoned all the other men of his order, and they gathered together in one place, all from the highest degree to the lowest. Teudoric said, "This deed of Tonuvenna shames us, and unless this rivalry is brought to an end the dead in Britain will be more than the living."

The bards debated together; and when they had done so they set out in a body to seek the mighty brothers. So it was that as the two hosts were preparing to do battle, all the bards in Britain came and ranged themselves between them, and forbade any man to strike a blow. Teudoric called to Belinos and Brennios, "Put aside your weapons and accept the judgment we shall give; or every bard here shall make such satires on the two of you that your flesh shall melt from your bones with shame!" Then for fear of the bards the two sons of Dunvallo disarmed themselves and came to hear the judgment.

Teudoric said to them, "When your father Dunvallo Malamud was High King of this Island there was peace and prosperity, and no man dared harm his neighbour. Now because of your strife it is hard to remember those days. It is shame to the sons of such a father to set his deeds at nothing; and shame to the people of Britain that they can make no choice who shall be their King. Therefore this is our judgment. Let us send into Gaul and ask the druids to judge between you, for they are very wise and have no kindred in this dispute. They will not favour one of you over the other, but will give good judgment." The brothers agreed to that, and each departed with his host; and each sent a messenger to his mother, to bid her end her penance.

Druids came from Gaul to make a choice between the brothers, and those were the first druids to come into the Island. They took counsel with many people, and made observation of the brothers, and then they debated long together.

When they had done so they called the Council of Britain together, and the two princes also, to hear their decision. "Here are two noble men alike in every merit, except that Belinos exceeds his brother in one thing: that he is the father of a son. Therefore since they are equal we divide the Island equally between them, so that Belinos shall rule Logris and Cambria, Brennios Albany and Cornwall. And the

Crown of London shall be bestowed on Belinos, since he, in this one thing, outdoes his brother."

The elders acclaimed this judgment, and Belinos and Brennios accepted it as they were sworn to do. Belinos said to his brother, "This is a swifter choice than battle would have made between us; for since at our birth you took hold of my ankle, if you were second to me it was by very little."

"In boasting you surpass me," said Brennios, and his eyes flashed. "In other things you find it hard. I will own I have found no adversary like you, but from the first you followed me close; for it was I who drew you after me into the world."

For an instant they faced each other like cats with flattened ears, then all at once they began to laugh. "No, let us not begin again," said Belinos, "for neither of us can ever defeat the other. But together, my brother, we hold all the strength of this Island!" Then he went to Brennios with his arms stretched out, and they embraced and laughed together; and the love and comradeship that they had known for most of their lives was restored.

For a time while each brother ruled his own realm there was peace in Britain. Belinos ruled well in his father's place, for he found that he had more pride in giving good judgment than in doing such deeds as bring glory to a warrior. But Brennios' prowess in battle increased daily, and he found his chief delight in feats of war.

Drustan, King of the Picts, made war on him in Albany; thirty thousand warriors came behind him, and Brennios met him with three hundred men of his warband. Drustan sent to him saying, "There is no honour in defeating this handful. I will send out ten champions, and let champions of yours do combat with them."

Brennios answered, "Be sure to send ten you can spare."

The ten Pictish champions came out in their chariots, and Brennios came alone against them. They threw their javelins, but with the shield-feat he caught them all on his shield, and then he threw his javelin with a curving motion, so that it pierced all ten of his adversaries and left them dead, and came back to his hand. After that ten other champions came out to fight him with their swords; but he moved his body so artfully between the sword-blades that they did not graze his skin, and with every blow of his sword he killed a champion. When the next ten came he commanded his charioteer to drive across before them with the fastest gallop his team could make, and while he did so Brennios stretched out of the back of the chariot and threw his keen spears between the spokes of the chariot wheel, and each found its proper mark. That is called the chariot-wheel feat, and Brennios killed ten men with it.

Drustan was watching, and he said to the ten warriors beside him, "He has lost his spears; you will not find him so sharp-toothed now." They went rushing at Brennios; but as every warrior cast a spear at him he caught it in flight and threw it back, and he killed all of them.

With these feats and others he slew every day a hundred Pictish warriors; the blood of the Picts was curdled with fear of him, so that when he raised the hero-scream and led his warband against them they scattered before him like birds, and those that lived were glad to flee. "Next time you have a mind to hunt such deer," they told Drustan, "you will go alone."

Brennios won great praise throughout Britain for that victory. But after it certain Kings who were subject to him began to murmur among themselves, "Why should a man who can perform such deeds be second to any in the Island?" And they said to him, "You are the Chief Dragon of the Britons; why should your brother be High King, and not you?"

Brennios began again to brood on that, until it seemed to him that his preeminence in battle gave him the right to wear the Crown of the Island. Then he gathered an army, and prepared once more to make war on his brother. When Belinos heard of it he summoned his warband and his subject Kings with their warbands, and he went to Tonuvenna and said, "There is a battle to be fought between Brennios and myself."

"Shall I go to the stone again?" she said.

He answered, "There is no need of that; but a time will come when you must choose between us."

Then he led his host against Brennios. But not all the men of Albany would fight for Brennios, for some of them considered he was breaking his oath, and the bards and the druids were all with Belinos. The two armies met in a great marsh in Albany; and for all Brennios' valour and warrior's feats, he could not overcome his brother's host. All day they fought in the marsh, and at night they rested and bound their wounds; and the next day and the next night were the same; but on the third day the army of Belinos was victorious, and the men of Albany fled.

Brennios said to his charioteer, "I never knew defeat until today, and shame will not let me stay in Britain. Drive me to the sea." So his charioteer took him to the coast and Brennios found a boat to take him out of Britain, and it was not known where he had gone.

Belinos mourned, crying out, "No man ever had such a brother as I have lost; my grief that Britain was too narrow for the two of us!"

He took Cornwall and Albany under his own rule, and governed Britain alone, and did so well. Britain had peace and prosperity in his time. He caused roads to be built throughout the Island, and they were considered to be holy places, so that all who travelled them did so in safety. In his reign druids came to Britain in great numbers and began to teach men their learning; it began to be the custom for the sons of Kings and noble men to be taught by druids in their youth. Also Belinos ratified all the laws of Dunvallo Malamud, his father, and at his urging the bards formed them into triads, and the Triads of the Law have been remembered since that time. And the people of Britain began to say that Belinos, son of Dunvallo Malamud, was a King not much less great than his father.

Brennios had gone into Gaul, and he was the guest there of many Kings in turn. He told no one his name or his kindred because of shame at his defeat. When he was asked it, he would reply, "Whatever name I earn from you, that shall content me." It was not long before his fame as a warrior was as great in Gaul as it had been in Britain. Whenever he came to a place where he was not known, he was welcomed for that fame and for his fine looks and bearings, but wherever he stayed for a day he was honoured for his wit and fluent speaking, and wherever he stayed a week he was loved for his gaiety and his courtesy, for his generosity and his greatness of heart. Therefore his name among the Gauls was Manocan, which means "noble, courteous."

At last he settled among the Allobroges in the north of Gaul. Andebrogorix their King gave him lands and cattle, and noble men began to gather about him. When a neighbouring King made war upon Andebrogorix he said to Brennios, "I am old, and my hand does not grasp my spear so firmly as it did. Put yourself at the head of my host and lead them to battle."

Brennios did so, and with him in the forefront the Allobroges were victorious; and in the battle he did such deeds as astonished the warriors who followed him. They spoke everywhere of his marvellous feats, and no warrior in Gaul had such songs sung of him as Manocan.

From that time on Brennios had no equal in the King's esteem, and not one of the nobles grudged him that preeminence. And the women and maidens of Gaul saw the perfection of his form, his bright eyes and burnished hair, and considered he had no equal for beauty and manliness. The daughter of

Andebrogorix said to her father, "I never saw a man so pleasing to me as this warrior. Among the Kings of Gaul there is none so princely, nor one that I love so well. If I cannot have Manocan for my husband I will have no other."

"If that is so you must have Manocan!" said her father. He called Brennios to feast with him, and when they were sitting together he said, "I have neither son nor sister's son and my daughter is my heir. It would please me to see you her husband, and to know that you would be King at her side."

"That would please me also," said Brennios, "if I were sure that the maiden's heart went with it."

"You must find that out by wooing her," said the King. "Her consent may not be impossible to win."

So Brennios courted the daughter of Andebrogorix and did not find her hard-hearted, and she became his wife. When Andebrogorix died they ruled together over the Allobroges, and Brennios was a good King to them, famed for his hospitality and openhandedness. Many noble men came to seek out one whose name was a byword for generosity throughout Gaul. The honour he had as Manocan was sweet to Brennios for it was all of his own winning and balm to the defeat he had suffered in Britain.

Nevertheless there were times when his heart yearned over Britain, and men from the Island of the Mighty found a welcome in his house, and a seat at his side. There was such a man who came, and he praised Belinos the High King so greatly that Brennios' heart was stirred to hear it. He said to his guest, "This you describe is a worthy King indeed. What does he look like?"

The man said, "I never saw him, but I need not praise him the less for that. A King is seen best in his deeds. Not since Brutus of Troy has there been such a King as this in the Island, except only Dunvallo, his father; he is so courteous, so honourable in all

his dealings and so noble that the people of the
Island call him Belinos Manocan!"

At that the warmth Brennios had been feeling
towards his brother turned to heat, and his smile left
him; but he said as if he jested, "When will this
emulation have end!" His warriors and his guest
laughed. But the heart of Brennios was sore after
that feast.

One night when they were in bed together his
wife said to him, "A man such as you are should
rule a great kingdom."

He murmured, "I had such a kingdom once."

"How did you lose it?"

"There was war between my brother and myself, and now he rules what was mine."

Until that time he had not told his lineage in
Gaul, and his wife was astonished. "Who is this
brother?" she demanded.

Brennios was unwilling to say more, but she
would not be contented. Every night for many nights
she questioned him until at last he told her. "If you
go to the court of London you will see in the chief
place there one who is like me in every feature, for
we were born at one birth: he clung to my ankle as
we came from the womb."

The queen was amazed, and cried, "Is the High
King of Britain your brother?"

"He is; and my name before I came here was
Brennios, son of Dunvallo Malamud."

Now she grew indignant. "How is it that you
have no part of that Island, and he is High King over
it all? What was there to make such a difference
between you?"

"Indeed the druids who judged between us found
us matched in every way, except that Belinos was
the father of a son; and so they gave him the
kingship."

"Now here is injustice! You too have a son now,
and so you are as good a man as he. I think it would

be right for you to go and claim the kingship, or at least your rightful share of the Island."

Brennios turned the matter aside with a jest, and was not willing to talk of it again. But his wife was roused on his behalf, and there were few days in which she did not urge him to claim his inheritance in Britain; until Brennios began to forget that he had not told her all the story, and to feel himself that he had suffered a wrong. At last all the rivalry he had ever felt for his brother was wakened in him again. Then he sent to neighbours and allies, and gathered a great host of the men of Gaul, and prepared to sail for Britain.

When Belinos heard that a great fleet of ships was crossing the Narrow Seas to Britain, he made haste to gather his army and led them to the coast to meet the invaders. When the foremost of the ships came in sight he called a herald, a man of keen sight, and bade him tell what manner of man led the host. The man gazed with narrowed eyes across the waves, and he said, "Son of Dunvallo, I see a marvel; for there is a kingly man on the foredeck of that ship, and when I look at him it is as if I see yourself."

Belinos said, "My brother would be more welcome if he came with fewer attendants." He sent word of Brennios' coming to their mother, and she made haste to his side. He asked her, "Have you come to welcome Brennios home?"

"Maybe I shall do so," she replied grimly, "but the chief reason for my coming here is to arm you for his presence; for he does wrong in bringing foreign men against Britain." So she armed Belinos with her own hands, but when she looked at him she remembered how they had stood in their twin glory before her on the day they came to manhood, and she wept. "Perhaps I can reason with him," she said, "before you come to battle together let me go and speak with your brother."

"As you wish," Belinos replied. "It is no pleasure to me to fight with him; but since he laid hold of me in the womb he has afflicted me."

When the ships of Brennios's fleet came to shore the men in them leapt out into the foam and onto the beach, and the charioteers fetched the horses out of the ships. Brennios's charioteer said to him, "We will not have much time for exercising our horses, by the look of that host gathered there."

"I see them," said Brennios, "and my brother at the head of them."

"That is a fond brother you have, so eager to welcome you with such a host. . . ."

Now a woman in royal garments, tall and stately, came out from the host of the Britons. Her tunic was of green brocade, her mantle of crimson brocade, and both were fringed with gold a handspan deep. Her shoes were so covered with gold the colour of the leather could not be seen. The combs and pins in her hair were of red-gold, and her ornaments of gold and pearls. Her head was high and her carriage upright, and though she was white-haired she moved swiftly down towards them.

"Here is their herald," said one of the Gauls; and another jested, "No, it is their champion, their foremost hero; it will be hard to find a challenger!"

Brennios turned and struck the man so that his teeth danced in his head and his eyes changed places; he saw with a squint all his life after.

"An ill Fate on any who show her discourtesy!" said Brennios. "Stay here and I will meet her alone."

He went to meet Tonuvenna, and she waited for him on a grassy place above the beach. His heart was stirred painfully when he stood before her; he began a formal greeting, "The blessing of the sun and the moon on you, Mother." But his words stumbled in his mouth. "Mother, when last I saw such a look as yours, it was across a shield-rim."

Tonuvenna did not embrace him, but folded her arms within her mantle and regarded him sternly. She answered, "I was never the mother of a man of

Gaul. Certainly you resemble a son I had; but my son was a man of the race of Brutus, and a fierce defender of the Island of the Mighty against its enemies. Ask Drustan the Pict what a strong door he found my son. If Brennios were to return, if I were to see him again and he were in such health as the man I see before me now, I would rejoice: but he has not come back today. Your outside is like to Brennios, *Manocan of Gaul*; but within such as you his soul would shrivel!"

When he heard these words Brennios could not speak for grief. Then his mother said, "Is it the sun that makes your eyes water, or the sight of the spears and chariots of the men of Britain? Or maybe the salt water you have crossed has stung them?"

"It is none of these things," replied Brennios, "but there is a cold wind blowing here."

"Strangers find our winds sharp, though our kinsman coming back to us find the welcome kind."

At that Brennios cried aloud in sorrow, and Tonuvenna was so moved that she had to turn her head aside from looking at him. She cried, "No woman was ever the mother of two sons so matched in excellence as the sons I bore! No woman ever had such pride as was mine. But now the people of Britain will curse me, who brought forth these two that afflict each other and afflict the Island!"

Brennios said, "Lady, will you tell me who armed the High King for the battle before him?"

"I armed him myself; for if I did not do so and there was truth in the report that his brother was here, his death would be in it."

Then Brennios was stricken with shame to be leading a foreign army against the men of the Island of the Mighty, and with grief at his mother's greeting. He cast aside his three-bossed shield, threw down his spears and unbuckled his sword, and took the helmet from his head.

He stood before her then, and in a voice low and rough he said, "May my right arm lose its strength if I raise it again against a man of Britain! Mother, bring me into my brother's presence, and let me have the greeting of a kinsman from him; and speak to me more kindly than you have done."

Then Tonuvenna came and put her arms about his shoulders and wept as she embraced him, and he wept also. Seeing this Belinos left his place and came down to them, and he held out his hand to Brennios. He said, "Too long have I lacked a brother; there is not your equal in the Island of the Mighty, and unless I have you to stand against I do not know my own height. Though we have fought too often, if you are not there to share it with me there is not taste in the wine, and the best singing sounds flat. Let us make peace, and at every feast where I am you shall have the Champion's Portion."

"And when you come to feast at my house, I will have the thigh and direct them to give you the hindquarter; for if the Champion's Portion is mine the King's Portion is yours. If ever again I contend with you for that, let the earth swallow me and the sea smother me, let the sky with its shower of stars fall and crush me. Let us be reconciled; we are men, and no longer boys."

With that the mighty brothers embraced, and from the whole host of Britain there rose a great sound of rejoicing. The host of Gaul was moved also; but the chief men of Gaul said to Brennios, "We followed you for glory; where shall we have it now?"

At that Tonuvenna declared, "Too long have my sons been like wayward horses who fight in their harness and threaten the wreckage of the chariot, when if they would run together, where would be a team so well-matched as they are? Why should you seek your glory in fighting each other? If you join together, in the world there would be none who could stand against you. From this hour the whole world is yours to win renown in."

And so it happened that Belinos and Brennios

together conquered Gaul and Germany, Greece and Italy, and Brennios ruled in Rome itself long before great Julius. But Belinos returned and took up again the rule of Britain, and he was one of the greatest to wear the Crown of the Island. There was in that time no King to equal Belinos, as there was no warrior who surpassed Brennios. The brothers never turned upon one another again; and their strength was a blessing to the Island of the Mighty and no longer a curse. In their time Britain knew law and wealth, and safety from all her enemies.

OR of all the Plagues that have afflicted Britain," sang Venogad, "there is none so bitter as contention between our Princes. Therefore as it befits men of authority to honour valour, so it befits the soldier to recognize authority. Let the Emperor call the General his brother, as Belinos embraced Brennios; and as Brennios at last saw kingship in Belinos, so now March salutes it in Arthur. Thus today as in the old tale shall Britain be blessed in the strength of her mighty men, and no foreign enemy shall withstand us."

His hand had not fallen from his strings when the storm of applause broke. Arthur's men were on their feet, Gai and Bedvir first, and it was not only the bard they were acclaiming. Arthur stood, holding out a ring from his own finger to Venogad, and there was a brightness in his eyes. Then he turned and offered his hand to March. The older man stood and held out his own, but instead of taking it Arthur embraced him; and before their followers they clasped each other in their arms as heroes of old had done.

Arthur said, "Mighty brother, not since Brennios was there such generosity. These are tears of remorse that I looked for rivalry from you."

"When I saw it I never blamed you for it. Plenty of Generals have been proclaimed by their armies. But I was not born for the purple; I never envied Vortigern's burden."

The door behind them opened, and a woman entered carrying a baby. She walked up to her husband smiling, and he took the child and said to Arthur, "We have waited a long time for God to give us a son, and now he has done so. Here he is. His sisters call him Arthois; but his name in baptism is to be Artorius. Chief of Dragons, give him a godfather's blessing: and may he some day serve you as loyally as his father will all his life!"

EOPLE who did not understand the Celts' religion were apt to call them a very superstitious people, when it would be fairer to say that they had and expressed a deep respect for the world around them. Few glimpses of their beliefs are so intriguing as that of the way in which an individual might be given a personal superstition—the "ban" or the "bidding." These taboos (though they could be things which were commanded as well as things which were forbidden) were sometimes attached to particular roles —Kings could be hedged with them; but the examples we have are usually of those given to heroes. He may have them from his conception or birth, or be given them at his attaining of warrior status; they are commonly given by a parent or teacher, but not always—bards and women were able to "put bonds on" a man at any time, as Grania put Diarmiad "under bonds" to elope with her. A hero whose father visited his mother in the form of a bird was forbidden to kill birds; this reasoning is clear, but some taboos are more difficult to understand.

The hero's life and power are bound up with the keeping of these commands. Bran's death, following upon his entry into a house, is an obvious example. (Perhaps this ban was because his father was a nature god, so his demigod power depended on contact with the earth.) In some stories the hero knowingly infringes his taboos and so precipitates his death; in others he is compelled to break them, and in a frenzy of despair foresees his ruin.

Reverence for the human head could very well be regarded as a tenet of the Celts' religion rather than mere superstition. Headhunting was common to all Celtic societies, for possession of a man's head guaranteed the subservience of his ghost. This transfer of spirit power to the one who held the head made such trophies very acceptable offerings to the gods (especially to the battle-goddesses; in Ireland the heads of the slain were called "the mast of Macha") and they were often hung in sacred groves, particularly on oak trees. The homes of Kings and men of rank were decorated and guarded with severed heads; even the representation of a head, on a pillar for example, or a sword-hilt, was a powerful amulet.

Old heads when displaced by newer trophies were never discarded, but preserved in cedar oil and stored carefully in special chests or rooms, and were brought out sometimes for display to guests! After battles a literal head-count was taken of the slain, and the Ulster hero Conall of the Victories boasted that he never slept without the head of a Connachtman beneath his knee.

For the same reason the head of a great man was a source of comfort and protection to his own people if it remained in their possession. It could ward off Plague and ensure prosperity, also defend a territory against invasion if buried—"concealed"—near its borders. If a King died out of his own lands it was vital to bring his head home, though his body might be buried where it fell. There is a Welsh elegy, composed well into the Christian era, for a King who died in battle in England, and the bard begins every verse, "This head I bear at my knee. . . ." The Celts found power inseparable from intelligence and eloquence, so it was obvious to them that the life of a man was in his head. Indeed the tongue was sometimes dedicated in place of the head, and tongueless heads were worthless offerings—as more than one dragon-slayer has found!

EVA, great City of the Legions, had remained safe from the Saxon barbarians, and had kept both her dignity and her people. When, in the autumn of 491 A.D., Arthur summoned the Princes of the West to gather there, she gleamed with imperial grandeur.

Her people filled the streets to enjoy the spectacle; the columns of well-drilled cavalry, the officers with glittering belts, the trumpets and the shining horses. They yelled themselves dry-throated in greeting the bearers of the names all Britons knew so well: Coroticus the son of great Cunedag, Dunvallo his son, their own Princes Cadvallon Longhand and young Maglocun and smiling Eugen, and the kinsman of these Votadinian Princes come from their old homeland in the North, Marianus of Manau Votadini; Agricola of Demetia with his son Vortipor, Cato, the fourteen-year-old Prince of Dumnonia with his regent Constans at his side; Gai and Bedvir, famous in song, beautiful Gueneva, and Arthur himself, the Pillar of Britain. The citizens of Deva acclaimed them all, then went to moisten their dry throats, to gossip about the Princes and speculate on what brought them to such a gathering.

Now night had fallen; girls dreamed of Princes and officers, young boys dreamed smiling of the day when they too would be heroes, and their mothers of a peaceful future when no heroes would be needed; while in the Residence those they had cheered were entertained by Cadvallon and his brother Eugen.

Amid the splendours of the stately room, warmed by braziers and lit by a hundred lamps, the Chief Dragon of the Island sat silent and smiling, turning his crystal cup in his hand, well pleased with the beginning of his Council of Princes. He had learned by now to know when men were ready to respond to his rule, when events would yield to his guiding hand as easily as his warhorse. Tomorrow they would discuss campaigns against Britain's western enemy, for he had reports that the past alliance of Saxon and

Irish was being renewed. Already he was confident
of victory, confident too that his plans for the remoter
future would succeed; his plan to alter the commands of the Votadinian Generals.

Bedvir sat by him, but they did not talk; on his
other side Gueneva conversed with her kinsman
Constans, Governor of Dumnonia. Arthur's eyes travelled consideringly over the company. Grey-haired
Coroticus talked with his unknown nephew Marianus,
the excellent Agricola with Eugen and Cadvallon;
they were no doubt discussing Cadvallon's campaign
to win back the grain island Mona from the Lein-
stermen. Eugen's son had been sent to bed, but the
other boys, much of an age, were sitting together on
one couch, their gruff voices occasionally audible
above those of their elders.

Arthur's smile strengthened as his gaze rested on
Cato, whom he loved for the sake of his father
Gerontius, forever gloriously young in death; on one
of the others his eye lingered thoughtfully. A youth
of some promise, intelligent and forceful; but one
who already insisted on his title of Maglocun Guletic.
Near them Gai was laughing with Dunvallo, most
trusted of all Arthur's subject Kings. They were not
talking of war, rather it seemed answering the teas-
ing of a couple of elegant ladies. But women could
not interest Arthur on such a night; his gaze passed
indifferently over them, even Gueneva, though as
she exchanged small family news with Constans her
face was softened and her beauty for once lit from
within. It was another glow that warmed his smile.
Within that room he saw united the magnificence
and order of Rome, the valour and brilliance of Celtic
Britain; and his vision of a new Empire, strong and
united, peaceful and secure, seemed that evening
too substantial to be called a dream.

Servants moved among them, refilling cups and
replacing sweetmeat dishes and bowls of fruit. At
Arthur's nod Riderch moved to the stool set ready
for him. Though the Votadinian princes were the

hosts, no bard had a better right than his to entertain the company; and for such an audience only one tale was possible. So Riderch tuned his strings, while the company grew quiet and settled into seats; and he called on them to hear the story of *Great Bran*.

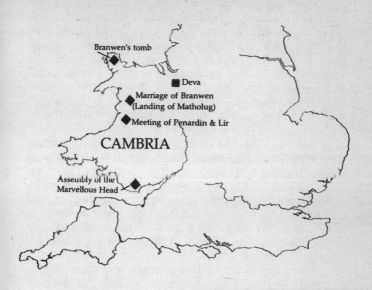

Branwen's tomb

Deva

Marriage of Branwen
(Landing of Matholug)

Meeting of Penardin & Lir

CAMBRIA

Assembly of the
Marvellous Head

ENARDIN White Throat, sister to the High King of Britain, had no equal in her life time for beauty and wisdom and royal nobility. Upon a day in summer she was walking with her maidens along the shore of the great bay in the west of Cambria, and the wind was sporting with her garments of green silk gold-embroidered, and her hair yellow as pollen, so that the maidens laughed to see the beauty of the sight: and then they saw a chariot coming towards them, and it came over the crests of the waves.

The rider in the chariot was a fairer man than they had seen. The foam that broke at their feet was not whiter than his skin, nor the sunlit sea so bright as the colour of his eyes, and his hair was as dark as a night with no moon. His rich garments were all sewn with pearls; the chariot he rode in was of silver, and the horses to it were one red and one white, and in the Island of Britain there were no horses like them.

When the chariot came to shore the man sprang out and came to Penardin saying, "Hail, Penardin of the white hands and gold-encircled neck! In my home beyond the waves I heard of your fame, and in that land of sweet songs none were so sweet to me as those wherein I heard your name. Though all is happiness there from morning to night, still longing for you seized me and I had no comfort but to seek you. As I rode towards this shore I saw the wind sporting with your hair and your garments, and I saw that your beauty is greater than the fame of it. Take my hand and come with me to my land, for that beauty will not fade there; there you will have more delight than in dwelling here, and death shall never find you."

The beauty of the stranger's face and form were great, but the quality of his voice held enthrallment; the music of the sea was in it. Penardin's mind was filled with amazement, and her heart with love and desire.

She answered him, "If I were not of the line of Brutus I would go with you, though I do not know your name. But my brother is High King of the Island, and it is foretold that a son of mine shall succeed him; that boy should be born in the Island of the Mighty. If you were to come and live with me in my brother's house, there would be no need of bride-gifts between us. Though this Island is not so fair as the land you tell of, it is very fair, and you will be honoured of its noble people."

The man said, "Though I shall not remain forever in this land, yet I will come with you to your brother's house and dwell there as long as I may, for I consider what a marvel a child of us two would be. As for my name, it is Llyr."

So the man from the sea became Penardin's husband and lived with her, and three children were born to them. Bran was their first-born, Manadan their second son, and last the lovely Penardin bore a daughter they named Branwen. Seven years passed, and nine more, and at last Llyr said, "Little fawn, dearest wife, jewel of the women of this world, I can stay no longer here among the transient dead. I must return to the Living Land, and though your people are dear to me I must be with my own." Then with tears they parted, and Llyr kissed his children tenderly, and to his son Bran he said, "I put a bidding on you, that because you are my son, from the time you are a man you shall never be contained in a house, a ship, or a chariot, but whether there is earth or water beneath you, your feet shall feel it. And there shall be no mortal to equal you for might, whether in your lifetime or after."

Then Llyr harnessed his horses of red and white to his silver chariot, and he departed as he had come. All the people of Britain mourned his going, and the grief of Penardin and her children was greatest. Yet after a while Penardin's sorrow abated, and she went to the house of another husband, and by him she was the mother of a son, Emnisien.

Never has there been, nor will there be, three in this Island to match the three children of Llyr. For loveliness and gentleness and courage there was no maiden the equal of Branwen of the shining hair, and dark-eyed Manadan has had no like for wit and wisdom and cunning skill in many crafts; but Bran was greatest of the three. He was of extraordinary size, yet his shape and his features perfect in proportion; in battle invincible, but not eager for destruction; in judgment famed for justice, in all things for generosity. When his uncle died there was no other among the gold-torqued Princes who could be chosen to be High King, for there was not one who did not love and honour Bran. Therefore he was exalted with the Crown of London, and he was the greatest King that there has ever been in this Island; never shall this people know again a ruler so good, so wise, so mighty. From the time he was a man he did not enter a house, and sleeping and waking he was in the open between earth and sky. All the children of Llyr had powers not given to mortals, but Bran was more gifted in this than either Branwen or Manadan.

Their half brother Emnisien was a youth of keen wit, handsome appearance, and of a proud and angry nature. His kin loved him, Branwen most tenderly, and there was no creature in the world so dear to him as she. He loved and admired all three; and yet he envied them bitterly for all their excellent qualities, and most for their immortal birth. From a boy Emnisien lived with a storm in his heart, and when he came to manhood his best delight was in stirring up strife. Where Emnisien was there was discord; he could make an infant quarrel with its mother's breast, a bard find fault with his harp. Only Branwen could soothe his contentious nature.

In spring Bran was holding his court in Cambria, and Manadan and Branwen were with him. At that time the beauty of Branwen was at its greatest; it was of no more use to adorn her hair with rubies than it was to adorn her throat with pearls, for the whiteness of her throat and the redness of her hair outdid the colour of jewels. The High King was sitting on a couch of silver on a hillside above the sea with his companions about him, when they saw four ships sailing towards the shore, and they were very curious at the sight. The sails of the ships were of fine linen brightly coloured, the sterns and mast-heads were gilded, and there were banners of silk on the wind above them.

"These do not come in a warlike manner," said Manadan.

"They are the more welcome for that," said Bran. "Come, let us go down and find out who they are."

He went down to the beach, and his companions came in a troop behind him. Manadan stood on his one side, Branwen of the dark copper hair on the other. The ships came up to the beach, and the herald called out to ask who they were and why they were come. From the foremost ship a man answered, "We are men of Ireland, and Matholug, King of Ireland, is in this ship with me. He has a gift to ask of Great Bran, and unless it is granted he will not come ashore."

"Let him ask it, and if it is not against my honour or the safety of this Island, and if it is mine to give, he shall have his request."

"He asks that Branwen, most illustrious maiden of the Island of the Mighty, shall be his wife."

Bran laughed and said, "That gift is not in my power to give; let him come ashore and make his request of Branwen."

So Matholug came to the shore, a handsome curly-headed man, young and of a princely graceful carriage. He said to Branwen, "Daughter of Llyr, fairest and noblest of the women of all the islands, your fame has filled my ears until I have no desire for any company but yours. I faint with love of you, Branwen of the burning hair and chiming voice,

Branwen of the delicate steps and eyes like candle-
flames. If you will not consent to be my wife I will
have no other. I will never hold a spear or mount in
a chariot again, never sit at a feast or talk with
friends, but lie between the pillars of my house and
take neither food nor drink until I die."

Branwen looked at him, and a great tenderness
for him filled her. She said smiling, "That were a sad
Fate for so fair and well spoken a man! I will learn by
my mother's example, and not refuse a suitor who
comes from the sea. I will be your wife."

So the marriage was agreed, and while her brothers and the chief men of Ireland discussed the terms
of it, Branwen and Matholug walked together beneath the blossoming trees. Since the year was near
its turning to summer, it was necessary to make the
marriage feast quickly, and Bran sent out messengers to summon Emnisien; but Emnisien had gone
hunting and could not be found. Therefore though it
grieved Branwen the marriage was held without him.
The feast was spread in the open because of the
bidding that was on Bran, and cubicles of wood
finely carved and hung with rich cloths were built
among the trees for the bride and groom and the
noble guests. There was great merriment there, with
abundance of wine and roast pork, with music and
song and telling of tales, with much swearing of
friendship between the men of Britain and Ireland;
and after the feasting Branwen and Matholug slept
together.

After the wedding the new-married couple stayed
with her brothers, for all four took delight in each
other's company; and the horses and men of Matholug
were billeted around the place where they were. So
it happened that when Emnisien ended his hunting
and came to seek the company of his brothers and
sister, he could find no place to picket his horses for
the number of the horses of the men of Ireland. He
summoned a groom and said, "Whose horses are
these, which leave no place for mine?"

The groom answered, "Lord, these are the horses of Matholug, King of Ireland, and of his men. But give me your horses, and I will find a better place than this for them."

"And why are the horses of Matholug, King of Ireland, picketed about the place where my brothers and Branwen are?"

"Lord, they came on a happy errand. Matholug came wooing your sister Branwen, and she has slept with him; and that is the cause of all the rejoicing."

When he heard that a great bitterness filled Emnisien. "That was ill done of them!" he cried. "To give so illustrious a maiden in marriage without my knowledge or consent! Though I am not a child of Llyr I am their mother's son, and I had a right to be considered in this."

"Indeed, your brother Bran sent men to seek you, but you could not be found; and Branwen much desired that you should return."

"It would have been better for them to delay the feast until then."

"That would have been to wait until Beltain was past, and there would be ill luck in that; maybe the marriage could not have been made."

"Nor would that have been a bad thing. Are there not worthy men enough in Britain, that my sister must choose a foreign man for her husband, and leave the Island of the Mighty?" The slight he felt himself to have suffered darkened his heart, and a cruel anger filled him. He went among the horses of the men of Ireland and hamstrung every one of them; he cut off their tails to their rumps, their lips, their eyelids, and their ears down to their heads. Then he went away satisfied, and said, "Though the bridegroom held the feast before Beltain, he has not escaped his bad luck."

The wild high neighing and the trampling of the maimed horses brought the Irish grooms and charioteers to them, and the sight filled them with horror and rage. The charioteers swore, "If we had in our hands the man who did this, a day would not finish his dying!"

They killed the mutilated horses, and each went to the man whose charioteer he was and told him of it. The nobles of Ireland went together and demanded of the British grooms, "At whose hand have we suffered this outrage?"

They answered, "The brother of your King's wife did this, because of the insult that he suffered when his sister was given to the King of Ireland."

"By the Old Sow," they cried, "if that is an insult it is hard to do him honour!"

They went to Matholug and said, "Lord, it is a pity we came here; outrage and insult have been put upon us all." And they told him of what had been done to the horses. Matholug was amazed.

"I cannot believe that they should wish to insult me!" he declared. "If they had done so, why did they give me so excellent a lady for my wife, and one that they love as they love Branwen?"

"It cannot be guessed why they have done it, but it is done. Moreover we have been told that your marriage to the lady is seen as an insult to Britain, and you can see by that in what scorn they hold you."

All Matholug's joy turned bitter, and utterly downcast, he said, "Let us return to our ships. At least for a little while I have enjoyed the love of Branwen."

Their servants began to gather their belongings. Bran heard, and he came himself to Matholug, asking why he should leave them so suddenly. The King of Ireland said, "I sought this marriage because of the love I had for Branwen, and so that there should be friendship between our two peoples; but there is no friendship for me here. If you wished to insult me I marvel you did not do it when first I came, and if you hold me in such scorn I marvel you gave me your sister."

"By my head," said Bran, "I do not understand you!"

Matholug told Bran of the maimed horses, and Bran was filled with sick dismay and grief for the poor creatures, and incensed with anger at the insult to his honour, so that Matholug was a little soothed to see it. The King said, "This was not done with my knowledge, much less by my authority. Moreover, if a man suffers injury while he is my guest, the insult and the shame are mine!"

"That may be so," said Matholug, "but still the injury and the loss are mine."

"At least you shall not suffer loss," declared Bran. "For every horse you have lost you shall have two from my herds, and your men shall have the choosing of them. Also I will make face-payment to atone for your insult; a staff of gold as tall as you and of a weight equal to yours, a dish of gold as broad as your face, and the same in silver for every man with you. Accept this reparation, for the sake of Branwen and her love."

Matholug was cheered at that, and accepted the compensation offered; and a feast of reconciliation was held. But Emnisien was at that feast, and being angry he bore himself haughtily to the men of Ireland, so that his presence was a provocation to them and lessened the value of the reparation Bran had made. There was less merry talk at that feast, and a cloud was on Matholug whenever he looked at Emnisien.

Manadan said, "You are not so good a talker as I have known you, brother. If the reparation we have made does not satisfy you, tell us so; for we would not have our sister's husband suffer grief."

Matholug replied, "I am not dissatisfied; nevertheless your brother has spoiled the gaiety of my wedding."

Bran perceived that he still smarted from the outrage he had suffered and from the insolence of Emnisien, and his great heart was stirred. There was

never another so bounteous as Bran; on an impulse
of generosity he said, "Because of the love and honour
I have for you, I will make you a gift. I will give you
the Cauldron of Rebirth, that is the chief treasure of
the Island of the Mighty. The property of that magic
cauldron is this, that if any man of yours suffers
death and you put him in the cauldron with a fire lit
under it, on the next day he will come out of the
cauldron whole and strong."

"By my head, that is a gift worthy of so great a
King as you are!" cried Matholug; and his smile
returned to him, while Manadan gave his brother a
startled look. After that the feasting between the
men of Ireland and the men of Britain was as cheerful as it had ever been, and Bran was content.

A year Matholug and Branwen stayed in Britain,
and at the end of the year they took ship for Ireland.

When the ship that Matholug and Branwen were
in was midway between the two islands they saw a
marvel; a man driving a chariot over the waves with
no more care than if they had been a flowery meadow.
He came alongside the ship and said, "King of Ireland, that is a fair woman you have there, though
not so fair as her mother was. My blessing on the
two of you; may there be harmony and plenty in
your house, and loving companionship between you.
But here is a warning for you, King of Ireland: if
ever you give three blows to Branwen, she must
leave your house and return to her brothers in Britain." When he had said that he shook his reins and
his horses leapt into a gallop faster than the flight of
seabirds, so that they were soon out of sight. Every-
one in the ship exclaimed at the marvel; but as for
the man's warning, Matholug said, "It will be easy
for me to avoid that."

In Ireland the two of them lived happily, and a
son was born to them whom they named Gwern. He
was a very fair child and a sturdy fellow, and there
was great rivalry to have the fostering of him. However, at his birth Matholug's kinsmen went to a

druid and asked, "Is this a good day for the birth of a son?"

"It is not," said the druid, "for the child and his mother will bring destruction to their kindred and people." From that day on the nobles sought to do Branwen harm.

Matholug and Branwen were sitting together, and a servant brought them apples. Branwen put out her hand to the dish first and took an apple, and Matholug said laughing, "You have taken the one I chose!" He struck her hand lightly with the palm of his hand.

Branwen shook her head at him and said, "Take care; that was a blow in jest, but you never struck me until today."

The chief men of Ireland began to speak to Matholug against his wife, and to remind him of the insult he had suffered in Britain. When he was unwilling to hear them they talked the more of these things among themselves and to the people, especially of the maiming of the horses; and in their talk they made the outrage large and the generosity of Bran small, until the people were stirred up against Branwen.

The King and Queen were playing chess, and while she considered her move Branwen touched one of Matholug's men. Matholug rebuked her with a jest, and gave her a tap on the hand with his hand. Branwen looked at him laughing. "Once in jest and twice in play; take care of the third time, my Lord!"

Matholug's kinsmen and the nobles never ceased reminding him of the insult from Emnisien, and of the harm it had done his name in Ireland; until Matholug began to listen to them and to feel the sting of it again. Most fierce against Branwen and her brothers were Matholug's foster brothers, for they said, "Our reputation suffers because of your shame, and because you suffer it willingly." They spoke scornfully to him, and called him unfit for kingship. From that time Matholug's heart began to harden towards Branwen, because of the mockery he suffered for her sake. As for the reparation, they said, "Gold and silver cannot buy the honour of Ireland."

Matholug smarted under the sharpness of their rebukes and chiefly from the scorn of his foster brothers and kinsmen; and he put the blame for it on Branwen. The time came when the people of Ireland were so stirred up against the Queen that there was not one good word spoken of her from one end of Ireland to the other; and they rose up against the kingship of Matholug, for they said that so long as he kept his wife he dishonoured them. The nobles came to Matholug and said, "Here is a revolt. You cannot have your wife and the Kingship of Ireland together."

Matholug said, "What must I do to retain the Kingship of Ireland?"

"You must put Branwen from your chamber and take away her foremost place from her, and see that your son Gwern is kept from her. If you offer the people of Ireland this compensation, they will not take the kingship from you, but will hold you in honour again."

"I shall do it," said Matholug.

When Branwen was told she came to him and protested, "I have not deserved this!"

He replied, "Nor did I deserve the insult I had of your brother."

"That is not generous: to remember the deed of my brother Emnisien, and not the bounty of Bran!"

At that Matholug grew angry, and he gave her a blow on the cheek. Fire came up in Branwen. She said, "That is the third blow, and given in good time. I will return to the Island of the Mighty."

Matholug would have been content with that, but the elders said, "If she does so her brothers will know of this, and they will come to make war on her behalf. She must remain in Ireland."

So Branwen was not permitted to leave Matho-

lug's court; but she was set to work with the cooks
at the worst labour, and the butcher was bidden to
give her every day a blow of his hand when it was
the bloodiest. For in his heart Matholug knew he
treated her unjustly; but the greater his shame, the
more it increased his cruelty to her.

Three years Branwen worked ill clad and barefoot among the cooking troughs. Her white hands
and delicate feet were burned and scarred, her wine-
red hair was defiled with grease and ash. The servants of Matholug used her as roughly as they were
bidden, but her courage and her dignity did not
leave her, and there was not one of them who saw
her weep, or who ever got a discourteous word from
her. Nevertheless her state was bitter to her, and she
yearned after her son, Gwern.

One day as she was alone in the court and
labouring at the spit, one of the women who had
come with her from Britain passed by. This woman
lamented, "Alas for you, Lady, you have never deserved this harsh Fate! It is well for your noble brothers that they do not know of it, for they would suffer
grief and shame if they did."

Branwen said, "It is not well they do not know,
for if they knew of it I should not suffer this long, nor
be kept from my child."

The woman said, "You speak truly. Yet Matholug
has forbidden the passage of ships between Ireland
and Britain lest rumour of your shame crosses the
sea. Who will tell your brothers of it?"

"You might do it, if your courage served you."

"How might that be?"

"There is not much need of courage either. I
shall put the form of a bird on you, and you could
fly to Britain, and take your proper shape there, and
give news of me."

The woman was amazed; but for love of Branwen
she was willing to do as she wished. Then Branwen
straightened her back from the spit and touched the
woman, and she was transformed into a bird that

fluttered about Branwen's head and perched on her hand. Branwen said, "You shall wear this form until you come into the presence of my brother Bran; and when you are there you shall have your own shape and tongue again, and can tell him of my Fate. I put a protection on you, against storm and misdirection and the swift hawk; go now to the Island of the Mighty."

The bird that was a woman flew out of the court and away from the hall of Matholug. With strong wings she sped over the land; she crossed the coast of Ireland and the heaving sea, and came to the shores of Britain. There she rested; and then she flew until she came to where beside Thames Bran was holding his court. Manadan and Emnisien and all the chief people of the Island were there. The bird perched on Bran's shoulder, then on his hand, and then at his feet; and there returned to the shape of a woman. All those who were there cried out in astonishment, and Bran said, "Are you from the Earthly Paradise? For it is not customary for mortal women to travel as you do. However, you are welcome here."

The woman replied, "Though I am welcome my news will not be. I am a woman of Britain who went to Ireland with your sister, Branwen. It is Branwen who put the form you saw on me, so that I might tell you of the Fate she has suffered, how she daily labours in Matholug's cooking troughs and suffers every day a blow on the ear from his butcher."

At that there was a great outcry; and when the woman had told her story it was not diminished. When he heard it Bran was moved to deep anger; his wrath was terrible. Without delay he summoned the warriors of the Island, and they were a great host. He bade them follow him to Ireland to rescue Branwen and avenge her shame; and then he led them forth, he and Manadan and Emnisien. They came to the sea, and the host went into ships, but because of his bidding Bran did not do so. He walked between Britain and Ireland, and the water bore him safely; the greatest wave broke no higher than his thighs. Also just as it had been hard for the chariots to keep pace with him though he went on foot, so he strode before the ships, and they could not overtake him.

Watchers saw them, and came to Matholug where he stood in the porch of his house. "Lord," they said, "a great number of ships is approaching Ireland, and before them goes a man of such stature and splendour that we never saw the like; and this man wades through the sea drawing the ships after him, and the waves do not cover his thighs."

Branwen was standing nearby; she said, "That is the host of the Island of the Mighty, and my brother Bran going before them. Since manhood he was never confined in a house or a ship."

Matholug was terrified when he heard that, and so were the nobles of Ireland. "Let us get the Shannon between us and him," they said. The King and the host fled into the west of Ireland, and the household with Branwen among them went too. As they went they broke the bridges over the rivers to hinder the host of Britain from following them. Yet the Britons came on, though the finding of fords hindered them, until they came to a river that though narrow was very deep, and there was no ford.

"This hinders our pursuit of that false son of the sow," said Emnisien, and Manadan suggested that they build a bridge.

"No," said Bran, "but he that is chief, let him be a bridge."

With his feet on one bank he stretched out and grasped the other with his hands. Hurdles were put upon his back, and then the whole host of Britain, men and chariots and horses, passed over that bridge. The crossing of the river took a day, and all that time Bran lay grasping the two banks. That deed of his shall never be forgotten, nor the words he spoke: he that is chief, let him be a bridge.

When they heard how the men of Britain had crossed the river, the nobles of Ireland were dismayed. Matholug called a council; he told them, "If this man comes to the Shannon, our bodies will be a bridge for him."

"Let us offer him terms," they advised.

Messengers were sent to Bran; they greeted him with great courtesy, and they gave him an affectionate welcome from Matholug, saying how it was not his wish that friendship should lessen between them, and how if he had his will only good fortune should befall Bran. "This is Matholug's offer," they said. "He will give the Kingship of Ireland to Gwern, your sister's son. This he will do in your presence, as reparation for the wrong done to Branwen. As for him, he will dwell where you send him, either in Ireland or in Britain."

Manadan laughed, and Emnisien gave the heralds a look that they trembled at. Then Great Bran answered them, "These are good terms for a man who cannot get better, and if I cannot take the kingship from him another way I shall take counsel concerning them. Until that time do not come back for my answer, unless you bring a different offer."

"Lord, we will go and come again with the best we can get; do you wait for us here?"

"I will," said Bran, "if you come quickly."

The messengers sped back to Matholug, and told him that Bran would have none of the terms he had offered. "Men," said Matholug, "what is your advice?"

The nobles answered, "Lord, we have none."

"You have had plenty before this," said Matholug." It was by obeying your counsel I came to this, and I lost the best wife that ever a man had when I did so." He said to the messengers, "Ask Branwen to come here." The messengers went to her, and she came as she was, grimed and barefoot and ill clad.

"Lady," said Matholug, "unless you help us Ireland will be destroyed. Go to your brother Bran and persuade him to accept the terms we have offered."

And all the council said, "Lady, do this for us; entreat mercy of Bran."

"I do not know why you call me 'lady,' " she said, "such courtesy to your cooks is not your custom. Yet I will go to my brothers; and if I find my son Gwern there, maybe I will do as you ask."

They made haste to obey her, and the boy was sent to the host of the Island of the Mighty. Branwen arrayed herself like a Queen, lest the sight of her poor state increase her brothers' anger past her power to soothe it. Then she left the camp of the men of Ireland, and went to the men of Britain, and into the presence of her brothers. They were overcome with joy to see her, and she to see them; but before they were done with embracing her Branwen was asking if her son was there. The boy was fetched; he ran to his mother and clasped his arms about her neck and Branwen laughed and wept for gladness. Bran and Manadan were glad at the sight; but Emnisien was not. He remembered that this was Matholug's son.

Then Branwen entreated her brothers to accept the terms offered to them, and not to make war upon Ireland, but they were reluctant to do so. Manadan said, "Are we not to have revenge, and you reparation for the wrong done to you?"

She answered, "The ash is out of my hair, and Gwern is restored to me: that is all the reparation I desire. To see Ireland laid waste would be grief and not pleasure to me, nor would it profit my son. As for Matholug, let his loss of the kingship and the fear and shame he has suffered be your revenge; for remember, he has been my husband. If you would gladden me, have mercy on him and Ireland."

Therefore through the intercession of Branwen Bran agreed to accept the terms Matholug had offered, and he and Manadan were not displeased at it though Emnisien was. The Irish praised Branwen and would have been glad to do her honour, but she

did not leave her brothers. A great feast of reconciliation was prepared, where the Kingship of Ireland
was to be conferred upon Gwern. The men of Ireland were anxious to please Bran and his brothers,
and they thought to do so by building a new hall to
hold the feast in, that should be larger and fairer
than any hall in Ireland, in honour of the children of
Llyr. For though Matholug knew of the bidding on
Bran, he did not tell them of it. The hall was built,
and it was large enough for all the host of Britain to
be seated on one side, and the host of Ireland on the
other, nor was there a fairer building in the world.
And on the day of the feast, they sent messengers to
ask Bran to come there.

Bran came, and he saw the hall in which the
feast was prepared, and he was dismayed; also he
saw how large and handsome it was, and understood that they had intended to do him honour. His
heart was moved at that; to any who showed courtesy and generosity, it was the nature of Bran to
return them tenfold. Therefore he thought it a worse
thing to slight the men of Ireland than to go within a
house, and he forbade those who were with him to
speak of his ban. So for the first time and against his
father's bidding, Bran was contained in a house.

The men of Ireland sat on one side, and the
men of Britain upon the other. When they were
seated the terms of peace were concluded between
them, and the Kingship of Ireland was conferred
upon Gwern. But since he could not wield authority
until he was a man, he was to be in Britain with his
mother and her brothers until then. When this was
done the child came back to his mother where she
was sitting between Bran and Manadan, and they all
made much of him; for to look on Gwern was to love
him, for all men of good heart. But as he looked at
the children of Llyr and the child between them, all
the anger and love and envy in the unpeaceful heart
of Emnisien rose up in a rage together.

"Why does the boy, my sister's son, not come

to me?" he said. "Even if he were not the King of
Ireland, I would be glad to show love to him."

The boy looked doubtingly, for from this uncle
he had had scant notice; but Branwen thought his
heart had changed, and was glad. "Go to your uncle," she said. Gwern walked up to him smiling, and
Emnisien took the child's shoulders between his
hands. When he looked at him, with the eyes of
Matholug in the face of Branwen, rage and sorrow
filled him; he said in his heart, "Though they call me
a harmful man, a deed they would not think possible is the deed I shall now do."

He said to his nephew, "You bear yourself like
one of good blood; and so you should. Have you
been told that you are born of immortal blood? For
your mother is one of the children of Llyr."

"I have heard that," said the child.

"Well," said Emnisien, "now is the hour shall
see it tested!" And he rose up with the boy between
his hands and the hearth at his feet, and before any
there could guess his purpose he cast Gwern into
the blazing heart of the fire. For the space of a breath
the company sat frozen. Then Branwen screamed
out a wild and terrible agony and made to leap into
the flames where her son writhed in the fire before
her; but Manadan and Bran each caught her by an
arm and held her back, while with their other hands
they reached for their shields. The men of Ireland
rose up with a roar to see their King murdered.
Then there were cries and shouts and confusion as
every man seized his weapons and the hosts of
Ireland and Britain fell upon one another. Around
every one of the hundred pillars of that great house
men fought and stabbed and cursed and groaned
and died.

Bran set Branwen between his shield and his shoulder and took his sword in his hand, and every man
there looked to see him bear her easily out of that
place, with no man able to withstand him. But there
was a roof between Bran and the sky, and a floor

between him and the earth; his ban was broken and his great strength gone. Still he and Manadan stood together and fought fiercely, and so did all the host with them; and the heaps of slain began to mount in the hall.

Then the Irish fetched the Cauldron of Rebirth and set it over the fire where Gwern had died, and they cast the bodies of the slain of their people into the cauldron; and however many it held there was always room for more. Then the men of Britain knew that all those warriors would return to the fight next day as strong as ever, and despair fell on them; for there was no such deliverance for them, since Bran had given away the cauldron.

Emnisien saw it, and the danger in which his brothers and Branwen stood, and the slaughter of the men of Britain, and there was darkness before his eyes. "This is my doing," he said, "this peril of my kindred and such destruction of the men of the Island of the Mighty. Alas that I was born, to do such harm to what I love. And shame on me, if I do not help them now, though I die for it." He cast aside his weapons and stripped off his breeches to go barelegged like an Irishman, then he crept in among a heap of dead bodies. Presently two servants came and cast him into the cauldron among the dead of Ireland. Though the cauldron could not be filled, Emnisien found it was not so big within as the stretch of his limbs. He set hands and feet against it and pressed outwards; he pressed with frenzied strength, until blood burst from his nose and ears; and the Cauldron of Rebirth burst into four pieces, and Emnisien's heart burst with it.

Then such victory as there was went to the men of the Island of the Mighty, but there was no gladness in it. For besides Bran and Manadan there were only six men left alive of the host that had come there, and Bran was mortally wounded in the thigh. Of the men of Ireland not one lived. As for Branwen, she sat in desolation, unable to speak.

Then Bran said, "A maimed King is a blighted land; therefore another and not I must be King of the Island of the Mighty. So this is my command to you; strike off my head and take it with you to London, and bury it there in the White Mount with my face looking to the sea. For so long as my head is concealed there, no foreign people shall take away the Island from the Britons. But wherever you rest on your journey, so long as you pause and feast there you shall have no remembrance of sorrow, and my head shall be as good company to you as ever I was while I lived. So you may continue, until you open a door that looks upon Cornwall; but after that you may delay no longer; you must go to London and bury the head. And now farewell, for it is time you made your crossing."

None of the company left had the heart or the courage to do his bidding save his beloved brother Manadan. So he it was who struck off the noble head from the rotting body. And great was their grief at it. Then they took the head, and the seven men and Branwen went into a ship; the other ships that had borne them to Ireland were left upon its shore, for there was no need of them. Branwen sat silent, her hair falling over her face, and if ever she raised her head she had the look of one who gazes at visions in a fire. They came to Cambria and disembarked, and on a hillside above the sea they rested, each a little apart from his fellows, for their hearts were heavy.

Then Branwen rose up and looked about her, and spoke; it was the first sound she had uttered since her scream when Gwern was cast into the fire. She looked at Manadan and the six men, all that remained of her brothers and the host they had brought to succor her; she turned her head and gazed over the sea to Ireland, and about her at the Island of the Mighty.

Then the tearing sound of her keening filled the air, and she wailed, "Alas! Alas! Alas that I was ever

born. Better if I had endured my shame in Matholug's
kitchen. Better that Gwern had lived. Two fair islands have been laid waste, because of me." Then
her heart broke with grief, and she died there. Such
was the death of Branwen, daughter of the won-
drous Llyr and the god from the sea.

With much mourning Manadan and his companions made her a tomb of stone, and after that
they went on their way towards London. They came
soon to a rich hall that faced the sea, and they rested
there. As they ate, three birds with bright plumage
came from over the sea, and perching in the porch
of the house they began to sing. When they heard
the singing the seven men forgot all their loss and
grief, and the head of Bran woke, and began to talk
with them.

Seven years they remained there feasting, and
the birds of the Great Queen, which make glad all
who hear them, sang to them every day. All that
time the head of Bran was as good company to them
as it had been when it was upon his shoulders, and
they were happy. At the end of seven years the
birds rose and flew west over the ocean. "Go now
into Demetia," said Bran. They went into the south
of Cambria, until they came to a hall upon a hillside
above the mouth of Severn, and they went into it.
There were three doors to it, and one of them at the
eastern end.

"See," said Manadan, "the door that looks
towards Cornwall, the door we must not open."

There they resumed their feasting, and under
the protection of the head of Bran all was merriment, with wine and song and lively talk, and after
it each night sweet sleep. Eighty years they were
there, and they did not grow older in all that time,
any more than do the people of the Living Land; nor
did any remembrance of grief come to them.

At the end of eighty years it chanced that one
morning a man of them woke before his companions. They slept in their places about him, and on its

pillar the marvelous head slept also; while he sat alone he felt a restlessness, a need—for what he could not name. He looked towards the door in the eastern wall. Beyond it the sun was rising, and all around it there was light. Then a great yearning and hunger seized him for what lay beyond that door; he rose and went to it, and he opened the door that looked upon Cornwall.

As soon as the door was open, remembrance of all his grief fell on him, so that he cried aloud and fell to his knees. The light streaming in roused his companions, and they woke to recollection of their sorrow. But though the sun fell upon the head of Bran his eyes did not open, nor did his mouth ever speak again. Manadan came out of the house, and he gazed across Severn, at Cornwall and Logris beyond, and his eyes were full of tears. "Now time takes us back," he said, "and we must finish our task."

That was the end of that fellowship, that is called the Assembly of the Marvelous Head. After it those seven men went to London, and they buried the head of Bran as he had directed them, in the White Mount looking down Thames to the sea. Then they went their ways, and Manadan went his way alone, grieving for Bran and Branwen. In the west of the Island is Branwen's grave, looking towards Ireland; in the east great Bran is concealed. And so long as his watchful head is there, no foreign people shall take this Island from us; but only the Britons shall rule in the Island of the Mighty.

ETWEEN Gueneva's lowered lids there were tears for Branwen, loveless and childless, dying of heartbreak and shame for the destruction her brother had caused; Bedvir sat silent with downcast gaze, thinking of the fate of Manadan, left alone to grieve for her and for his great brother. But Arthur's thoughts were of the wise and mighty King, even in death the talisman of his people; and his eyes were shining.

ELTIC warriors won fame first as "chariot-warriors," later as "battle-horsemen." Their armies contained infantry, but this force was not tactically central as it was for Romans and Saxons. The horse was essential to Celtic warfare, and no bard ever forgot it: they sang of the swift chargers, of how they were fed and how their coats shone, of their swooping down like eagles. It was the power and mobility of mounted men which gave the British their best weapon against the Saxons, so long as they kept the breeding grounds and the land to support their mounts. In Arthur's time the ancient warband had become a force of three hundred accomplished "battle-horsemen," owing allegiance to one leader, able to strike swiftly and hard. He was above all a Commander of cavalry, and that is how he went into legend—his warband transformed in time into an Order of Chivalry.

In earlier times warriors went to battle in chariots, although they might dismount to fight their single combats. They also fought enemy infantry on foot, the chariots standing ready to carry them out of danger when needed. Julius Caesar described this tactic with admiration: "Thus they combine the mobility of cavalry with the staying power of infantry." Others who faced the Celtic chariots speak of them with less detachment, describing instead the terror of the charge, the havoc the chariots caused as they hurtled across a battle front while warriors hurled javelins from them. Chariots had not been used on the continent for a long time, and the Romans were appalled to encounter them in Britain; Cassivelaunos apparently commanded 4000 of them. One legend, however, is untrue; there were no scythes on the wheels.

Chariots gave these flamboyant warriors plenty of opportunity for the displays of skill and daring that they loved, and a hero's "chariot-feats" are often mentioned, though tantalisingly the story-teller often says which feat it was, but does not describe it— obviously his audience would have known them well. We know that in battle a warrior might run out along the yoke-pole and cast his spears from there; another wonderful piece of bravado, though for games rather than war, was to bring the team from full gallop to a rearing halt, then dash forward along the shaft to balance between them. If in battle the chariot was an early form of tank, in play it seems to have foreshadowed the motorbike!

The Celtic chariot itself was pared down to the minimum, to little more than a platform between two wheels, and immense skill and courage were needed to drive one. To charge across uneven ground, and to control a team in the din of war, all the time remaining aware of the warrior's needs, must have been a daunting task. In battle charioteers were protected by a taboo, and also perhaps by the fact that they were not members of the warrior caste. Even so they were highly honoured, and the close friendship between a hero and his charioteer is important in many stories, providing not only emotion but humour, in the contrast between the talk of the privileged commoner and the high flights of his aristocratic comrade. On campaign it seems that they did the duties of groom, squire, and doctor as well; and one of the duties of a charioteer was to taunt his warrior into fierceness, if he seemed too mild!

Most chariots were drawn by two horses: a team of four may have been for royalty. Chariot teams and cavalry chargers were probably all of native British breeds—what we would call ponies; strong, lively, intelligent animals, quick and neat in manoeuvres. They too were given their share of glory; their names and attributes were recounted, and in stories they sometimes have superhuman powers to match those of the hero. The Welsh *Triads of the Horses* commemorate many of them—the Slender Grey (perhaps an Arab?) was one of the Three Be-

stowed Horses of Britain. They went into battle
with richly decorated harness—many pony ornaments have been found, including a cap with curving horns. But the necklaces of severed heads one
Roman describes were no doubt the most impressive horse-trappings, if not the most beautiful.

For all the bloody descriptions, except in story,
battles between Celts probably cost very few lives.
It took a long time to train a warrior, and even the
aristocrats with their death-and-glory ethos were
not to be slaughtered needlessly. Battles went to an
established pattern, beginning with boasts and insults, through a great deal of aggressive display, and
usually ending in duels between champions, which
decided victory for that day at least. Even these did
not always end in a death. If tempers ran too high
and real bloodshed threatened, druids or bards could
intervene to stop the fighting. The deliberate extermination of entire villages and tribes practised by
the Saxons was unheard of among the Celts.

Only against opponents who did not obey the
same rules, or in a really desperate situation like
an invasion, was widespread killing unavoidable.
Then the Celtic warriors proved themselves as good
as their glorious words, winning deathless fame by
their fierceness and their gallantry. Warriors
naked but for torc and belt often led the assault,
while hopeless situations and desperate odds never
deterred them; they would fight, said Strabo, "even
though they had nothing on their side but their own
strength and courage."

I t had been a hard day's riding, and most of Arthur's comrades were relaxing by the hearth; but he himself was walking with the youngest of them on the city wall, enjoying the last burning of the sun among the autumn woods, and the molten glow of the quiet river with its wing-folded ships.

With a sweep of his arm at the fire-crowned oaks and beeches Arthur declared, "There's a sight to shame the hair of any lady a poet ever praised! Look there, and you'll find a match even for Gueneva," and when the young man studied them seriously, then said, "No," he laughed and put an arm across his shoulders, walking him on.

In the west the clouds ended as at a shore, but they were flocked above, and the Emperor, turning his face up to their fretted gold, was lit with glory. Youth had left Arthur early, but there could be no regretting it; the assured vigour of his prime was better suited to him. At his side the young man walked silent, dark head erect, grave and attentive. When they paused again to look over the old city, Arthur gazed long, but the eyes of his companion soon returned to his face.

"She's a tough old town," Arthur mused, "how many times sacked, and always recovering?"

"Phoenix of Britain, Eternal City."

"From most people I'd call that mockery. Don't you care for this place?"

"Yes. But Camalodunum is my home. You must expect me to be partial."

As always, his deliberation made Arthur laugh. "You're such a Roman, Medrod. Camalodunum! I've a mind to tell the Bishop I suspect you of being a Stoic." His attention returned to the town; in a moment he said, "When we've really beaten them—when there's peace—I shall make my court here."

For once Medrod looked startled. "Why here? Why not London?"

"Better placed to keep the Saxon settlers apart.

And I haven't a strong Underking here. The Cornovii, the Votadini, and the men of the North, hold the other three corners of the compass: I'm most needed here in the east. Besides, I like Camalod." He did not speak of his other reason: that London was London, and he wished his city to be remembered as his.

"What does the Queen say to that?"

"She doesn't know. What should she say? Look, the colour's gone from the river. How quickly the ships' lanterns brighten. Let's go down."

On the stairs down from the wall, though, he paused again; and as he looked over the city then it was hard to say whether his face was that of a father, a son, or a bridegroom. Watching him, Medrod's grey eyes unveiled and lit with affection, while his rarely relaxed austerity melted into a smile of real warmth. It had not left him when he walked behind the King into the room where their companions were.

The King walked to the hearth, clapping his hands and saying, "Well, Horse?" The old hound groaned welcomingly, rolling onto his back; his master picked up his paws and looked at them, then let him go with a pat. "No more frontier inspections for you. You're getting too old for this ride. Well, friends, what entertainment now? Where's Dumnoric?"

Gai answered, "Gone to bed to nurse a cold: we've no bard."

Bedvir, bringing a cup to Arthur, said, "You can't say that, when Medrod's here. Give him the harp," and he smiled at the young man, expecting a denial.

But Medrod said equably, "If people want singing, they'd do better to ask you; but I can tell a few stories, if anyone wants to hear one of them."

"One at least," said the Emperor, settling into a chair. "Come, harper, tune your strings; what will you tell us?"

The young officer said nothing for a moment,

concentrating on his instrument. Then he said, "Since we're here, where I was a boy, I shall tell you of the hero I loved best then. I used to think this was his city, and I'm still reluctant to give up the idea. Anyhow, it was certainly the first the Romans put their mark on, and they are in the story too, so it's still appropriate. So, lend an ear, friends; here is the tale called *The Sons of Troy.*"

Camalod
(Camulodunum)

London

THAMES

Landing of
Julius Caesar
on Tanatus

Third battle of Cassivelaunos & Caesar
Treachery of Androgos

First battle of
Caesar &
Cassivelaunos

WHEN Cassivelaunos was High King in Britain, great Julius was Emperor of Rome. He was a man unequalled in might, and when he had conquered Gaul all the world was his, save Britain. He went up and down surveying his lands, and he came to the north coast of Gaul. There he stood and looked across the sea, and he saw the cliffs of Kent like a greater wave above the white waves. He said to the men about him, "What land is that I see beyond the sea?"

They answered him, "Lord, that is the Island of the Mighty."

Caesar said, "There also shall I rule."

"Lord," they said, "that will not be easy; for the name that land bears was not given it lightly."

"Nevertheless I shall rule there," said Caesar.

He caused a great fleet to be built, and summoning his legions he embarked them in the ships and set out for Britain. But when they came near the shores of the Island a great wind arose, so that the ships could make no headway against it, and though for a day they struggled to go forward they were driven back onto the shores of Gaul. Caesar was displeased; within a few days he set out again, and again when they came near the Island the great wind blew. The order was given that they should take down their sails and drive the ships forward with oars, and they strove to do so; three mighty men laboured at each oar, but the wind piled the sea up against them, and though the oars thrust the ships forward the waves thrust them back further, so that for all their labour the Romans found they made greater speed back to Gaul than to Britain.

Julius Caesar said, "Do the waves fight for the men of this Island? This is a greater army than Pompey had."

Yet he was still resolved to rule in all the world, and a third time he attempted the crossing. Then the wind blew so hard and the waters sucked so fiercely at the keels that it was only by good fortune that the

fleet was not wrecked. Great Julius was angry; he
sent for wise men and demanded, "What is the
cause of this wind that drives my ships back from
Britain?"

"Great Caesar, it is said by the people of that
Island that it is under a protection from invasion by
a foreign people, and that except by the invitation of
their King such a people could not come there. You
will never set foot upon that Island unless you do so
by guile."

"Then I shall be guileful," said Caesar.

He summoned Dividiag, a merchant who had
frequently been to Britain, and said, "What manner
of man is the King of that Island, and what thing is
it he loves more than any other?"

Dividiag answered, "King Cassivelaunos is a noble and warlike man; for accomplishment in the skills
of a warrior and the craft of battle there is none like
him. He is of a proud and fiery temper, and whatever he has sworn to do he will not turn back from;
no man has heard a false word from him. In speech
he is eloquent and witty, and prudent in judgment,
and his manners are courteous and pleasing. It is his
nature to be generous and hospitable, but if a man
has proved himself his enemy he will find Cassivelaunos harsh and implacable. In person he is handsome, well proportioned, and like a fine stallion in
his bearing. Also he is young, and fond of all sports
and games; and apart from his kindred and friends,
most in the world he loves his horses."

When he heard this Julius sent out messengers
to all parts of his Empire, with commands to bring
him the finest horses from every part of the world.
They did so, and it was a great number; but the
finest horse there was the Slender Grey. He so far
surpassed the others, that the sight of him was worth
the possession of all the rest. He was so swift he
would outstrip an arrow shot from his back: so strong,
he would gallop a day and a night without rest: so
hardy, he would do that without food or drink and

suffer no ill of it after. As for beauty, he had no
match in creation; from the crest of his head to his
plumed heel every hair of him was perfect. With all
this, he was so gentle he would step through a
meadow of larks and not crack one of their eggs, he
would bear a sleeping infant on his back and it
would not wake.

Julius Caesar had a fine harness made for him,
and sent Dividiag with him to London. The man
took the Slender Grey to the Island of the Mighty
and to the court of Cassivelaunos. There were many
young noble men of fine appearance there, but
Cassivelaunos outshone them all, with his red-gold
hair, his tall shapely form, his bright eagle glance.
He welcomed the merchant, and asked why he came
there; and the man said, "I bring you a gift from
Julius Caesar, the Emperor of the World; for he
wishes to greet the only King who can be compared
with him for might and magnificence." Then he
brought the Slender Grey before Cassivelaunos. The
harness was all hung with little tinkling bells; he
sported with his silver bit and pranced as proud and
graceful as a summer wave on the shore.

Cassivelaunos was captivated by the beauty of
the horse; he came and took the bridle from Dividiag,
and said, "I swear by the gods my people swear by,
this is the King of the horses of the world! Your
master is no niggard, of his speech or his gifts. What
can I give him in requital of such a gift as this?"

The man said, "It would please him if you would
grant him space for his horses' forefeet upon the
land of Britain."

"By my head, he shall have that," swore Cassivelaunos, "so often as he requires it!"

When Julius heard this answer he laughed aloud,
and he embarked his army again. This time the wind
did not blow against them; and they landed on the
island called Tanatus.

When the news was brought to Cassivelaunos
he was angry with himself. "I see I spoke rashly,"

he said. "But I cannot take my words back." He was angrier yet when messengers came from Caesar: for they said that the Emperor was come to receive the submission of the people of Britain and their tribute.

"Even in requital for the Slender Grey he shall not have that!" said Cassivelaunos. "The Romans should rather honour the Britons, for they, like us, are descended from the race of the Trojans, and are our kindred. And Julius Caesar is a descendant of my forefather Aeneas; let him speak to me with the courtesy his first messenger used, for it was more fitting!"

When Caesar had that reply he said, "Not all people gave their submission when I first asked it, but none withheld it when they had fought me."

He prepared to fight the Britons, and Cassivelaunos summoned all the warriors of the Island of the Mighty. In Kent near the mouth of Thames the two hosts met; never had two such hosts faced each other within this realm. When Cassivelaunos looked on the ranks of the legions he said, "Though these are not Britons, still they are warriors."

And when Julius Caesar saw the Army of the Britons approaching, with the chariots of the champions going before, and the sound of the horns and the battle cries, he said, "Today's victory will not be easily won."

The Romans were dismayed by the fury of the onset of the Britons, and most of all to find women among the warriors, for that had never been the custom of Rome; but the Britons were astonished by the battle-craft of the Romans. For the sons of Troy were alike in valour and hardihood, and the battle hung even, so well were the hosts matched. Great Julius was armed with a sword called Yellow Death; and in the battle he did great slaughter with it, for its every stroke was mortal. If Yellow Death wounded so much as a man's finger he would die of it. When he did not have this sword the Emperor was a great warrior, and when it was in his hand there had not been found until that day a champion who could withstand him. Therefore a great heap of the dead of Britain began to mount about the place where he was, and the Britons were confounded when they saw the power of the sword.

Cassivelaunos had a young brother Nennios, and he was a better warrior than many with more hair on the lip than he had; and for high heart and courage he had no equal—when he rushed at his foes he never paused to count the number of them.

He saw the slaughter Caesar made among the men of Britain, and his anger was roused at it; he said to his charioteer, "I cannot watch the Emperor killing the men of this Island any longer; let us go and put a stop to it."

"That will not be easy to do; he is a good fighter, besides having a strong guard about him. Also he has a powerful sword in his hand."

"If I do not fight him, I will never eat pork or drink wine again!"

"Alas for those words," said the charioteer, "for you may never do so again if you do fight him."

"Are these taunts to raise my fury? Before the Gods, I will not leave this battle unless I do so with Yellow Death in my hand! Drive at the Emperor now, and do not turn aside for other combats!"

The charioteer set the horses to a gallop and Nennios raised the hero-scream; his warrior's fury fell upon him as he did so. A glow of light burst from him; his hair sprang out of its braids and the pins that held it, and stood about his head hard as bronze. His sinews were knotted and his veins bulged, a sweat of blood ran down his face, his skin darkened and became like cured leather for hardness, his lips writhed back from his teeth and there was foam on them. He trembled violently with the intensity of his frenzy, and the heat of his body was so great that the wood of his chariot began to smoulder, and the shafts of the spears he held burst into flame as he threw them.

Romans fled from the sight of him, but the
Emperor's guard stood firm. Nennios hurled his burning spears among them and charged into their midst,
then he sprang from his chariot and drawing his
sword began to fight them. There were skillful warriors there, and Nennios was wounded by them in
neck and side and thigh; but he did not heed his
wounds, and he killed all the guard. Then he fell on
great Julius. There was a bitter battle then, for there
were not many warriors equal to the Emperor, but in
his frenzy Nennios overcame him and wrestled Yellow Death from his hand. Then he sprang back into
his chariot, and his charioteer drove him swiftly out
of the battle; and as the battle-rage left Nennios all
his wounds began to bleed, so that he leaned on the
side of the chariot for weakness.

His driver said, "Those wounds are not bee
stings."

Nennios answered him, "They would not much
concern me; but I have a cut on the arm from this
viperous sword. Take it to my brother, for I shall not
wield it today."

When the chariot halted Nennios got out on the
grass and took three steps and died. The weeping
charioteer took Yellow Death and went to seek
Cassivelaunos, and when he reached the King he
said, "Your brother sends you the Roman's sword;
he has no need of it himself."

When Cassivelaunos heard of his brother's death
he raised a great cry of rage; the Romans blanched at
the sound of it, and when they saw him shake
Yellow Death above his head they fell back.

"There will be no withstanding him now," said
Caesar. "Sound the trumpet; we must forego victory
today."

The trumpets were blown, and the Romans fled;
they did not pause until they were in their ships.
Thus the Britons were victorious; but Cassivelaunos
did not pursue the Romans, he turned back to where
his brother lay, and wept over him.

They buried Nennios in a rich tomb, and Cassivelaunos mourned long for him. His companions said, "Nennios won great glory and kept his people safe. For what else does a warrior live? Long years could not have brought him more glory than he has."

"No," Cassivelaunos agreed, "but the loss of his company is bitter to me." Nevertheless in time he was comforted and took pleasure in the company of good friends.

Beltain grew near, and the year's turning; there was white blossom on the thorn trees, the cuckoo called, and deer cried from the hilltops. Cassivelaunos found his heart light again, and all his grief forgotten; he rode out alone on the Slender Grey, and he was singing as he rode. The harp of the wood played the melody for his singing, the gold iris stood along the bank of the bright river, the scent of the meadow came to him. "Before the Gods," said Cassivelaunos, "to be the man I am and riding the Slender Grey on such a day—a good Fate is mine!"

Soon after he had said that he came to a lawn of grass between the wood and the river, all studded with bright flowers, and there were eight young women sitting on the ground plaiting garlands. The sound of their talk and laughter was sweeter than the singing of larks, and in their midst was one in a tunic of purple with silver brocade on her slender arms, and she was fairest in that fair bevy. The sight of her struck Cassivelaunos with wonder, so that he stopped the Slender Grey and sat gazing at her. Her hair was like the blackbird's wing for darkness and softness, her brow and shoulders and arms white as the meadowsweet, her face the colour of delicate appleblossom, white and pink; her lips were smooth and red as clover, her bright eyes the colour of the harebell. Her delicate slim fingers twisting the flower stems and her bare feet on the bright grass were like moonbeams. For grace and elegance of bearing she

was like the swan, for gaiety and sweetness of tongue
like the linnet.

When this lady raised her head and saw looking
at her the tall warrior in a gay chequered tunic,
red-gold hair about his shoulders and the noblest
horse in the world under him, her eyes sparkled
with her smile and two dimples came in her cheeks.
She said, "Here is the King of the horses of the
world, and the King of their riders on him!"

At that whatever of Cassivelaunos's love had
not gone out to her did so; he dismounted from the
Slender Grey and walked towards her. "Lady," he
said, "his name is the Slender Grey, and mine is
Cassivelaunos; I am King of the Island of the Mighty.
And I marvel that I do not know your name, for the
fame of you should have reached me."

She answered, "My name is Flower."

He replied, "Indeed you are well named, for
surely you are the most delicate, the loveliest flower
of all the women in the world."

He sat down beside her among her attendants,
and they fell to talking; sweet was their discourse.
All that day they spent together, walking beside the
river or under the trees, or at games with her gaily-
dressed maidens. Then when sunset was near Flower
said, "King of my heart, I must leave you. For we
will be reproached if the dogs are loosed and the
gates closed, and we are not within them."

He said, "If you were willing to be my wife,
who else is there whose consent I must seek?"

She answered, "Alas, though I should be willing, you would need my father's consent, and that
you would not get, not though you are High King of
the Island. He has sworn to admit no suitor to me,
even should the Great Son of the Great Mother come
wooing he should not have me: for my father cannot
have a son-in-law and his life together. For he is
Ugnach the Giant, and if I marry his death is in it."

"I will seek his consent for all that."

"Alas, do not do so; for I fear it would end in

your death, and there would be no joy in my life
after that."

But Cassivelaunos kissed her and bade her be
courageous, and to tell him where her father's hall
was; then they parted. Flower went with her maidens to the stronghold of Ugnach the Giant, and
Cassivelaunos mounted the Slender Grey and rode
to his home.

When he came there his companions looked at
him and said, "This is the face of one who found
sweet fruit out of season."

"Sweet fruit on a thorny bush," replied Cassivelaunos. "Who will come with me to find the house
of Ugnach the Giant, and to fetch his daughter out
of it?"

Seven men armed themselves to go with him,
for love of Cassivelaunos and the honour of the
exploit. Cassivelaunos took Yellow Death from its
place and put it in the sheath of bronze his armourer
had made; then he mounted the Slender Grey and
led his companions the way Flower had instructed
him.

The house of Ugnach the Giant stood on a rocky
hill within a wood; the palisade about it was oak
trees rooted in the ground, with thorn plaited between them and rocks piled behind. The gate was
closed, and Cassivelaunos beat upon it. A din of
harsh voices answered him, but all the voices spoke
as one, and there was a fearsome baying of hounds
behind. "Who asks admittance?"

"Cassivelaunos, of Beli's sons, the High King of
the Island of the Mighty, and a noble company with
him."

"The gates are shut, the dogs are loosed; you
cannot come in."

"Here is a niggardly house, that shuts its gates
while the sun is high and offers no welcome to
travellers. Who denies us entrance?"

"We are four brothers and four sisters, and we
are the Porter of Ugnach. Without the bidding of

Ugnach we will not open, not to a learned man or a noble man or to a craftsman, not to a bard; and not to the High King of Britain."

"Nevertheless we shall pass the gate."

"Here are eight of us and the seven threefold dogs; if you passed the gate you would not cross the court, and the gate will not open."

Then Cassivelaunos rode the Slender Grey at the gate, and though it was twice the height of a man the Slender Grey jumped it as if he were a colt at play. So soon as he was in the court Cassivelaunos struck away the bars of the gate, and his companions rushed in. Immediately there was a hideous clamour in the court, and seven hideous dogs rushed to the attack; each dog had three bodies and three heads, with a spiked bronze collar around each of its three throats, slimy foam running from its jaws and bronze claws on all its twelve feet. A hard battle had those champions; but worse was the battle of Cassivelaunos with the Porter of Ugnach.

The four brothers and four sisters were scaly-limbed and ghastly, with swarthy skin and red eyes, and blue nails dripping venom. This multiple creature came prancing and hopping at the King, darting out its sixteen arms with their poisonous talons, eight purple tongues lolling on eight chins. They had one soul and one life among them; they could not be slain separately, but so long as one lived they all had life and force together. They struck at him from all sides, and leapt high in the air to fall upon him; but with his great strength and skill, and the nimbleness of the Slender Grey, and the mortal power of Yellow Death, Cassivelaunos defeated them, and sheared off all their eight heads, so that the Porter of Ugnach fell dead. And when it was done, he found that his seven companions had slain the seven hounds; so he led them into the hall.

Ugnach the Giant was sitting before the hearth. His feet were in the embers, his head was bent forward in the height of the roof. He was the most

hideous creature those men had seen, with his bowed
legs and his belly sagging onto his thighs, his brown
warty skin, his matted hair like straw raked from
cow-byre. His hands hung to the ground, and there
were nine fingers upon each of them. His ears
drooped to his shoulders, his lower lip hung upon
his breast, and he had no upper lip; his black gums
and yellow pointed teeth were not hidden. His eyes
were yellow and rheumy, the sweat on his face was
like a pig's grease, his breath had the stench of a
foul bog; the fire shuddered before it.

Cassivelaunos said, "My Flower had a fair
mother, if this is her father."

Ugnach said, "Here is a cursed loutish guest, to
kill my servant and my little pet dogs."

"Those were ungentle playfellows to keep for
Flower; and a churlish ungraceful host you are, to
bar your doors in the morning and offer no hospitality to strangers."

"The company of strangers does not please me,
and less than others do I love the men of Britain,
and less yet the sons of Beli, and least of all my
daughter's suitors."

"Yet here is a man who is all four of those
things, and one who will not leave your house until
his request is granted: the hand of Flower in his
hand, and her lips to kiss!"

Ugnach rose from his seat with a howl at that,
and the great ugly bulk of him filled the room to the
roof. Cassivelaunos stood like a flame before his
darkness, and Yellow Death gleamed in his hand.
Ugnach struck at him, but he avoided the blows, so
that the giant's fists smashed great holes in the floor-
paving; and then the High King ran close to him and
pierced him in the side with Yellow Death. Then
Ugnach gave a bellow and a shriek, with a blast of
breath so foul that the seven men with Cassivelaunos
fell senseless, and the Slender Grey reared scream-
ing. Flinging up his arms the giant stretched to his
full height so that the roof burst off the hall and it

was filled with light and clean air; and he fell sideways in death, and the walls of the house were smashed down. The back wall of the hall where the men of Britain were fell, and it revealed a little enclosed lawn about an apple tree, and there was Flower with her maidens. Cassivelaunos sprang over the giant's limbs and went to her, and they embraced; then he set her on the Slender Grey before him and bore her away, and his companions brought her maidens.

He said as they rode, "Within three days there shall be such a feast in my house as was never seen there yet, and then shall come the time I long for, when I shall stretch my side at your side and my arm around your head."

But Flower replied, "It is not fitting I should be your bride so soon, for my father's blood is on your hands, and his head will see me as I pass your door. Therefore give me a place where I can live with my women, and in a year and a day you may fetch me from there, and I shall be your wife."

Cassivelaunos did as she asked, and gave her a fine hall richly furnished; there she dwelt with her attendants, and the noble people of Britain came to do her honour. All who saw her marvelled at her beauty; she was esteemed throughout the Island of the Mighty, and the High King visited her constantly, and the love between them grew past measure. And after the slaying of Ugnach, Cassivelaunos never fought with Yellow Death in his hand again, but it was laid on the breast of his brother Nennios in his tomb.

Julius Caesar was in Gaul, but he had not forgotten his resolve to rule over Britain. He caused a tower to be built on the coast, and every day from this tower he looked towards the shores of the Island, while he gathered another army and another fleet. This time his purpose was to sail up the Thames and attack London, for he knew it was not the custom of the British to make war in this way, but to fight in the open field, and he hoped thus to gain the advantage over them. However Cassivelaunos heard word of his intention; he caused a great barricade of stakes to be planted across Thames from the north bank to the south, and each stake had the girth of a champion, and their ends were sharpened.

On a day of early spring the Romans came up the river with a fair wind. A host of Britons was gathered on either bank, and when great Julius saw them he laughed, saying, "Our stroke will go past this shield!" But the tide was high and covered the stakes, and he was not aware of them until there was a great rending as the ships were impaled on the barrier. The belly was torn out of each ship, and the water rushed in. Then there was a great commotion, cries of men and groaning of wood, and confusion as the ships that had been behind sailed into the wrecks of those that had been before. Many Romans in their armour drowned, and the warriors of Britain were waiting for those who escaped from the river; there was great slaughter that day, and those who were not slain or drowned fled with all the speed they could.

The ship that the Emperor was in was not harmed, and the captain of it made haste for the sea again. Julius gazed at the ruin of his army, and a great rage filled him. He said, "What is this Cassivelaunos, that he has twice done what no other King in the world has done once? By all the gods of Rome, I shall have revenge for this!"

The ship he was in put in for water on the southern shore of Thames, and when they came to shore great Julius and his guard rode about to refresh themselves, and there was little conversation to be had from him because of the anger that filled him. They came upon a fair hall between apple orchards: and it chanced that it was the place Cassivelaunos had given Flower, and she was at sport with her maidens among the trees.

When great Julius saw her and his eye took in

her beauty and her grace, he forgot all the bitterness
of his defeat and all his rage. He gazed at her in
wonder, and his heart melted in him; he had not
looked long before he was altogether filled with love
of her, and the place at her side seemed to him as
desirable as the foremost place he had among the
Kings of the world. He dismounted from his horse
and greeted her, saying, "Hail, Empress of the
World!"

She said astonished, "I do not know why you
should call me that, for it is not my name."

Caesar said, "It shall be. Jewel of the earth, I
will give you the foremost place among the Queens
of the world, and the noblest man in the world to be
your husband!"

"That I have already, for the world does not
hold the equal of Cassivelaunos!"

When he heard that Caesar delayed with words
no longer, but seized her and set her on his horse
before him; for he saw that he could have his desire
and his revenge together. Flower fought with him,
and her maidens ran to her aid, but the guard drove
them off, and Flower for all her striving could do
nothing against the great strength of Caesar. He
rode swiftly back to his ship, and the captain set sail;
and when Flower saw the coast of Britain grow small
behind her she lamented and covered her face in
despair. Great Julius said to her, "Here is no cause
for fear or grief! I shall do you no harm or dishonour,
but take you to Rome and make you my wife."

But Flower cried, "Alas for my sorrow! When
Cassivelaunos was at my side I did not know what
care was, but there is no goodness in life without
him. If I am not to hold him in my arms let me
perish, let me die before I kiss another mouth than
his!"

Cassivelaunos was rejoicing at his victory. He
gave Thames a thank-offering of fine armour, and he
prepared a great feast, and sent for Flower to be
present at it. But instead of Flower came the news of

her abduction, and the feast was forgotten, and rejoicing turned to outrage.

With controlled fury Cassivelaunos said, "Julius Caesar hopes thus to be revenged on me; but he shall not find it easier to take Flower from me, than to take Britain!"

"What will you do?" said his companions.

"I shall go to Rome, and no host shall go with me; and if I do not bring her back, I shall never feast with my champions again."

"Let us go with you."

"In this no man can help me; I shall have no companion but the Slender Grey. And if I do not succeed, give the Crown of the Island to another!"

Caesar had taken Flower to Rome, and provided a palace for her, built of white marble and ornamented with gold throughout. There was a multitude of servants to wait on her, garments of silk for her to wear, the best of meat and drink, but she would not be comforted. Caesar came daily to visit her, bringing gifts; but Flower turned her face from them all, saying, "Gold has no brightness compared with the hair of Cassivelaunos, and jewels are dull when I remember his eyes. There is no beauty or wealth in the world that can match his perfect form, or console me for the sight of the smile he would give me!"

Nevertheless the preparations were made for her marriage to Caesar, and when Cassivelaunos came to Rome he found nothing else was talked of in the city.

He had come in the guise of a craftsman, and the craft he chose was that of a shoemaker. The shoes he made were of the finest leather stitched with gold, and they were cunningly ornamented, with silk linings to them. There was no man in Rome who made such shoes, and the fame of him spread: for that Cassivelaunos is called one of the Three Noble Shoemakers of the Island of Britain.

The women who waited on Flower were preparing the garments for her wedding, and she would not wear the sandals they had obtained, but said she wished for shoes of the British fashion. They went to her steward and told him of it, and he said, "There is a shoemaker in Rome who is marvellously skilled in the making of such shoes. Let the pattern of her foot be sent to him."

The pattern of her foot was taken to him, and he made a pair of shoes from it; but they were found to pinch in the toe. He made another, and they were found to pinch in the heel. When the servants came the third time, Cassivelaunos said, "The patterns you have given me are at fault; I must come myself and take the measure of her foot."

They brought him to her palace. Flower would not receive him for she said, "I will go barefoot all my days sooner than be shod for this wedding."

When Cassivelaunos was told this, he said, "By the three rivers of Britain, it would be easier to fight with a threefold dog and an eightfold warrior than to bear the moods of such a woman!"

When the servants reported this speech to Flower, she was astonished. She said to herself, "This is a man of Britain, and for the sake of hearing one of my own speech I will admit him." They brought him into her presence; when she saw that it was indeed Cassivelaunos she thought her heart would burst for joy. When her servants saw her laugh they were glad, for all who served Flower loved her.

Cassivelaunos took his measurements and said to the attendants, "I have never made shoes for so delicate and perfect a foot; the leather I have brought is not fine enough for her use. If you were to bring the lady to my workplace, she might make her own choice."

They replied, "If she is willing we will do so."

It was very sure Flower was willing; she went there with them, and that was the first time she had left the palace given to her. She praised some leathers and rejected others, but she did not make a choice.

At last Cassivelaunos said, "In the room beyond this I have a horsehide, softer than silk and more supple than water: that is perhaps fit to go under you and keep your feet from the ground."

Flower's eyes sparkled. "I will see it," she said.

Her women were all comparing leathers and debating over ornaments, and she left them and went through the door with Cassivelaunos. There was the Slender Grey; and they mounted him together, and fled out of the city of Rome. And they had left the city before her ladies finished their debate and found her gone.

Then a great hue and cry was raised. In fury Julius sent out messengers, and gave orders the fugitives should be pursued; but however fast the news went, the Slender Grey was faster. He bore the lovers through Italy and Gaul without pausing for rest or food, so smoothly that they were no more wearied by that journey than he was, until they came to the coasts, and there they took ship. The rumour of their flight had not reached Gaul then, while the servants of Caesar pursuing them were not a hundred miles from Rome.

So soon as they returned to London the wedding feast for Cassivelaunos and Flower was made, for the year and the day were past. All the Kings and nobles of the Island were gathered together for it, with the bards and the druids and the foremost craftsmen. Cassivelaunos had new halls built to house them, for those there already were not sufficient for such a gathering: there was food and wine of the best for all who came, comfortable beds and good attendance, and Flower gave gifts to all the ladies.

The poets who had not seen her before that day were most eloquent in her praise, and all the guests hailed her as Queen of Britain. Then after the feast Cassivelaunos took to his bed the bride for whom he had waited so long, and had won from two enemies,

and for whose sake he is called one of the Three
Lovers of this Island. No love was sweeter than the
love between these two.

The feasting continued many days, and there
were sports and contests between the men gathered
there, horse races and chariot races and games, and
much jesting and boasting and contests of words.
But one of these jests turned to harm; for a man of
the High King's warband called Prasutag, and Cunagus a man of Kent, began a dispute over a horse
race. What began as merriment turned to rivalry, the
rivalry to anger, and the anger to fighting; and
Cunagus killed Prasutag in the High King's guest
hall.

When Cassivelaunos heard of it he commanded
Cunagus to appear before him for judgment, but the
man had fled into Kent and could not be found.
Then the High King bade the King of Kent to seek
out the man and cause him to come to London to be
judged. This King was called Androgos. He was
young and of a high temper, and Cunagus was the
son of his mother's sister.

"I will not send him to you," he said, "but I will
pass judgment on him myself."

"The wrong was done to a man of mine and in
my hall," replied Cassivelaunos. "The council of my
tribe shall hear his fault, and I shall judge him. Bring
him before me."

"I will not do so!" said Androgos; and he gathered the men of Kent and withdrew into his own
kingdom.

Then Cassivelaunos's wrath was kindled; he fixed
the penalty that Cunagus should suffer, and the
reparation he should make, and sent into Kent to
demand it. But Androgos felt that for his honour he
must protect one who was his kinsman, and he said,
"It is my right to judge my people."

The High King said, "Do I not wear the Crown
of London?" And waited.

When Cunagus neither appeared before him nor

made the reparation, his anger grew. He sent again to Androgos, saying, "If this man does not answer for his crime, the penalty for it shall fall upon his kinsmen, and I shall demand it of you."

Androgos retorted, "Then you must come yourself to collect it."

Now Cassivelaunos was out of patience, "If reparation is not made within one month, I shall do so."

The elders of the tribe were dismayed at this message. They said to Androgos, "It will be ill for the High King to make war upon us. Better if Cunagus is persuaded to accept judgment of him."

"The man is my kinsman and under my protection; I will not let Cassivelaunos judge him."

"Then you must make the reparation on his behalf, lest all Kent pays it."

"Is my honour nothing? It is my right to pronounce judgment on my people, and I will not be denied that by any man, though he is High King!" Nevertheless Androgos knew that he had not men enough to withstand Cassivelaunos if it should come to war between them. He said to himself, "It is not counsel I need, but allies." He pondered the matter: and he thought of Julius Caesar.

He crossed the sea and sought the Emperor, and found him in a house he had in Gaul, taking his ease. He said, "Hail, Caesar! I am Androgos, King of Kent in the Island of Britain, and I am come to offer you alliance."

Great Julius was surprised. He looked at the princely, well-made young man and said, "Twice I have fought in Britain, and it was your kingdom I fought in. You did not offer me alliance then."

"No. In each of those battles I killed many Romans and made trophies of their heads. Your people will vouch for my prowess."

"When did you learn this friendship for me?"

"When a slight was put on my honour, and the

man who is your enemy became my enemy also: Cassivelaunos, son of Beli, High King of the Island."

When the Emperor heard that name he rose to his feet, and the blood came and went in his face. "Indeed he is my enemy, for the two defeats he has given me and for the rivalry between us concerning Flower. Yet in all the wars I have fought, never have I had so noble an adversary."

"He is a man of prowess; but for all that I shall not take a slight from him. If we make alliance, we may defeat him."

"By the Shield of Mars, that would delight me!"

So they made alliance, and together led a host into Britain, and Caesar was eager for battle, for he thought that when Cassivelaunos was slain then Flower would be his, and all the world should call him Emperor. The High King led his host into Kent; but not all the men of Britain were there, for some Kings sided with Androgos and others with neither. Upon the banks of the great river of Kent he saw the host of Androgos camped, and a vast army of Romans with them, and Julius Caesar at their head.

In grief he said, "Alas for the words I spoke, when I gave the Roman his requital for the Slender Grey! And alas for the contention between guests and the crime of Cunagus, for the warfare between the men of Britain! For now the greatest warrior of the world has come the third time against us, and half of my spears are in his hand. Agrona and Andraste and Cathobadua, Queens of Battle, sharpen our spears today!"

Then uttering his war cry he shook his weapons above his head, and his charioteer set his four shining horses to the gallop; and the host of Britain raised a fearful clamour, and charged with him on their enemies. There was a bitter battle; few such battles have been fought in the world, by Britons or Romans. Crows and kites gathered to watch the feast prepared for them, and the air was harsh with their voices. Chariots were overturned, men and

horses slain, the noise of cracking wood and scream-
ing metal was heard on all sides, the ground became
a swamp of blood. Heads fell and limbs were hewn
off, entrails spilled, men and women had their souls
ripped from their breasts in violent death, and the
sound of their cries went up like thick smoke.

All day the struggle raged on the river bank,
and the waters ran dark. Cassivelaunos fought like a
foster son of the goddesses; no man lived where he
came, and there were no wounds on him. But there
were both Romans and Britons united against him,
and in greater numbers; and he could not prevail.

So victory went to great Julius and Androgos,
and the host of Britain fled from them. Cassivelaunos
went last of all the warriors. At every ford and
narrow place he turned and fought the foremost
Romans and the champions of Androgos until all his
host had passed in safety. Wherever he stood there
was a heap of dead; and soon they dared follow him
no more, and left the pursuit.

Then said Julius Caesar, "Now I am Emperor of
the World!"

"Not so," said Androgos, "for Cassivelaunos
lives, and you cannot call him defeated while there
is life in him."

Great Julius answered, "In all my life I never
knew so noble a man as this, so brave an enemy and
so worthy of honour. I would be glad if there were
peace between us."

"That will be when you have his head."

"That would grieve me. Go to him, and make
him this offer, that he shall have all that is now his,
if he will make the submission of Britain to me, and
give me the tribute that every other King of the
world gives."

"You will not get that from him."

"Then tell him all that is now his shall be mine,
the rule of Britain, and Flower, and the Slender Grey
too!"

Androgos went in search of Cassivelaunos, and

he found the host of the Britons, and Cassivelaunos seated on a hillside beside three hazel trees. He stood up when he saw Androgos, saying, "Here is the man who would give the Island of the Mighty to a foreign people. Once he was King of a noble tribe, now he is the Roman's herald."

"I am no herald; but I come to tell you the offer Caesar makes you. That if you make submission and pay him tribute, like other Kings, nothing that is yours shall be taken from you." He folded his arms and met the High King's eyes. "But I told him he would get none of it, unless he got your head first."

"He might have spared you your journey, seeing you gave him my answer; he will not get a better from me. Yet tell this Emperor of yours that he should not seek to shame the blood that is his also: for we are of the blood of Dardanus, the race of Troy, and no foreign people shall receive our tribute or our submission. This Island was given to our forefather Brutus and to his people forever: born of the fortunate breed of Brutus, we shall never be slaves."

"I will tell him that gladly!"

Cassivelaunos looked at him with anger and sorrow. "You will need to tell him; he would not know it by your example." Androgos's face darkened, and his heart burned in him. The King said, "My reproach on you, Androgos! There were few in the Island to compare with you for honour and valour, and you were admired of bards, of warriors, of women. Grief to us and shame to you, that for your own quarrel you would make this bargain, that for a lawbreaker you would betray Britain! It will be no good song that is sung of you."

Then Androgos wept, and went to his knees before Cassivelaunos. "My grief for the deed! High King, I would be reconciled with you."

Cassivelaunos looked down on him, and he was near to weeping also, but he said, "Shall Cunagus come to judgment?"

"Why should we contend over Cunagus, when the crows do battle for him now? But I will make this reparation for his crime; half the value of his cattle shall be given to the kin of the man he slew, and half to you. And by earth and sky I swear, I shall never bear arms against you again!"

They clasped hands and were reconciled, and all the host who saw it rejoiced. Cassivelaunos said, "Take my answer to Caesar; and propose to him a truce, that each side may tend their wounded, and give him my challenge to battle after that."

Androgos carried this message to Caesar. When he heard it the Emperor was amazed. "Am I to hear no more than that?"

"There is more, though Cassivelaunos did not speak it. We have taken requital for our honour of each other, and are reconciled; and when you fight with him again, you will find me at his side."

With that Androgos left Caesar and led his men to the Britons, and they were welcome: but the Romans were dismayed. Their officers said to Caesar, "Only with difficulty could we overcome this man, and that with a host of Britons at our side. Moreover the Kings that held aloof from this battle will not do so from the next."

"And more than that," said Caesar, "I no longer desire to be his enemy. By the Eagles of Rome, I swear, his defeat would grieve me like my own!"

He rose, and donned an armour of gold and his purple mantle over it, and he commanded his horse to be brought to him. Then he rode out with only his shield-bearer, and sought the camp of Cassivelaunos. When he came there the Britons looked with wonder on his pride and his splendour; and Cassivelaunos said, "It is a brave man who comes alone before his enemies."

"It is not my custom to fear. Nor is there need of it, when there are noble men to trust in." Then Julius dismounted from his horse and faced the High King, stern and imperial, and there had never been seen together two such men. "Why should Romans and Britons be enemies, the sons of Troy, twins in valour? When kinsmen long parted meet, feasting is better."

Cassivelaunos rejoiced to hear him; he said, "For the sake of our forefather Aeneas, let us swear friendship. As kinsmen you are welcome to Britain, and space on the shore for your horses' forefeet is yours so often as you wish it."

The Emperor offered his hand, saying, "I have had no friend I loved so well as such an enemy. Not since Hector has there been such a warrior as you!"

"Nor since Priam such a ruler as you. All that is mine I will share with you; save Flower and the Slender Grey!"

At that they laughed, and clasped hands, and swore friendship together; and the nobles of Britain acclaimed them. That night Romans and Britons feasted together, and a strong alliance was sworn between them, and great Julius conferred on every free man of Britain the citizenship of Rome. Thus met the two races of Trojan descent, and the divided heirs of Aeneas were united, and found in one another the equals they had not found before in all the world. While the earth endures that alliance shall be remembered; and while Britons and Romans are one, none shall overcome them.

HE company did not applaud Medrod as they would have done a bard, but their praise was warm enough to ruffle his composure a little. Arthur said, "Not so Roman after all! The most correct of my captains has gifts unknown to me."

"I told you I had an old-fashioned tutor who taught me, 'eloquence is fitting for noble men.' " Medrod rose, and went to pour himself some wine.

"And indeed, you told the old tale well. Still, I think no dark Flower can compare with our ladies. But you favour dark girls, do you?"

The faintest shadow flickered in Medrod's face, but his back was to the room. "When I was a boy, it was the Slender Grey I dreamed of. Then when I got older, I used to think how much better I'd have managed Androgos's part in the story."

"Not the King's?"

"I didn't aspire so high: nor think he could be bettered. Come, Bedvir, take the harp. Sing to us now."

HE Celts loved finery, and their story-tellers took pains to describe the elegance of their heroes and heroines as well as their beauty. Even when they could not be fine, they were personally fastidious; writers of other nations noted that even the poorest people were scrupulously clean, and their clothes never dirty or ragged. Most of their garments were wool or linen, but they wore finer materials when they could, and liked to think of figures of legend as dressed always in silk and brocade. Colours were as bright as possible, heightened in imagination to brilliance, and they were fond of combining them in checks or plaids. The Celtic languages have a vocabulary for colour which is wide, vivid, and precise; it is impossible to render it in English.

This vanity was not limited to their clothing. They were proud of their hair, which they often dressed elaborately and sometimes bleached or dyed, and especially in Britain and Gaul men were proud of their long moustaches, though they did not usually wear beards. Both sexes used cosmetics, and men frequently adorned their breasts and arms with elaborate tattooing. This may have marked both their warrior status and their tribe. The people most famous for their use of this decoration were the Celts of Northern Britain, the Picts—that is, the Painted People. The tattooing was done with woad; this is the origin of the belief, started by the Romans, that the Britons "painted their bodies blue."

The most beautiful and enduring result of this love of adornment was their exquisite jewellery. This included articles like mirrors, caskets, and cups, as well as personal ornaments. Indeed, some weapons owed nearly as much to the jeweller as to the smith—though these may have been intended as offerings to the gods rather than for use. Most Celtic designs are abstract, though they sometimes suggest highly stylised animals, or faces; an example is the famous strapwork, an intricate interlacing pattern also found in carvings and later in manuscript illumination. The commonest metal was bronze, but if gold and silver were not as plentiful as tales would suggest, they were not, in fact, rare—Britain was famous as a source of gold, also of pearls, which were obtained from mussels. Other jewels too were used when available—rubies seem to have been their favourites. These and other luxuries, like the wine for which they had an insatiable appetite, came along the busy trade routes from the lands to the south and east of Europe. The Celts, however, surpassed in the art of enamelling, and it was enamel which most often supplied the touches of brilliant colour so dear to them.

Among the variety of brooches, rings, and so forth, the most important ornament was the torc, a heavy neck collar, perhaps the badge of a free tribesman and worn by men and women. A golden torc marked the wearer as of high rank, maybe within the "nine degrees" of royal blood whose members were eligible for kingship. In that case the common phase "a gold-torqued Prince" meant one who might become King.

NOW was swinging through the patch of spilled light and patting against the window like a flock of moths; large light flakes, that would not outlast morning. Arthur let the curtain fall and turned back to the warm room, filled now with the agreeable disorder of a household at leisure, where he alone was restless.

Here at the Queen's villa there was no shabbiness, but elegance and the sheen of care. Of all the lodgings of the court, only this had the look of a home. Gai was stretched asleep on a couch, Medrod talking to young Cato, Bedvir to Cato's mother. Riderch and ancient Merdyn sat with a chessboard between them, though Merdyn dozed more than he played. Scattered among the adults were the children of the household, his own two sons among them. Arthur moved towards Gerontius's widow, preparing some remark about Cato's coming first campaign; but catching an embarrassed glance from her he instead asked grinning what she had been saying about him.

She looked confused, but Bedvir nodded towards the Queen and said, "Only, what a pity it is Gueneva has no children."

"Yet, that is," said the Dumnonian lady hastily, "after all, she is still young—though nine years—"

Arthur gazed at his wife. There was a tray of wax on the table beside her, into which she and Gai's two little girls were pressing beads, making a copy of the floor-mosaic; at her feet Bedvir's Ambros played and made his bid for a share of her attention. Her bare feet were tucked between the rug and the warm floor, her rich hair, unpinned and repinned by the girls, was lopsided; she was as absorbed in their task as the children. On a stool by her chair the elder of his own sons, Ambrosius, sat reading, fingers in his ears against the children's chatter.

"Yes. A pity. But then, I never expected my heir to be my son." The lady glanced up and muttered something to herself, which he did not notice. His eyes moved from Ambrosius to ten-year-old Lucius, seated as usual by Riderch. "Which is as well, since I seem to have a scholar and a harper. Fine things to be; but my successor will need to be a soldier too."

Cato's mother got up from her place and crossed the room to speak to Gai's wife. Arthur sat down, and Bedvir said, half in jest, "What you need is a sister's son. Can't you find one?"

Arthur answered, "I think I have, now."

His friend grew attentive, and followed his gaze. "Medrod?"

"I think so . . . though it's too soon to name him. Ah, I'm bored!"

The last words were spoken loud enough to reach the bards, who raised their heads, the white and the grey. "Come, Riderch," said the King, "I'll deliver you from that boy, if asking a story of you is deliverance. Have you one?"

"Indeed. A new one, if you would like to hear it." He turned his stool unhurriedly, and nodded Lucius away to his father. "Did this house not once belong to Severa, whom Vortigern put aside for the Saxon woman? And was she not of the line of our Emperor Maxen? So it seems a good place to tell, for the first time, this tale I have made. And the name I have given it is *The Sovereignty of Britain*."

MAXEN the Prince was a noble of great Rome, and highly esteemed of all the Romans of his time for he was as handsome as Paris, with eyes like the night for darkness and the day for brightness, and in nobility and prowess in battle he was the equal of Hector. No guest lacked good cheer in Maxen's house, those who came to him for judgment went away praising him, and in battle where he was there was breaking of shields. He was an eagle among counsellors, a stag among warriors, and the hawk of the ladies of Rome.

He was heir to the Emperor; but it chanced that the Emperor died while Maxen was making war in a distant land, and another of his kinsmen, called Gratian, took the throne by treachery. Now this Gratian was a low, crooked, ugly, craven, lying, niggardly man; those who lodged in his house grew lean there, those who waited at his gate for justice grew grey there; there was no more wit and courtesy in him than there is marrow in a dry bone, and as for getting a gift from him, it would be easier to get a pup from a she-wolf giving suck. When Maxen heard that such a man had taken his place, he was very angry.

"By the Seven Hills of Rome," he swore, "I will not suffer so base a wretch as this to sit where great Julius sat!"

He and his army returned with the best speed they could to Rome. News of it came to Gratian, and he was dismayed; he called his brother Valentian to him and wailed, "Alas, I am in peril of losing all I have gained; what shall I do?"

Valentian advised simply, "You must meet Maxen in battle; it cannot be avoided. Besides, with much gold you bought your soldiers, and it would be a pity to get no use of them. But keep in the rear of your army, so that if you are defeated you may more easily escape; and so will I."

Gratian followed his brother's advice; but Maxen

rode in the forefront of his legions, and so eager
were they to win honour in his sight that with the
first fury of their onset the army of the usurper was
utterly overthrown. Gratian and Valentian fled into
the eastern Empire; Maxen entered Rome, and he
was received there with great joy.

No man was ever more fitted to be Emperor
than Maxen. He dispensed justice wisely, and was
so virtuous a man that Saint Martin himself was his
guest; he held court with splendour and gave with
an open hand. Thirty-two Kings were subject to him,
and they all came to Rome to do him honour. He
entertained them well, with feasting and pleasures.
There was a day when he rode out hunting with
them, and they hunted from early morning until the
day grew hot. Then Maxen said, "It would be good
to rest for a time, and to shelter ourselves from the
heat."

The thirty-two Kings being agreeable, each man
drew apart from his fellows, and the dogs lay down
on the grass among them. The Emperor's servants
set up their spears and spread cloths over them for
an awning, and in the shade beneath it they spread
a bull-hide, and he lay down upon the bull-hide and
composed himself to rest.

Then Maxen slept, and he dreamed: and this
was the dream of Maxen.

It seemed to him that he woke, and rose, and
left his companions, and that he journeyed with
marvellous swiftness until he came to a great mountain. The greatest mountain in the world it seemed
to him; its sides were purple and brown, its shoulders were white, its head was blue. Nevertheless he
passed over it and beyond there was a fair land
through which he moved with marvellous swiftness,
and in all this time in his dream he did not encounter any people.

At last he came to a noble seaport at the mouth
of a river where a mighty fleet was assembled. All
the sails were set and they were of silk and brocade,

the pennants were silk gold-embroidered, the sterns of the ships were wonderfully carved. The waves lifted the ships, the wind spread the sails and the pennants, while the sun shone glittering upon the sea and the bright silks, and that dancing of the ships was a sight that filled Maxen's heart with joy.

In the midst of the fleet was the largest and fairest ship of all, with the likeness of a dragon upon it, and between that ship and the shore was a bridge. This bridge was of ivory skillfully carved, but it was no thicker than a wand nor broader than a handspan, and it bucked and rippled like an eel. Nevertheless Maxen thought he would try to cross it, for he had a strong curiosity to enter the great ship. And as soon as he set his foot upon the bridge it became still; he walked over it with no more difficulty than he trod the stones of Rome. No sooner was he standing on the deck than the fleet set sail and bore him across the sea.

When they came to harbour Maxen left the ship and made his way through the land, and he saw he had come to the fairest country in all the world. He came at last to a city on a great river, and that city was more splendid than any he had ever seen, save Rome herself. The city had many gates, and each gate seemed matchless to him until he had seen the next. Maxen walked about the city admiring it, until he came to a great hall. The gate was open, and the door was open, and Maxen went in.

Within was a room of such splendour that his eyes dazzled at it. The pillars of the room were one of silver and the next of gold, the windows glittered and the tiled floor shone. It was bright with the light of many lamps, and a fire burned on a hearth with bronze pillars in the midst of it.

Beside the hearth were two great chairs, one of carved ivory, the other of red-gold. In the ivory chair a hoary-headed man was sitting; his face was handsome and his presence august, and a dragon was carved on his chair. He wore a robe of golden brocade, and a circlet of gold and rubies on his head. A maiden sat at his feet; and when he looked at her Maxen heeded the brightness of the room no more, for she outshone it all. She wore a flame-coloured silken tunic, with ornaments all of gold set with white pearls and red rubies, even to the golden sandals on her dainty feet. Her white skin was clear and delicate as the petals of a new flower, her hair was shining auburn, her eyes under fine black brows were the blue of violets, and her lips the colour of the rowan berry. There were no words to tell of her loveliness; it was without fault or blemish, she was as bright as an angel of heaven.

The silver-haired man said, "Welcome, Maxen, Emperor of Rome!" And that was the first word he heard spoken in his dream. The King bade him sit, and Maxen sat in the chair of gold. The venerable man said to the girl, "Fetch the cup to the Emperor, that he may drink."

The maiden arose; calm and stately was her bearing, and full of grace and pride. She brought a cup of fine workmanship to Maxen, full of dark wine to the brim. He drank, and when he put the cup back into her hands she said, "Hail, King and Emperor!" and she smiled at him. At that the whole of Maxen's love went out to her.

He began to speak to her; but as he spoke the hall and the old man and the girl all vanished from him, and he woke. About him was the stamping of horses and the yelping of the dogs, and he lay under the canopy on the bull-hide with his thirty-two subject Kings about him.

Then Maxen rose up in haste, and his companions, seeing his consternation, gathered about him asking the cause of it. He told them his dream, and they were astonished.

"And now farewell," said Maxen, "for I must find the place of my dream and make that lady my wife, or I shall have no joy in the world."

They were dismayed at that, and caught his

bridle and his cloak to restrain him. They persuaded
him earnestly that he should not go in such haste,
but return to Rome and take counsel; until at last
Maxen recollected who he was, and heeded them.

Returning to the city he called the Senators and
Bishops to him, and recounted his dream to them,
and they were amazed. But they said, "Nevertheless, Lord, do not go yourself to seek this lady, but
appoint men to do so, and yourself remain here.
That will be more fitting to your dignity, and moreover, if many seek her the lady may more easily be
found."

"That is a hard thing," said Maxen, "to send
another wooing for me!"

But he consented at last to do as they asked,
because of the duty and love he had to his people,
although the longing of his heart was like the longing of the birds when they fly after the summer.
Many messengers were sent out, and they searched
in many lands, while the Emperor remained in Rome,
tormented with fear and hope. For the love he had
felt for the maiden when she smiled on him did not
lessen, but it consumed his spirit as well as his
body, and there was not an hour when he did not
think of her. Yet he did not rule his people less well
for that, nor show himself less cheerful and courteous towards them.

The men he had sent out searched diligently for
the place and the lady of the Emperor's dream, because of the love they had for him; but it was not
God's will they should find what they sought, and
at the end of three years they returned to Rome with
no good news. There was not a man of them did not
grieve to take news of his failure to the Emperor, but
Maxen greeted each kindly, and thanked him, and
rewarded him, though he had no tidings of the lady
he loved best. But when he was alone he covered his
head with his mantle and wept.

Then for eight days Maxen lay on his bed, and
when men ate he was not with them, and when

they drank his lips were not wet, nor did he know
how time passed while he thought that he would
never see the lady of his dream.

On the ninth day noble men of his following
came and said to him, "Lord, leave this grieving: it
is not worthy of you."

Maxen answered, "Why should I not mourn for
the lady I love? It is fitting to grieve, for she is the
only lady fit to be my Queen and she is lost to me.
Why should I not grieve?"

"Yet though your loss is heavy, to turn aside
from all other things for it is not worthy of a man of
your lineage and fame and valour and wit and judgment, and one who is Emperor of Rome besides.
Nor should you neglect your people for your own
sorrow!"

Then Maxen was ashamed, and said, "I have
well deserved that rebuke." He rose and took his
place again, and did his duty as before. All the same
his heart wasted with love of the lady, and the
Romans were distressed for him because of it.

While Maxen was Emperor in Rome, the High
King of the Island of the Mighty was called Octaf.
He was growing old, and he had but one child, his
daughter Elen, a woman of good counsel and judgment, and the succession was hers. However, Octaf
had many kinsmen, and each thought his right to
the Crown of London was better than any other,
and each led a strong warband. Octaf feared that if
his daughter were made Queen they would make
war on her, and if one of them were preferred to the
others they would make war on him, and however it
began the end would be that they would all be at
war among themselves, and the outcome would be
woeful for the Island of Britain.

So Octaf called the elders together and said,
"There is a host of gold-torqued Princes in Britain,
and each is ambitious to wear the Crown of London."

The elders said, "That right belongs to your
daughter Elen, and there is none so fit for the rule of

the Island: we would choose her to succeed to your place."

"Yet I do not see how her right might be defended, if all these lesser Kings joined against her, nor do I see how Britain can be preserved from great spilling of blood. Therefore, give me your counsel."

The elders debated together, then returned to Elen and her father. They said, "It would be best if Elen took a husband to share her throne who would be an ally strong enough to curb these lesser Kings. And as for where such a man might be found, the Emperor of Rome is a man both noble and mighty, and he has no wife. Send an embassy to Rome, and offer him your daughter and the Sovereignty of Britain with her."

"That is good counsel, if my daughter is willing."

"I am willing," said Elen, for being the only child of Octaf she was well versed in statecraft and moreover held dear the welfare of her Island. "Let the embassy be sent." And she added, "But send me word privily of the bearing and countenance of this Maxen."

Accordingly some of the elders journeyed to Rome, and there they came before Maxen, and he greeted them courteously. They said, "Hail, Emperor of the noblest city of the world, and descendant of our forefather Aeneas! The High King of Britain has sent us to you, and he offers you his daughter to be your wife, and the Sovereignty of Britain with her!"

"I must take counsel concerning that," said Maxen. He withdrew from them and called the Senators about him, and told them of the embassy.

They answered, "This is a fair offer, and you should accept it. For Britain is a rich and mighty land, and since the time of great Julius has been near in friendship to Rome."

"Yet if I do so, I must forget the lady I love best."

The Senators looked at each other, and at last

one said, "Lord, we grieve for your sorrow. But consider: it was in a dream you saw this lady, and much seeking could not find her. It may be there is no such woman in the world. And such a man as yourself must have a wife."

"Alas," said Maxen heavily, "I fear you speak the truth and that I will never see that lady. But still my heart is set on her, and it would be a grievous wrong to the daughter of the King of Britain, to take her for my wife and to keep my love from her."

"It would do the lady no wrong, to take her in honourable marriage and make her Empress of Rome besides. And it would be a benefit to our people."

Then Maxen saw that it was his duty to accept their counsel, and to make that alliance; and so he consented. The Senators and the elders were relieved, but Maxen's heart was heavy, though he hid this from the Britons lest he seem to put a slight on their King's daughter, and he entertained them with great splendour.

Without delay the Emperor set out with the embassy to travel to Britain, entrusting the rule of Rome to the Senate for his absence. He heeded little the lands they passed through, because of his sorrow and care, until they came to the coast of Gaul. There was a great fleet assembled to fetch him over into Britain, and when he saw it Maxen was astonished. He said in his heart, "I have seen no such ships as these, except in my dream!"

The fleet carried them into the mouth of Thames, and up to London. When they were come there Maxen looked at the city, and his heart began to beat; he said to himself, "This city is like the city of my dream!"

Then he was taken to the King's house, and he saw it like the court of his vision, the fairest King's house that mortal ever beheld; he was led into the hall with the pillars of silver and of gold, and the hearth and the walls and the floor of the hall were all as he had dreamed them. In a chair by the hearth sat the venerable man in a robe of golden brocade, and that was Octaf, King of Britain; and by him in a chair of red-gold sat a fair auburn-haired woman, his daughter Elen.

And when Maxen saw her, and saw that she was the lady of his dream, he saw no other thing: he thought he would die of gladness. Elen saw that he was the handsomest man of any she had known, and the noblest, and the look he gave her melted her heart; she was at once filled with love for him. She rose and went to him. "Hail, Empress of Rome!" he said: and they put their arms about each other, and sat down together in the chair of red-gold. And that night they slept together.

Now Octaf had a sister's son who was called Conan Meriadoc, and he was the foremost of the Princes of Britain for nobility and valour and pride. When he heard that Elen had been given to Maxen, and the Sovereignty of Britain with her, he was very angry. He said to the warriors in his hall, "My uncle has put a shame on us, to send for a man from across the sea and to bestow both Elen and the Crown of London upon him. Were there not gold-torqued Princes enough in Britain? By my head, I will not see this foreign man set over the Island of the Mighty!"

He gathered his warband, and sent his challenge to Maxen, whereat Maxen gathered his legions and prepared to lead them out. At that Elen said, "Alas for this! Is bloodshed to come to Britain after all? And Conan Meriadoc is the man of most prowess in the Island, and the most generous, and the most great-hearted. Woe that war should come between us!" Then she said to her husband, "Flower of all men of the world, dearest Maxen, I have not received my maiden-fee: and since I was found a virgin, grant me this for it, that I may go between you and Conan and seek to avert this war. For if you two should come to battle, whoever should have the victory, the loss of Britain would be great."

"Dear one, you need not ask this as a gift, when to do so is your right," replied Maxen. So Elen took an escort and went to seek the host of Conan Meriadoc; and when she came there, he came to greet her.

She embraced him saying, "Foremost of the Princes of Britain, and dear to me as a brother, what is the cause of your anger, that you come thus with your warband?"

He answered, "Octaf your father has put a slight upon the men of the Island, to bring a foreign man to rule over Britain."

"Conan Meriadoc, you speak without counsel. This is not any foreign man, but the Emperor of Rome, who is chief of all the rulers of the world, and one of our own blood besides. There is no man on earth fit to be compared with him, except maybe yourself."

"He may be all you say; but by what right is he to rule the Island of the Mighty?"

Then Elen drew herself up frowning, and looked haughtily at him. "By the right that is mine!" she said. "As my husband and my ally he will share my throne and rule beside me according to the laws of the Britons. And if any man of our people finds shame in obeying those laws, the fault is his own!"

Conan Meriadoc looked a little ashamed at that, for he honoured Elen and loved her. Seeing that she had moved him Elen said more gently, "Best of my kinsmen, do not harm Britain and grieve me by your enmity to the man I love most in the world. Indeed, Maxen was ordained to be my husband." And she told him of the dream of Maxen. He was astonished to hear it, and the story went round among his people, and was the cause of great wonder.

"By my head," said Conan Meriadoc, "the half of this tale was not told me! Though I will not swear to forego battle, I will go with you and speak with this Emperor, and make my own judgment of him."

Elen asked no more. Accordingly Conan Meriadoc

went with her, and she brought him before Maxen. When Conan saw how noble a man the Emperor was, his heart went out to him: and so did the heart of Maxen to Conan, for they were alike in excellence. Conan Meriadoc said, "Here is my hand, Emperor of Rome; and my friendship until the earth swallows me, the seas drown me, or the stars crush me. I should have known that the judgment of Elen and of my uncle could not err."

"Indeed it cannot," said Maxen, "for they told me you had no equal, and I see it is so!" From that day there was the friendship of foster brothers between the two of them.

Then Maxen and Elen lived together in great bliss, and when they ruled over Britain the Island was prosperous and well governed. Elen caused roads throughout the Island to be set in repair, and new roads to be built; they are called the Roads of Elen because of that. She was one of the Illustrious Queens of Britain, and Maxen was honoured of all the people. And because of his love for Elen, and the good fellowship he had in Britain, it did not come into Maxen's mind to return to Rome, but he remained many years in the Island of the Mighty.

However, because of his long absence a new Emperor arose, and took the rule of Rome from Maxen. This Emperor sent a letter to him, and there was no more in it than this: "IF YOU COME, AND IF EVER YOU COME TO ROME!"

Then Maxen sent a letter in return, saying only, "AND WHEN I GO TO ROME, AND WHEN I GO!"

After that he called Conan Meriadoc and all the Princes of Britain to him, and assembled an army, and they set forth to win back Rome from the man who governed it. As for Elen, she remained in Britain to govern it.

First Maxen and his allies conquered Armorica and made it a realm of the Britons, as it is to this day. Then he conquered all Gaul and Spain and Germany and Italy winning back all that had been his, to the very gates of Rome. But Rome he could not take. A year he camped about the city. Although the false Emperor could not drive him away, neither could Maxen capture the city from him, and at the year's end he was no nearer entering Rome than he had been at its beginning.

Hearing of this, and grieving to be so long parted from her husband, Elen determined to go to his aid. She armed herself, and went about Britain, and she raised a great host. The army she gathered was the greatest army of Britons that had ever assembled: the most part of the strength of the Island was in it. When it had set sail, there were farmers and craftsmen and men of learning in Britain, but few warriors. Elen placed herself at the head of her army, and led it to Maxen before the walls of Rome. There was a joyful meeting between them, and the Emperor and the Princes marvelled at the host that followed her. For that deed of hers, she is called Elen of the Hosts.

Now Conan Meriadoc asked that he might lead the assault on Rome, and bring Maxen the head of the false Emperor, for much he desired the praise of that deed; and Maxen granted it. Conan led the army that had come with Elen against the city. They were fresh and unwearied, and so great was their valour and their might that the army of the usurper was overthrown, and Rome was won. Yet not a man or woman of the city was harmed, except the false Emperor: and Conan Meriadoc brought his head to Maxen. Thus was his city restored to him, by the prowess of the men of the Island of the Mighty.

Then Maxen took his place as Emperor again, with Elen the Empress at his side; and the Senators and Romans rejoiced at it, for their other Emperor was never so goodly a man as Maxen. As for the Empress, they marvelled at her majesty and beauty, and loved her also.

Maxen said to Conan Meriadoc, "You have made me an Emperor again; it is fitting I should make you a King," and he bestowed the realm of Armorica on him. Then Conan took leave of Maxen and Elen, and went away with the host of Britons behind him, and all three grieved at their parting, that should be as long as life. For Maxen and Elen never left Rome, nor returned to the Island of the Mighty; but they ruled together in Rome in great glory, and there they lived all their days, and there they died.

But Conan Meriadoc went to Armorica and governed it, and he was a worthy King; his heirs rule there today. The Army of Britain that went with him settled the land, and scarcely a man of that host returned to Britain. That was a Plague of the Island, and a great cause of the later weakness of Britain. Elen's host was one of the Three Levies that departed from the Island of the Mighty and did not come back; the others were the host that Erp the Pict led against the Northmen, and the hosting of Bran into Ireland. Yet though the results of it were grievous, still the Hosting of Elen was a glorious deed.

HE silence was broken by Arthur's sigh. "Glorious. But grievous indeed. So, Bedvir: is that the history you learned in Armorica?"

"No; but I liked it better."

The King looked at his Head of Song, ready with praise and reward; then he changed his mind, and restrained Lucius from going to him for triumph and tragedy still illuminated the bard. Slowly the audience stirred, and turned to other things. Only the two bards sat silent. Merdyn watched the younger man, a queer smile lit by ancient knowledge on his lips. Riderch sat gazing at nothing, heavy-lidded and unsmiling. But he was lost in the glow for which a bard lives, and which comes so rarely; the knowledge that he had made something that would live, and grow, and never need him again.

ELTIC Kings were the chosen leaders of their people, rather than men with an inherited right to their place. A King's heir was chosen sometimes in his lifetime, from among a wide "royal family," usually three generations with a common ancestor; so that in theory a King could be succeeded by a great-uncle or a cousin as well as by a son. The uncle/nephew relationship was especially important, here as elsewhere. In practice no doubt only men in the prime of life were considered.

Originally kingship was sacred, involving the "marriage" of the representative of the people with their divine protectress. This memory survived long, in strange enthronement rites, in a historical King who is called the "Spouse" of Ireland and most of all in stories of a destined King's "vision" in which a young woman representing Sovereignty offers him a cup in symbolic marriage. The King's real wife was often identified with his mystic bride, so Kings who lost their wives to a rival, whether by seduction or kidnapping, were "robbed" of their kingship until they regained her. The sacredness of the King hedged him with many taboos, and one was universal—the King must be physically perfect. (There are hints that he had to be displayed to the women of the tribe to prove this.) Loss of such perfection meant abdication, and rivals for the kingship need not kill each other—it was enough to maim, or even scar, an opponent, and he would be disqualified.

In later years the secular duties of the King (defined as "judgment, hospitality, leadership in war") became more important. Kings administered the law, but did not embody it, and might themselves be taken before "the King's judge." Hospitality was essential because status, much more important than rank, was determined by the number of a man's dependants, or clients. These were also the men who would fight for him. In a Welsh story Arthur says, "We are noble men so long as we are resorted to."

It seems that some tribes in Gaul and Britain only elected a King for such emergencies as war. Of course histories and stories deal with such times—the Romans were bound to encounter Kings and Queens. But the High Kingship, alas, existed only in the bards' imaginings. Maybe in the face of Caesar the Celts had begun to develop a stronger and more united organisation, but in Britain the process was not completed and in Ireland it came much later. That status was conferred on Kings of legend by later story-tellers, possibly inspired by the Roman Emperors; and almost certainly by such as the Emperor Arthur. In fact it seems that Vortigern (whose name is a title meaning Great Prince or Overking) was almost certainly the first High King of the British!

SUMMER NIGHT: warm shadowy woods crowning the hill, flowers and silky grass below them, the birds of night singing in the deep blue twilight; thin clouds making gauzy shadows across the moon, and beyond them the white blossom of the summer stars. A tranquil scented night, and Britain at her loveliest. And the two rivals for her beauty face to face.

There were no lovers under the trees of Mons Badonicus, but a host of men and horses, the best strength of the Island. Three warbands: Urbgen of Glevum with his battle-horsemen, the men of Dumnonia with Cador leading them, and Arthur's own picked band of champions, the Flight of Dragons.

They had been nine hundred when they withdrew there, dragging the Saxons after them like a dog with its teeth fast in a cloak, and they were hardly fewer now, though they had beaten off a dozen attacks. Plenty of them had been shocked at the retreat, had raged to find themselves besieged on this hilltop—here, in Dumnonia, in lands never threatened before!—but they were coming to understand Arthur's reasons better.

After three days the Saxon army was growing ragged, its supplies eaten, its spirits sunk by all the unsuccessful assaults, exposed in enemy country: more the prisoner now than the captor of the British host, for they dared not turn away from it, though Aquae Sulis lay temptingly in sight. Terrible as they were in battle, the barbarians were not soldiers. Already the Britons had seen many signs of straining discipline, even some raiding parties going off that had not returned. While they, practised campaigners, coming there with saddlebags stocked to maintain men and horses for several days, were fed and rested, in good heart, their horses fresh, the initiative theirs.

Still, the army below them was no marauding band out for plunder, led by impulse, but all the strength of the Saxons south of Thames. Aelle of the South Saxons, oldest of their Kings, was the acknowledged leader; but the real power lay with Oesc of Kent, who had broken his treaty with Britain. Hengest's heir, who had lately named his newborn son after the great Gothic King Eormenric, dreamed of a final victory over the British, and he had persuaded the other Kings to war. His White Horse standard was prominent in the moonlight.

But it was not that which Arthur had chosen to watch, nor Oesc he had selected for his own opponent in the coming battle. Through the dipping branches of a hawthorn, he watched the Golden Dragon banner which told him where he would find Cerdic of the Belgae.

"He owes me a death," he said to Gai and Bedvir. "Fourteen years has he owed me a death for Gerontius. And I owe Cato his head. If I sleep on that Golden Dragon tonight, I'll sleep sound."

Gai clicked his tongue. "Can't they have it to wrap his corpse, then?"

Arthur laughed sharply. "Let his body lie in a ditch, let the crows and the kites bury him. I'd not dishonour the barbarian kings in death, not even Oesc the Oathbreaker: but Cerdic is a traitor who'd give his own people to the heathen."

Bedvir had moved a little away, and now came back. The King turned to him. "What is it?"

"Fire on the walls of Aquae Sulis. A small one, and beneath them I think."

"Medrod can handle it. Are there any of the Dragons farther on than this? Come then, let's go and hear Dumnoric."

They followed him up the hillside towards a small clearing, through lines of drowsy horses. Deeper among the trees it was dark, for no fires burned, but where moonlight slipped between the branches it touched gleams of breastplates and helmets. All Arthur's warband had gathered to hear his household bard sing them, according to custom before battle, the song called "The Monarchy of Britain."

A little earlier Arthur had gone round among them, speaking to every man of his Flight of Dragons. There were men there from every region of Britain, and others, like Bedvir, from beyond it, even an Irishman from Dal Riada, even two men of Saxon descent. But in their prowess they were akin; strong comradeship bound them, and their devotion to Arthur. As for the King, he was never so happy as when among them. Now they greeted him in a shout with the name they had been first to give him, "Pendragon! Chief Dragon!" and they made room for him and his friends, while he smiled and did not try to quiet them. Friend and enemy, let them hear his name, let them remember he was there: let them hear the laughter.

Dumnoric sang, his beautiful voice true on every note, each word clear, the harp music in perfect counterpoint, its sweet plangency like pure water, like light made audible. Arthur felt his eyes stinging. Love swelled in him, made his throat and sides ache, shortened his breath: a love whose strength he could never express, not though he had the Harp of Teirti and the skill to sing to it, not though he could gather all Britain within his cloak. It was not the words of the song that moved him, the obscure familiar words, not the music nor the voice of the singer. It was rather that here they were all one, standing together to listen, as was the custom on the eve of battle, to the bard whose duty it was to sing the ancient poem that custom too ordained. This was Britain. This was what they would fight to defend, when day broke and the battle came.

When the song was done, before a man moved to depart, Arthur spoke. "Combrogi . . ." His speech was not so firm as usual. "Combrogi . . . fellow countrymen. This battle tomorrow may be the most important we have fought since Lindum; may be more than that. Let us remember who we are fighting, and why; remember what brought us here. Pardon me, Dumnoric, if I ask a story too of you. There is time before morning. If I had the skill, I would tell it myself. . . ."

"King and Emperor, I understand. Britons, harken, while I tell a tale you all know: the story of *Vortigern the Traitor*."

ALBANY

Hengest's Hall ◆

LOGRIS

CAMBRIA

Landing of Hengest's great fleet ◆

Vortigern's death
in his stronghold ■ Glevum
◆

✕
Mons Badonicus;
the Battle of Badon

The Night of the ◆
Long Knives

London
■

First battle of
Vortimer & Hengest
✕
Third
battle:
Saxons
driven to
their ships
✕
✕
Second battle:
deaths of Horsa & Catigern

VORTIGERN was a Prince of Britain, but he was not content with his rank. He desired to be High King of the Island of the Mighty, and he cared nothing how he gained that place nor how he kept it, so long as it was his.

In those days Britain had few warriors, because of the loss of the host that had followed the Emperor Maxen and won Rome for him. So Vortigern went to the Picts with gold in his hand, and hired a strong band of them to fight for him, nor did he consider that it shamed him to have men who served him for pay, but only that no man in Britain should have so strong a warband as he.

There was little need of warriors in the Island then, for it was peaceful and well governed. The King of Britain at that time was Constans the son of Constantine who was the son of Maxen, and Vortigern's wife Severa, a noble woman, was sister to Constans. Because of the bond between them Constans trusted Vortigern; but Vortigern cared as little for kinship as for honour, and thought only how he might kill Constans and take the kingship. There came a time when he was a guest in the King's house; and he caused his Picts to murder Constans, and contrived that the blame of it should fall on the King's own guard. The King's son Ambrosius was at his foster parents' house, and a band of Picts went there secretly to kill the boy; but his foster parents had fled with him into Armorica. Vortigern was angry and fearful for it meant his plot was betrayed to Ambrosius and he lived in dread of the King's son all his life after.

But no others knew of his perfidy for when Severa learned of the death of her brother she mourned bitterly, and Vortigern too made a great show of his grief. Then because of his strength, and because Severa was his wife, the Council chose him to be High King of Britain, and Vortigern was glad.

However, after a year the Picts who served him

began to increase their demands on him, and to threaten him with disclosure of his crime unless he increased the amount of gold he gave them; and Vortigern was dismayed, and did as they asked. From that time he went in fear of his warband; the Picts bore themselves insultingly to the nobles of Britain, and he could not prevent them. Nor could he prevent the raids of Picts led by Drust, son of Erp, upon the shores of Britain, since his men would not fight against their own people. Because of all this the Britons began to speak against Vortigern, and to withhold honour from him, so that his pleasure in being King was less than he had hoped for.

There came a day when he was sitting alone in his hall in London, brooding on his fear of Ambrosius and of the Picts, when his porter came to him saying that two foreign men desired speech with him. Vortigern asked who they were.

"Their names are not known to me," said the porter, "but they are young men, and well made, of proud bearing and courteous in their speech. They have no horses, and each bears a great axe with him."

"Let them be admitted," said Vortigern, "but let them leave their axes at the door."

The foreign men came unarmed into his presence. They were of great height and strongly built, yellow-haired and bearded, with tunics of wolfskin and the wings of sea birds on their helmets.

The elder of them said, "Hail, great King! My name is Hengest, and with me is my brother Horsa. We have come across the sea with our followers seeking you."

Vortigern said, "You are welcome, if your errand is good."

"Judge of that, Great King. We are Saxons, and it is the custom of our people that when the numbers in the land grow too many, then the young men must go and seek their living in another place, and the King's sons must lead them. We are the sons of the King of our people, and the god Woden is our ancestor; we do not come of common blood. Therefore we left our home with three keels of warriors. We had heard of the Island of Britain, that a mighty people live there, generous and valiant, among whom warriors are honoured, and so we set our course here. Great King, if you choose to maintain us and the men with us, we will serve you for the honour we shall win, and such gifts as you think we deserve."

Vortigern was delighted with the look and the warlike bearing of the brothers, and with Hengest's speech. He said, "It was truly told you that war is understood in this Island, and warriors are honoured here; also men of wise speech and good judgment, such as I perceive you are. I will take you into my service, you and the men with you, of whatever number."

"King of the Britons," said Hengest, "we are three hundred."

"A fortunate omen!" said Vortigern. "It is the custom of our people that a King shall have a warband of that number that he feasts at his table. You shall be my warband. Do you keep faith with me, and I shall keep faith with you.

"Never doubt us," said Hengest.

Alas for the folly of Vortigern! Thus was the greatest Plague that ever afflicted this Island brought upon it, when by permission and invitation the barbarians came into Britain. The blindness of Vortigern, who took the sea wolves for house dogs, called them over his threshhold, fed them and warmed them at his hearth! Thus did those pirates, those wreckers of cities, those red ravagers, enemies of God and men, gain a foothold on our shores; thus began all the loss and bloodshed and wretchedness the Britons have suffered since then.

Yet the fire which was to scorch the Island of the Mighty from shore to shore seemed at first only a little glow to warm the hands of Vortigern. The first thing the Saxons did to serve him was to fall without warning on the Picts he had hired, and to slaughter every man of them; and the King was heartily glad to be rid of them and the fear of their knowledge. He praised and thanked the Saxons and rewarded them, and he gave rich gifts to Hengest and Horsa. But when the brothers were alone, Horsa said, "It is well to be warned. This King shows us early how he rewards those who fight for him."

"Let us thank him for the lesson," answered Hengest grimly.

In those first days the Saxons were not offensive to the Britons, but they kept the laws and bore themselves discreetly. There was good order among them; they were obedient to their leader, and he was obedient to Vortigern. He never refused a task nor named his own reward, but he gave thanks humbly for gifts he received. If he gave counsel to the King at any time, he did so with deference. Vortigern was delighted with his warband, and swore no King had ever been so loyally served; and the Council also found no fault with them, and much to commend.

When next Drust, son of Erp, led the Picts in an assault upon the shores of Britain, the Saxons met them where they landed. There they proved themselves fierce and hardy warriors, as skillful in battle by land as by sea; they drove the raiders back more swiftly than the wind had driven them south, and for that they were everywhere acclaimed and honoured. Vortigern gave a great feast for them, where oxen were roasted and rich mead was poured without stinting, and he sat at the feast among them. He gave gifts to all of them, and richest to Hengest and Horsa; to Hengest he gave an arm-ring of gold, a princely gift. That was the first time Hengest heard himself praised by bards, and he found it sweet. He sat at the King's side, and carried his head high. Vortigern said to him, "It will be long before the Picts harry our lands again!"

Hengest looked into his mead-horn and consid-

ered a while; then he said, "This time we were a
surprise to them. The next victory will be harder to
win."

Vortigern looked at him dismayed and pouting.
"It is your modesty speaks. Your men will not be
less valiant for being known, nor less strong of arm."

"No; but they are fewer than they were, and the
King of the Picts will come in greater numbers." He
looked musingly along the hall. "If we were to be
waiting at the places where they land we could drive
them off, despite our small numbers. But I know
that you wish us to remain here, because of Ambrosius."

Vortigern was alarmed at that, for he had not
spoken to them of that name. He said, "Why should
I fear Ambrosius?"

"Indeed, I do not speak of fear to you. But if
half that I have heard of this man over the sea is
true, you are wise to be wary of him."

"I shall not forget him. However, he is no man,
but a boy."

At that Hengest turned an astonished face to
him, and said, "I would not have guessed that! He
will be a worthy enemy, then, when he is grown."

Vortigern made no answer to that, and Hengest
said no more, only smiled to himself. The King
brooded all night on what he had heard, and won-
dered that Hengest had known so much, when himself he had heard no rumour of Ambrosius's prowess.
He said to himself, "The Britons do not wish me to
know how the boy grows: it is true they do not love
me, and I perceive I must not trust them. It would
be well for me if my faithful warband were stronger."

Accordingly next day he sent for Hengest and
Horsa, and said, "It seems to me it would be well if
some of your people were stationed about the coasts
to guard against the Picts: but I would be sorry to
lose your company. Are there other men in your
lands, who would take service in Britain?"

Hengest answered, "There are many such, val-

iant men, who would be glad to serve so great a
King. But they might wish to bring their families
with them, should they come; for those with us
were the young men without wives."

"Send a message to them; and if they will come,
I will give them lands to dwell in, for the maintenance of their wives and children."

Horsa said, "I will go myself, and tell them of
your offer."

Then Vortigern was content, and praised himself for wisdom; and the brothers left him, well
pleased. Hengest said to his brother, "Long life to
this Ambrosius! If we use him with care, he will
serve us well."

So Horsa fetched more Saxons into Britain, and
Vortigern gave them lands about the Wash for their
own; and in a while more yet followed, until Hengest
had a great army at his command. The British began
to grow uneasy at it, and the Council protested to
the King; but the more they did so, the less he
trusted them, and the more he clung to the barbarians. There had been little love for Vortigern in the
Island of the Mighty before the coming of the Saxons, but there was even less now.

Nevertheless the people were glad of the might
of the Saxons when it happened as Hengest had
foretold, and Drust led a great army of Picts against
the east of the Island. It was a greater host than had
ever been gathered, and a multitude of ships carried
them; also they made alliance with the men of Ireland, who came at the same time to attack the western coasts. But the Saxons had no match for fighting
at sea, and they utterly destroyed the Pictish army;
while the men of Britain fought the Irish, and they
had such a victory over them that after it heralds
came from the King of Ireland, to ask for a treaty
and a lasting peace with Britain. There was great
rejoicing at that, and many praised the barbarians
for their valour: though others said, "Why should
they not fight bravely, to defend what is theirs?"

Vortigern made the treaty with the King of Ireland, and sent his daughter to be married to that King's son, and he was well satisfied. He made another feast at which he honoured the chief warriors of the Saxons, and Hengest most. At the height of the feasting he said to the Saxon, "Preserver of Britain, for the deeds you have done, you must name your own reward."

Hengest replied, "I have wealth enough. I fight for honour, not for riches."

"Honour you have; but it is my honour to reward you."

Hengest considered long; then he said, "My people call me Earl; it would please me if the Britons would call me Prince."

Vortigern laughed uneasily; for he knew that the Britons would not give such a title to a hired barbarian, and would call the asking presumptuous. "Indeed it would please me also; but it is not a gift in my giving. Ask another thing from me."

"Perhaps they would honour me more if I had a city as your Princes have. Give me the right to build such a stronghold on the land you have given us.

Vortigern was confused, thinking that in his simplicity the Saxon did not know the greatness of the things he asked. He said, "That also is not in my giving, but a matter for the Council. Wealth and cattle and land I can give you; ask what you will of them." And he was shamed at twice denying what was asked. Hengest saw it, and smiled; but he said humbly, as if the last thing he asked only as a token to save his pride.

"It is long since I saw my wife and children. Give me as much land as may be enclosed by a single thong, to have for my own and not to hold of you, so that I may build a house for them."

Vortigern granted that gladly; and after the feast he praised the modesty of Hengest's asking to the Council, and said, "It is well if so small a gift does not shame us!"

But Hengest sought for the largest bull-hide that could be found, and when he had it, he cut it into one strip of exceeding thinness and tremendous length: and within that single thong he enclosed a very great piece of land. And on it he built a mighty fortress, and within the fortress a hall for himself. Because of that trick Hengest played on Vortigern the Saxons still call the land that belongs to one family "a hide."

When Vortigern heard how he had been tricked he was mortified, and for the first time his anger was roused against Hengest. Horsa said to his brother, "You will need a strong charm to win the friendship of the King again.

Hengest laughed, and said, "I have one that may be sufficient."

When his hall was built he went to Vortigern and begged pardon for the deceit he had practised, calling it a jest, because his asking had been twice refused, and saying it had not been his wish to offend the King; and he begged him to come to the feast which according to their custom he would make to hallow the hall. Vortigern considered, and decided that it was not for his dignity to seem to care much for what Hengest had done, and that the reproach of twice refusing a gift would be increased by it; so he consented to be his guest, although he was more distant with him than had been his custom.

Accordingly he went to the feast: and the acclaim he had there, the fervour with which the barbarians exalted him, were sweet to him after the fault the Britons were wont to find with him, and the scantiness of the praise he had from them. With the honour, and the good entertainment, and the wine and mead that was provided abundantly, he began to melt a little towards Hengest. And when the feast was at its height there came to pour his wine for him the Saxon's daughter, Ronnwen.

When Vortigern saw her he forgot his anger, and his bitterness, and whatever honour he had left,

for the maiden was more beautiful than any woman
he had ever seen. She was tall and splendidly formed,
with the warm blood shining through her soft cheek
and hair that gleamed like polished gold falling like
a mantle to her slender waist. The colour of the ruby
was on her lip, the ray of lovemaking in both her
blue eyes; she spoke beguilingly to Vortigern, and
when she smiled at him two dimples of sport appeared in her cheeks. Wherever she moved after
that the High King's eyes followed her; what he saw
was so lovely and enticing that he was aflame to see
more. From that hour he thought no more of Britain,
nor of his wife, imperial Severa, nor of his sons; he
thought no more of God, he was so consumed with
desire for the pagan woman.

"By my head," he said to Hengest, "I do not
know what man is worthy to drink of the cup that
girl would offer him!"

"She is grown fair enough, and fit for a husband," said Hengest indifferently. "I must seek among
my young men for one who would not disgrace me
as a son-in-law."

Vortigern saw the eyes with which the Saxon
warriors followed Ronnwen, and the fire mounted
in him. He cried, "Seek him among the Britons! For
if you would give me your daughter, I would think
no price too great to offer for her!"

Hengest feigned surprise at that. "Her rank is
not great enough for you," he said. "Moreover I
know it is a custom with you Christians to have no
more than one wife, and that you have. Do you ask
for my dishonour?"

"No indeed!" declared Vortigern. "I will put
away my wife, and make your daughter my Queen.
As for her rank, it is in her beauty. And lest any
complain of that, I name you from this moment my
Magister Militum, my commander-in-chief; and the
daughter of such a man is not unworthy of such a
marriage."

Hengest exulted, but he shook his head doubt-

ingly, saying, "You will maybe regret what you have
spoken." And when Vortigern swore he would not,
he still would say only, "I must talk with my kinsmen about this." Nor would he give any more answer that night, for all Vortigern's urging.

The time seemed long to Vortigern that he must
wait for an answer, for every sight he had of Ronnwen
increased the fierceness of his lust, and the girl took
care to fan the heat of it with her looks and smiles.
At last Hengest and Horsa came to him and said, "If
you will increase the lands we have here, and give
us Kent as her bride-gift, we will give you Ronnwen
for your bride."

And Vortigern was so besotted with the woman
that he consented to do all they asked. He divorced
Severa, his wife, and sent her back to her kinsmen,
and without the consent or knowledge of its ruler
Curangon he gave the Saxons Kent with all its
harbours, as a bride-gift for the pagan woman.

Then all Britain was thrown into an uproar. The
three sons of Vortigern, Vortimer, Catigern, and
Pascent, rose up in a rage and left him; Curangon of
Kent protested vehemently at the wrong done to
him and to his people; the Council reviled him furi-
ously; and from every altar the priests thundered
against him, for casting aside his Christian marriage
to take a wife who was a heathen. But Vortigern
cared nothing for any of them, since Ronnwen was
his.

Indeed, Hengest had become a great man in the
Island; and the might of the Saxons weighed on the
minds of the Council, until they said to each other,
"The harm this marriage has done cannot be un-
done; and at least we have a sure shield against the
Picts." And they accepted Hengest among them, as
was now his right by his rank.

The Saxon used his power discreetly, and did
not offend Vortigern; but all the while in subtle ways
he and Ronnwen worked on the King's fear of
Ambrosius, so that he was never at ease without a

strong guard of Saxons about him. Many times he commanded Hengest to send men to Armorica to kill the noble youth, but each time he but feigned the attempt, and told Vortigern that the deed was impossible, because of the wit and prowess of the young man. When there was talk of increasing the strength along the coasts Vortigern would not consent to a lessening of the Saxon army about him. Hengest said, "There is need of more strength in the North; and you cannot be in danger here, in the midst of your people, with·so many noble men of Britain and their warriors about you."

Vortigern paled. Hastily he said, "Call other men from your old lands if there is need, but I cannot consent to your going."

"It will not be hard to call such men; and I will give the command of them to Ronnwen's brothers if it pleases you, for I know Octha and Ebissa can be trusted."

Vortigern gladly agreed, and gave Octha and Ebissa the command of all the lands between Humber and the Wall. But that roused all the people of Britain against him; they could endure no more. The nobles and the chief men held many debates together, and they went to Vortigern and said, "These dogs of yours are good hounds, and effective against foxes, but their bellies are bigger than we knew."

"Speak your meaning," said the King.

"It is this: there are too many Saxons in the Island, and the burden of them is too great. Bid them depart."

"By my head," said Vortigern, "am I to send from me so loyal a man as Hengest, one who is my Magister Militum and my father-in-law besides? I will not do it!"

"If you will not part with the Saxons," they said, "you must part with the Crown of London!" With that potent alternative they left him. The end of it was that by the consent of all the Britons the kingship was taken from Vortigern and bestowed instead on Vortimer his son, because of his excellence both in counsel and in battle, and because of the blood of his mother, Severa.

Then Hengest said to his brother, "The young King is not like the old. Soft speech will not serve us now; let us use our axes!"

And throughout the east of the Island the Saxons rose up and fell upon the Britons among whom they lived. They battered down the gates of the towns and slew their inhabitants, men and women and children, every last one; they slaughtered priests and bishops in their churches, and threw the altars down. And they left nothing whatever that was of Britain living.

Then the British speech was heard no more in those regions, for none were left alive to speak it: and the only burial they had was in the bellies of beasts and birds.

When they had utterly devastated those lands the Saxons turned west, and in the first fury of their attack they reached almost to the western ocean; all across the Island men fought to defend their cities, and flames went up from roofs. Thus did the Britons pay for the folly and treachery of their King.

Vortigern fled with Ronnwen to London, and even then he did not bear his sword against the Saxons because of his love for his wife. But Vortimer called warriors to him from every part of the Island, and led them to battle. The sons of Vortigern were young men of valour and prowess, with swords that were sharpened by their mother's wrongs, and the eldest of them was the greatest. There had not been such a Prince as Vortimer in the Island of the Mighty since the time of Conan Meriadoc, whether it was for the skills of a warrior, or the judgment of a counsellor, or the generosity and true speaking that befit a man of noble blood: he was beloved throughout Britain.

In those evil days a message was sent by the Council of Britain to Aetius, Consul for the third time in Gaul, to ask his help; and it said, "Hear the groans of the Britons! The barbarians drive us to the sea, the sea drives us back to the barbarians; we are either slain or drowned!" But no help came from Gaul. Vortimer said, "I do not grieve at that. This Island is ours, from the time of my forefather Brutus; and by our own strength let us hold it!"

Then there was fierce war in every part of Britain: bards fought beside noblemen, the sons of priests and lawyers and farmers became battle-horsemen, and everywhere the Britons fought mightily against the heathen. And because of their fury, and the leadership of Vortimer, they inflicted many defeats on the Saxons, driving them out of the west and the midlands of Britain, and pursuing them into their lands in the east. Nevertheless the Saxons were stern fighters, and the victories were not gained without struggle. But riding at the head of his warbands Vortimer forced Hengest and Horsa to retreat into Kent; and he said to Curangon, "Now shall you have your revenge, and take back what is yours!"

Three battles they fought in Kent. In the first at the river Derventio the Saxons were not defeated, but under the protection of Vortimer's host many Britons reached the safety of London. Then at the Ford of Horses they met, and there was a great battle: Horsa died there, and Vortigern's second son Catigern. Bitter was the mourning of their brothers for them. Many men were slain that day, and the waters of the ford were churned and red, but at the last the Saxons broke before Vortimer and Curangon, and made for the sea.

Then Vortimer raised a great shout of triumph, and led the Britons in pursuit; at the old fortress by Tanatus they fell upon the Saxons, and utterly defeated them. But Curangon fell there, fighting under the great arch in Rutupiae: yet he had his revenge in his dying, for the Saxons were overthrown and fled to their ships. Many drowned as they tried to launch them, and those who scrambled into them fell at once to their oars; and when the Britons saw the long ships in flight from their shores, they made great acclamation, and blessed the name of Vortimer.

Then Vortimer wore the Crown of London. Two years Vortigern lived in his son's shadow, and rage that he was no longer King burned in him. All that time he did not hinder the messages that passed between Ronnwen and her father, for he hated Hengest less than he did his son, and his only thought was of how he might take the kingship once again.

Ronnwen said to him, "Send a message to your son, and ask to be reconciled with him." He obeyed her in this as he did in all. Men went between them to make peace, and at last Vortimer consented to it. He came to be his father's guest, though he would not consent to eat with the pagan woman, or to see her face. But Ronnwen was skilled in poisons; and while Vortimer was under his father's roof she put venoms in his food, that took their effect subtly, so that three days after he had returned to his own house he fell sick. Doctors were summoned, but none could cure him; and soon it was seen that he was dying.

When he knew it Vortimer called his warband to him and said, "Bury me upon the shore from which the Saxons fled; and as long as I am concealed there, they shall never hold the coasts of Britain again." Then Vortimer the Blessed died, and all Britain mourned.

His warriors would have buried him as he asked, but Vortigern came to them weeping, and said, "Let me have the body of my son, to bury it!"

They debated together, and the last of the brothers, Pascent, said, "Grant what he asks: but let him swear to bury Vortimer according to his wish."

Vortigern took his oath to do so, and he bore away his son's body with a great show of grief. He built a noble tomb upon that shore where Vortimer had hung like Hector about the prow of the Saxon ships, and held a great funeral there. But the body he placed in the tomb was not the body of Vortimer: he placed an unknown man there, and buried his son secretly. So the grave of Vortimer gave no protection to the Island of the Mighty; and where that grave is, no man knows.

Then the kingship went again to Vortigern, and for some time he ruled discreetly; for he knew there was no love for him in Britain. Therefore when a message came from Hengest asking to return, and Ronnwen pleaded for it, he did not refuse. Nevertheless he remembered the revolt, and he said to himself, "I would not have my father-in-law so strong again." So he sent a message saying that his wife's kinsmen were welcome, but they should bring few men with them. Hengest agreed to that. But when he came, he came leading a great fleet of ships, and three hundred thousand Saxons in them.

At that even Vortigern was angry and afraid. He called the Council of Britain, summoned all the warriors of the Island to him, and prepared to resist Hengest's landing. But Ronnwen sent a warning to her father; and Hengest did not come to shore, but sent a message. He swore that only fear of Vortimer had made him bring such a host, and if it were true that Vortimer was dead they should not land with him. And he said he asked only for a treaty, that the Saxons should be permitted to live in the lands they had been given, and to guard the coasts from the Picts. "For," he said, "the war we made was only in fear of the sons of Vortigern, lest they drive us from the Island: as they did."

With Ronnwen's entreaties to sway him, Vortigern believed Hengest, and offered the treaty he asked for; and Hengest asked him to name a place where the Saxons should come to once again swear their faith to him. Vortigern appointed such a place, and prepared a great feast where Britons and Saxons would take oaths of friendship together. Hengest laughed when the message came to him, and bade Octha and Ebissa take the great fleet out of sight of shore. He said, "It is better dealing with the old serpent than the young dragon."

All the chief men of Britain assembled for the feast Vortigern had prepared, the Council and the nobles, Bishops and Generals and judges, three hundred men; and Hengest came there with three hundred Saxons, bound by the most solemn oaths of peace. They met with a great show of friendship and sat down to the feasting, every Briton with a Saxon at his side, and Vortigern between Ronnwen and her father.

Now it had been decreed that according to the custom of Britain no weapons should be brought to the feasting; the Britons had kept faith with that, and so had the Saxons to outward appearance. But the Saxon dress has long sleeves, and that enabled their treachery. For when the feasting was at its height, when there was song and good fellowship, when each Briton was talking courteously with the Saxon at his side, Hengest shouted out in the Saxon tongue "Nimmt oure saexes!" And every Saxon there drew a long knife from his sleeve, and killed the Briton at his side.

That was the Night of the Long Knives, when the flower of Britain died by Saxon treachery. As long as a British tongue can speak to tell the tale, the deed of that night shall never be forgotten. Shameless and base beyond words was that betrayal, to kill under a pledge of peace unarmed men and feasting companions. Dear bought was the lesson then learned, never to trust a Saxon, and least when he offers friendship. Let that night be remembered, so long as the race of the Britons shall endure!

Vortigern alone was left alive, left to buy his life with the rich southern lands of Britain. Kent was restored to Hengest, and he gave also the Forest of Anderida and all the lands of the Saxon shore, the south coast with its harbours, great tracts of land along the Thames, and many roads. London itself he ceded, in return for his life. Then Hengest let him

go, and took the knife from his throat. At that
Ronnwen rose and said, "Have you had all you
want of him?"

"Indeed I have," said her father.

"I am rid of him, then," she said, "and that is
good." And she walked away from Vortigern without a glance behind her, though he wept and implored her to stay; he never got a word from her in
all his life after that.

Still he feared the contempt of the Saxons less
than the hatred of the British, and for a while he
stayed with them, the shadow of a King, Hengest's
buffoon. He saw the great host of Saxons come to
shore, he saw the lands that Vortimer had won back
taken by them again, he saw the slaughter of those
Britons who had not fled. He saw the despoiling of
the fine houses and the devastation of the cities, the
ruin of the churches and the martyrdom of many
priests; and he grew sick at heart. But he would
have endured the sights longer, if Ronnwen had not
wearied at the sight of him; and at her command the
Saxons drove him out at last.

There was no welcome for him anywhere in
Britain, and he fled to his old lands about the Wye,
and barricaded himself in a fortress there. Then his
old fear came true at last; for Ambrosius came over
the sea, determined to drive back the barbarians, but
determined first of all to be revenged for Constans,
his father. He was grown to be a man of judgment
and a fine warrior, battle-hardened in the wars of
Gaul, and he led a host of Britons who had escaped
from the Saxon rising. When it was heard that he
had landed, men gathered to him from all Britain,
and implored him to lead them against the Saxons.
"For that I came," he said, "but I have a task to do
before that. Where is Vortigern the Traitor?"

In the fortress where he was hiding he found
him, and led his warband there. But Vortigern would
not surrender, nor would he fight, though Ambrosius
daily and many times in a day rode about under his

walls calling challenges to him. So at last Ambrosius set fire to the fort to drive him out: but even then Vortigern would not face him. He remained in the fort and perished in the flames; and so died Vortigern the Traitor.

"UT AMBROSIUS, when the fire had died, turned his face to the East where the Saxons were. And so must we, my brothers, for the birds know that dawn is near; and like trumpeters they call us, to make ready for the battle!"

Horses were led from their lines to stand ready behind the gaps through which they would charge, helmets were strapped, spear-thongs checked, girths tightened. Arthur stood by his silver mare, his eyes alive and dancing; Gai shook the silken dragon banner free of its shaft. A signal, and the quiet commotion of mounting. The well-trained war horses were as silent as the men, stepping carefully to their places. The host waited quiet for the day: for the day that would be immortal in song, the day that would end with Cerdic and Oesc and a thousand Saxons slain, the day that would win a generation's peace: for the victory of Badon.

Long swords were drawn, shining in the thin light. Arthur raised his arm; a trumpet sounded, and around the hill two others answered it. Moistened lips parted, ready for the yell. And suddenly all the birds in the wood broke into song, as day broke, as the Flight of Dragons burst from the trees, sweeping down behind the streaming banner and Arthur with his war cry, "Ambrosius!"

N THE islands of the Earthly Paradise, the Celtic heaven, the Celts expected peace, wine and conversation, music and lovemaking, with neither strife nor death; but in this world there was fighting. If one aspect of their intense delight in living was their poetic appreciation of the world's sweetness, another was their appetite for war.

Battle was, of course, the sport of the aristocracy, the warrior caste which justified its existence by fighting and was paid in goods and glory to protect the rest of the people; but there can be no doubt that these nobles did what was required of them with relish.

Life was glorious, but to hoard it was miserly, and they despised misers. The greatest heroes of legend went into battle in an ecstasy, in which their "warrior's glow" burst from them and its glamour transformed their appearance, often into something monstrous. This battle-frenzy has a parallel in the rage of the Norse "berserker": but it is more fantastic, and the sternness and stoicism of the Germanic people was wholly alien to the emotional Celts.

They had the reputation of being utterly fearless. Alexander the Great asked a Celtic chief if he feared anything (one imagines he was supposed to say he feared Alexander); but after deliberation the man replied that they feared the sky falling on them. Some Roman writers explained this fantastic courage as being due to a belief in rebirth—a belief, they said, so absolute that the repayment of debts could be deferred into the next lifetime! This was a Roman invention, but the Celts did believe in the immortality of the soul, and this with their reputation for daring led to the belief that they despised death.

The hero-tales however give a rather different picture. The doomed hero may go into his last battle recklessly defying the omens against him, but the furious courage with which he faces death is balanced by his poignant grief for all he is leaving.

THEN began the time that has never been forgotten: the reign of Arthur.

For Badon, for the victories that went before it and for the years of peace that came after, the Britons remembered him. No other name was so loved and honoured among them as that of the man who had gathered all Britain under one banner, and made one law obeyed. He was for them the measure of all Kings.

Long after his death, the bards were singing of him. As the years darkened, his glory shone ever brighter, and the sorrow of his passing was felt more bitterly. The fame of his deeds and the tales told of him grew, until they were as marvelous as any told of the ancient heroes. Yet he was a man, like any other. And touched by the gods, as who among us is not.

Here are a very few of the stories of the Chief Dragon. . . .

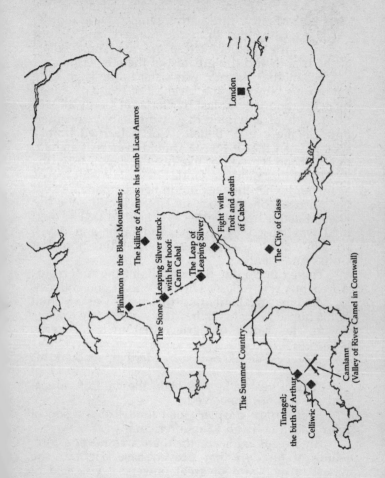

- London
- Plinlimon to the Black Mountains;
- The killing of Amros: his tomb Licat Amros
- The Stone Leaping Silver struck with her hoof: Carn Cabal
- The Leap of Leaping Silver
- Fight with Troit and death of Cabal
- The City of Glass
- The Summer Country
- Camlann (Valley of River Camel in Cornwall)
- Tintagel; the birth of Arthur
- Celliwic

F ALL the Kings of the Island of the Mighty, three are foremost: Dunvallo the Lawgiver, Bran the Blessed, and Arthur the Soldier. These are the Three Pillars of the Island; and the greatest of them is Arthur.

His mother, Igerna, was sister to the High King Ambrosius. She was the loveliest of women, wooed by many, and won at last by Gorlas of Cornwall. For the length of a winter they were happy together, until on the eve of Beltain, Gorlas learned from a wise woman that if Igerna should ever bear a child, her husband would not live out the day of its birth.

From that moment Gorlas never lay with Igerna again, and when he was not in her company he kept her prisoned on the rock of Tintagel with none but women about her. The neck of land to that stronghold was closed by a gate, and night and day a woman warrior was portress there so that none but Gorlas might enter.

There came a day that the High King Ambrosius Aurelianus was talking with his friend and counsellor Merdyn, and lamenting that there was no child of his house to be his heir. "It is not my fate to have a wife," he said, "but I grieve that my sister Igerna is barren."

"Maybe she is not so," Merdyn soothed his Lord.

"Seven years she has been the wife of Gorlas, and she has not conceived."

"Yet do not despair, for I foretell that a son of Igerna shall be High King after you."

Ambrosius rejoiced, for there was never a foretelling of Merdyn that proved false. He was the wisest of men and of great powers; it was said of him that he had no earthly father. He was the bard of Ambrosius, and he is called one of the Three Foremost Bards of Britain; the others are Guidion son of Don, and Taliesin the bard of Arthur. By his great knowledge Merdyn found the truth of Igerna's barrenness, and he was angry with Gorlas. He left the court of Ambrosius for a while, and no man knew where he had gone. Nor has any man ever known all the deeds of Merdyn, nor all his journeyings.

Gorlas had a mistress, and one summer's eve he set out to visit her; but before he reached their tryst he came to a lake, and by it was a troop of fair and merry people of unearthly beauty. They called to him, laughing, and said, "Come with us, handsome brown-curled man, to our court within the lake."

They took him by the hand and led him below the water, and there was a hall fairer than any he had ever seen, full of light and music. In the chief place was a dark-haired woman of great beauty, who rose and coming to Gorlas kissed him and bade him take the place at her side. Presently she led him away to her own chamber, and that night he lay with her.

On that same night a little after sunset a man with the likeness of Gorlas came to Tintagel, and the portress admitted him. The man sought Igerna, and so soon as he was alone with her he said, "Beloved, at Beltain it is not good for lovers to lie apart!"

Igerna looked at him both astonished and angry. She replied coldly, "I marvel that you speak so to me! Seven years and a winter have I been your wife, and since this night seven years ago not one word of love have I had from you. You have caused me to be reproached for barrenness throughout Cornwall and shamed me in my own house. Seven times has Beltain come, but not you to me. What miracle brings you tonight?"

He answered gently, "Alas, it was not my choice that you should lie down and not I at your side. A Fate has been on me, that I might neither enjoy your love nor tell you of the reason for it; hard I have found it. But tonight I am freed of my bonds; therefore let us forget sorrow."

And he talked tenderly and persuasively to her, until Igerna forgot her anger; and because of his sweetness she remembered her love for Gorlas, and welcomed him to her. They passed the night of Beltain together in great joy; and that night Arthur was conceived.

But when the sun fell across their bed and they woke, the man rose up in his own form, and Igerna saw that he was not her husband. And though he was handsome with an unearthly beauty she covered her face and lamented her dishonour.

"There is no dishonour here," said the man, "for I am a King among my own people, and the child that shall be born of this night shall bring you more honour than ever belonged to a woman of Britain. And while you go with child none shall know of it, lest Gorlas seek to harm you; for his death is near when you bear your son, and that is why he has kept from you." Then he kissed her, saying, "Have no shame of our love, for you had no sin in it." And he departed as he had come.

Three times the time that is customary the child was in her womb, yet Gorlas was in the fortress with her when her time came, and she feared his knowledge of it. But in the same hour that the child first strove to be born there came a red-eared white stag to the gates of Tintagel; its calling was sweeter than any music, and when it shook its antlers brightness fell from them. Gorlas and his companions spilled from the fortress in such haste to hunt it they heeded nothing else, and the woman warrior went with them leaving the gate open. Then Igerna fled into the woods to bear her child there. But she came upon a hut where were three old women and they cried out, "In your belly is a gold-torqued Prince!" and taking her in they tended her. The child was delivered without the pains of childbirth. The afterbirth they took and cast into a fire by the door.

Igerna bore a son, a boy strong and beautiful and bright as fire; when he came from the womb he raised a shout. The woman who received him first cried, "Here is a dragon! He shall be the terror of

Britain's foes!" Peering into the baby's face her sister said, "Here is the comfort of the weak, the Protector of Britain!" and the third prophesied, "Here is the King to surpass all earthly Kings, the glory of his people! His name shall be a joy and a comfort to the Britons so long as it is spoken." Then they gave the child to Igerna to nurse, and she was full of joy.

But Gorlas had returned to Tintagel and finding her gone he pursued her in great anger. When he found her in the hut with the child at her breast, his terror was as great as his rage: he snatched the baby from her and took him to the shore to drown him. Yet as he raised the boy in his hands to cast him in, fear of the deed came over him: so rather than kill with his own hands he took a little boat and set the child in it, and cast the boat out to sea.

The fire where the afterbirth had been cast had burned down, and among the ashes there was an egg; and out of the egg broke a worm. The worm ate the shell of the egg and the ashes and embers of the fire, and it grew to the size of a lizard, then of a cat, then of a hound, then of a horse; then it spread its wings and rose into the air. The dragon sped down to the beach, and found Gorlas coming up from it. It swooped over him and enveloped him in its fiery poisonous breath, so that he smothered and scorched in it, and so died.

After that the dragon flew above Britain, and many saw it and cried out in wonder and fear. But Merdyn said to Ambrosius, "The child I foretold to you is born!" The High King went eagerly to his sister, and he found Igerna in distraction and the child gone, and Gorlas dead. In sorrow and bewilderment he took her to his own house, and although Merdyn bade them be hopeful they were full of grief. As for the dragon, it came to land in the mountains, and found a cave among rocks, secret from men; and there it lay down to sleep quietly.

The little boat was borne to shore in the lands of Cunomor King of Cornwall, and the child was brought to him. He was amazed to see his beauty and strength, marvelling that a child so young should come unharmed from the sea. He said to his wife, "What shall be done with him?"

His wife was a sister of Igerna through their father Andblaud; her name was Morvith, and she also had lately borne a son. She looked at the baby and instantly said, "My heart yearns over him; give him to me, and I shall nurse him with our son Custenhin."

They named the boy Arthur, and he was raised in the court of Cunomor until he was seven years old. At that time he was the leader of all the boys in the place, even those of twice his age. At four years old he could outrun grown lads and cast a spear, at five he could ride a warhorse and swim the fastest river, at six he could leap up to the roof crest and down again and ride at the mark. The King and Queen were often in fear for him because of his daring.

When Arthur was seven Cunomor said, "It is time this boy was fostered!" He took the boy with him when he next went to the High King's court. Ambrosius saw him there, at sport with the other boys, foremost among the best, and his heart stirred in him.

He said to Merdyn, "Whose son is the little bronze-haired lad? For I feel my heart drawn to him, as if he were my own kin."

"That is no wonder," replied Merdyn, "for he is the son of Igerna your sister!"

Ambrosius was amazed and Merdyn now revealed to him the story of the boy's birth. Then Ambrosius summoned Arthur and talked with him, and he was delighted at the alertness and courtesy of the boy, and by the understanding that he showed. When he heard that Cunomor was seeking a foster father for him the High King said, "How would it seem to you to remain here and have your fostering of me?"

"What should I learn here?" asked Arthur.

"To be a King."

"That would delight me!"

From that time Arthur was fostered in the court of Ambrosius, and when his birth was made known Igerna, now married again, hastened joyfully to see her son. The High King was not the only one to have a hand in his rearing. Part of the year Arthur passed with Cunomor and Morvith, another part in the household of Igerna's husband, Rica, Chief Elder of Cornwall. No man in the realm had such wealth as Rica, nor dispensed it with such an open hand. He fostered the sons of many noble men; Gai was Arthur's foster brother there. Merdyn taught Arthur all the lore of Britain, and other learning he had of Saint Illtud who was his cousin. But Ambrosius, his mighty uncle, taught him the skills of a warrior, and all that was needful for a King to know; and the boy's heart belonged to him above all others.

When Arthur was near to manhood the Saxons made war again in the east of the Island. Ambrosius gathered his warband in haste and rode out at the head of them. Arthur saw it as he was returning from hunting with Gai, his foster brother, and Custenhin, his cousin. He said to Merdyn, "What news has come, to cause my uncle to lead out his warriors?"

"That the breed of Ronnwen are healed of the hurts he gave them, and rise again to plague us."

"By the Dragon born with me," cried Arthur, "it is time I rode with him!"

Merdyn replied, "Indeed it is; for the victory of the Britons follows at your heels. But the weapons to arm you are not in this court."

"Where shall I find them then?"

"Come with me," said Merdyn.

He took Arthur into Cornwall, and to a lake; it was very fair, with a wood of oak and hazel on its shore and an island in the middle of it. Merdyn said, "There is the place you will find your weapons. Go now, and I will await you here."

Arthur went down into the wood, and a girl met him on the path. She was tall and slender, the nine braids of her black hair fastened with silver pins, with a garment of green silk and a crimson mantle over it. Her brow and arms were white as the blackthorn blossom, and when she smiled at Arthur her red lips disclosed teeth of pearl, and the beam of lovemaking shone in her bright eyes. Arthur dismounted from his horse to greet her, and the brightness of his eyes and his smile was like her own.

The maiden said, "Who you are I know, and why you come. You shall have what you ask; and I will give you counsel that might gain you more, if I might have the thing I ask."

"And what is that?"

"Your company this night, and your side against my side."

"By my friend's hand, it is no hardship to grant that!"

He went with the girl into her green bower; and that was his first knowledge of women. In the morning she said to him, "And now for my counsel. Upon that island you will find a rock, and behind it the way to the place you seek; but so much I was sent here to tell you. Here is my own word to you. The lord and lady of that place will arm you, and whatever spear they offer you, whatever shield and helmet and dagger, accept them; but refuse any sword they offer you until you see an old plain sword with hilts of brass and a sheath of pigskin to it. Take that; for that is Caledvolc. That sword would draw blood from the wind, it would divide the thought from the word. So long as Caledvolc, the hard falcon of battle, is in your hand, there shall be no warrior who can withstand you; and while its sheath is at your side there will be no hurt upon you. Go now; and return to me tonight."

"Every word I shall remember, but none so clear as that!" said Arthur. He took her in his arms and gave her many sweet kisses before he went across to the island. He found the rock and the door, he found the hall Gorlas had seen, and there was the lady of surpassing beauty who ruled in the place.

She said, "You are welcome here. Long have we waited for you, Dragon of the Island!"

Arthur answered, "A blessing on this place, and on the lady of this place. I thank you for your greeting, but as for the name you give me, I have yet to earn it. It is a poor warrior who lacks weapons."

"Those you shall have," said the lady.

Weapons were fetched and she armed him, setting a helmet on his head and a fine shield on his arm, a dagger in his belt and a spear in his hand. But when she fetched him a sword all inlaid with bright enamel, and an enamelled sheath to it, he said, "That is not the sword for me."

"Then you shall have another," she said, and a finer was fetched; but Arthur gave the same answer, and so he did to every one however splendid, until they fetched out an old sword with a dark blade and brass hilts to it, in a worn pigskin sheath. That he laid hold of, saying, "This is the sword for me!"

"There is a good eye for a sword!" said the lady. "You have that from your father."

Then the lord of the place came in and greeted Arthur smiling. He said, "I think you were taught that asking; but take the sword that was mine, as is fitting, and smite the enemies of Britain with it." A horse was brought in, all of white with glittering red ears, and a red-eared white dog as big as a calf, and the lord put the bridle of the horse and the leash of the dog into Arthur's hand. Also he gave him a mantle, saying, "Here is one of the Treasures of the Island; for whoever wears this mantle sees everything and is seen of no one."

After that Arthur left the glorious hall, and on the shore of the lake Merdyn was waiting. When he saw Caledvolc in Arthur's hand he smiled, and said, "You are well armed indeed, if your father gave you his own sword!"

Arthur was surprised. "Was the lord there my father?"

"He was: the same who came to your mother in the form of Gorlas, her husband. It was well done to get Caledvolc of him; I would not have thought it could be done, unless by help of the lady or of her daughter."

Remembering the lovely girl in the green bower, a great dread filled Arthur. Slowly he said, "I had counsel. Who is the maiden here?"

"Then there is less wonder, for that is your sister, Morgen."

At that a great horror fell on Arthur, and when he saw the girl coming towards him he cried out, "No! No nearer! When I think of the sin we have shared, my heart is turned to ice!"

Morgen drew back angrily. "I see no sin," she said, "but great discourtesy! Go then! Break your tryst and lose the luck of it: for there is a price for your faithlessness. In might and glory no man shall equal you, and Britain shall never forget your fame; but this Fate also is on you—that you shall never have the love of a woman, and never one to keep faith with you, and never peace in the arms of one, until you lie in my lap again!" Then she whirled away from them and went down into the lake.

Merdyn looked grave. "That were ill fortune, indeed."

But Arthur raised his head and said, "How so? Are might and glory not mine, and a name to be remembered? It is time I sought them all; therefore tell me where I may find this battle!"

So mounting the red-eared white mare, and with the hound at his side, Arthur rode like the wind in pursuit of Ambrosius and his warband; and he found them, for the horse and the hound were two battle-smellers. The host of Ronnwen's people was great, and the Britons were hard pressed, until Arthur came. He went into battle as a reaper goes into a barley field; as a harsh wind comes to strip the orchard of its blossom, so was the descent of Arthur upon the Saxons. Back and forth he charged, Caledvolc a bloody scythe in his mighty arm, crushed bone and death beneath every hoofprint of the white mare, while the great hound hurled himself at any attacker who came from the rear. But soon none came—those that survived the battle-mad companions fled. Then on the ghastly battlefield Arthur and Ambrosius met, and dismounting from their horses they embraced.

Arthur said, "I have my weapons, Head of the Island."

The High King threw back his head and laughed aloud. "Dragon of the Britons, the word has spread!"

Thus was Arthur born of the gods, weaponed by them and blessed by them with glory and might and powers not human. But the Fate put on him by his sister flawed his strength and followed him all his days.

The time came when Ambrosius died, and bitter was the grief of Arthur. But in a while he came to remember his heritage. At Easter Arthur was acclaimed High King of Britain and there was rejoicing throughout the Island that they had such a mighty man to lead them. For there never was a King to compare with Arthur.

His court in Camalod was of great splendour, and there bards and warriors from all Britain gathered to him, men of art and men of craft and noble ladies, and all found a generous welcome. The laws were kept in Arthur's time; then the strong man dared not oppress the weak, and there was no dissension among the Princes of the Island. Britain knew safety from the foreigner. When Arthur rode to battle, gaily clad, with Caledvolc in his hand, his mare, Leaping Silver, under him and his dog, Cabal, at his side, there was no withstanding him. In twelve great battles he defeated the Saxons, and in the last of them at Mount Badon he crushed them utterly. He was winter to his foes, but summer to the Britons.

Many are the marvellous deeds of King Arthur; only a few are told here, for the measure of his glory is well told elsewhere. In the first days of his kingship a giant called Ritto sent an insolent message to him: "My cloak is trimmed with the beards of Kings, and I would have the beard of the King of the Britons, if his cheek could grow one!"

Arthur was incensed; with Gai, his foster brother, he sought the giant, but he climbed the mountain to the mouth of the cavern alone, and called mockingly, "Here is Arthur of the Britons; and his beard also, if your razor is sharp enough to get it!"

Ritto rushed out, the beard-fringed cloak on him, and they fought until Arthur was victorious. He came down the mountain with the cloak on his shoulder and the head of Ritto in his hand. Gai raised a shout, but Arthur only said, "Speak softly of the deed; it is not for my honour to kill a barber!"

The women of Britain smiled on Arthur, perfect in face and form, with his hair like shining bronze and the blue-green iris of each eye pleating about the pupil like the Cornish sea about a rock. Many was the tryst he kept with a garland of sweet-mouthed girls. Yet better to him than the love of women was the comradeship of his friends.

Dearest of all to him were Gai and Bedvir. Gai the Tall had been his foster brother in childhood. As a man in battle he was a joyous host at Arthur's side: courage was his heart and laughter his head. As for Bedvir, the Britons called him the Perfect Man. Beautiful and fair-spoken was he, the swift eagle of war. Between these two and Arthur was great love, and he did many deeds in their company. But he did not set his desire on one girl more than another, until one year at apple-harvest.

Riding alone he came upon a wood of wild

apple trees, and he was confounded, thinking it was an orchard of the Ever Young, because of the exceeding beauty of the maiden he saw there. She was straight and slender as a pear, though supple and graceful in her movements. Her unbraided hair was the colour of dark honey, and the sheen and ripple of it was like the sun passing over a field of barley; the eyes under her fine brows were the colour of violets, the red of the rose hip was in her lip. There were no words to tell of her beauty; a summer day was in her face. She wore a tunic of saffron silk with a bright enamel belt, and she held up the skirt to gather apples in the lap of it, showing her slender ankles and delicate feet.

Arthur watched her, marvelling; the girl turned her head and saw him, but she did not speak, only looked at him smiling and then veiled her eyes with her lashes. At that, love for her filled every limb of him, so that he blushed red and sprang from his horse to go to her. But she slipped out of his sight, and though he sought he could not find her, nor a sign of her passing. He cast about calling to her, and when he knew she was gone indeed anguish filled him; he felt there was no good in the world for him anymore, if he could not see that slim perfect girl again and take her in his arms.

He returned with haste to Camalod and sought Merdyn. He said, "Wisest of men, here is a puzzle for you! Who is the woman I saw under the apple trees, with the bearing of a Queen and the aspect of a morning in May, her auburn hair brighter than any gold I ever saw?"

Merdyn answered, "You have seen Gueneva, daughter of the giant Ogran."

"I must find her again," he declared, "for nothing will content me but to have her love."

Merdyn laughed, saying, "Are there not bright-eyed girls enough in Britain, that you must seek a tryst with a giant's daughter?"

"There is no woman in the world could content

the man who had seen Gueneva!" said the King. "Moreover, it is not my arm about her waist only that I desire, but to make her my wife and Queen of the Island of the Mighty; for nothing less is fitting for her."

Merdyn was dismayed but still he used soft words. Gently he said, "Though the maiden is indeed lovelier than any now living, though she has the beauty of Eve and of Helen, still the Chief Dragon of the Island must use wisdom in selecting a Queen. This lady is not the wife you should choose."

But Arthur answered hotly, "By the Dragon, I *have* chosen her! And if I do not have her I shall have none!"

"Even that would be better for you," Merdyn replied shortly.

Then a quarrel arose between the young King and his counsellor. Arthur would not yield. And Merdyn in his wisdom could not; nor would Merdyn tell Arthur where he should seek Ogran the Giant. He said only, "You will get no help from me in this matter; for by my counsel you will not seek this maiden."

"Then I will seek her against it, and find her despite you!" cried Arthur; and they parted in anger.

Arthur donned the mantle that the lord under the lake had given him, and went back to the wood of apple trees. Three days he waited and when next he saw Gueneva he followed her to her father's stronghold. They came to an old grey fortress hewn from the mountain, with nine gates into it and every one guarded by a giant. Now Arthur threw off his mantle, broke down each gate and slew every porter. He won entry at last to a vast hall where Ogran sat in darkness, and he a deeper darkness within the gigantic shadows.

Then a great rumble filled the chamber, and it was the voice of Ogran. "Who knocks so roughly, and why does he come?"

"Arthur of Britain, Chief Dragon of the Island,

and he comes requesting that your daughter Gueneva shall be his wife, and Queen of the Island of the Mighty!"

"A bold asking! But a guest is not to be denied. Come here, Gueneva!"

Into the room came three young women, and they brought their own light with them. Arthur caught his breath at sight of them for each was as like to the others as one drop of water is to another.

With malicious politeness Ogran said, "There are my three daughters, my three Guenevas. Which is the one you love? Choose now; but if you choose wrong, I shall have your head!"

Arthur gazed at the three Guenevas before him, and strove to see a difference, so that he might choose the only true soul he loved among the three. Yet he could not choose. He said to himself, "By my head, this is a harder trial than battle." Then Ogran laughed, and waved the girls away and they walked towards the door; and as the last of the three passed Arthur, he caught from her swinging skirt the scent of apples. Triumph filled him; he seized her hand and cried, "Here is the bride of my choice!"

The girl laughed and her sisters vanished away. But Ogran said, "A bad choice; your death and mine is in it. Yet take her since you choose her, and keep her if you can!" As he spoke he rose up and struck at Arthur out of the darkness. But Arthur cast his mantle about himself and Gueneva and drew Caledvolc and cut off the giant's head.

Then he fled with Gueneva, and she came gladly. When they were in the sun she cast her arms about his neck and kissed him, and said, "I feared the man did not live who could win me from my father!"

Arthur reassured her, "So long as I have Caledvolc in my hand, even a giant cannot withstand me."

So he took her to Camalod, and all his court marvelled at her great beauty. Only Merdyn did not rejoice. He said to Arthur, "Now you have what you have chosen. Well is she named Fair Enchantment; for no man now living shall see her equal. Yet she is one to cause the breaking of spears and therefore if you will heed me, you will not make her your wife."

"In this I will not heed you," declared the King.

Merdyn rose and said, "I have never prophesied falsely, nor advised you ill; yet since you prefer a girl's kisses to my counsel I will burden you with no more of it."

Arthur was grieved, yet in those first days it was hard for him to repent of what parted them, so joyous his victory over the giant, so sweet the company of Gueneva and the delight he found in her arms.

In Arthur's time Huarwor the hungry man came as a plague on the Island; he had never found a table that could feed him, yet at Arthur's court he was satisfied. Also there came Paluc Cat, that ate nine score warriors at a meal, until Arthur killed it; he covered his shield with its hide and its hairs gave spear-points for a host.

But of all his deeds, the boldest was the raid he made upon the Land of Promise, to capture the Cauldron of Plenty. He wished to win that Cauldron to be a Treasure of the Island in place of the Cauldron of Rebirth that Bran had given to Ireland. For Arthur felt a rivalry between himself and Bran.

Yet that venture was not much more fortunate than the hosting of Bran into Ireland. For they sailed to the shores of the Land of Youth, Arthur in his ship, Pridwen, and other ships behind; and Arthur went alone to seek the Cauldron and found it. But when he laid hold of it he found he could not so much as tilt its rim; and when he would have left it, he found his hands stuck fast to it. There he was held until the people of that place came to release him, and they freed him from the Cauldron only to bind him in Oeth and Anoeth. Manadan, great in craft, had built that prison; it is made all of human bones mortared together, and within it is a labyrinth of little cells. Its name means, Difficult and Very Difficult; Wonderful and Very Wonderful; Strange and Very Strange.

Three nights and three days Arthur lay there, and the Prison of Bone had held him forever, had there been lesser men in his company. But Custenhin, his cousin, and Bedvir found him, and getting on the roof of Oeth and Anoeth they dug down until they broke open the House of Bones and disclosed all its prisoners. They were curled like young bees in the cells of a hive. Arthur came out unhurt, but he did not speak for a night and a day; then he wept like a child, and after was whole again. But the host of the Otherworld fell upon them, and when that host was driven back, only six men remained to escape with Arthur in his ship. Seven times the fullness of Pridwen was the host that sailed with Arthur; seven men only returned. Yet though the victory was costly, it went to the Britons; and no other victory was ever gained by mortals in battle with the Ever Young.

It was after that raid that Arthur dug up the Head of Bran from its place of concealment in London. That is one of the Three Unhappy Disclosures, when the head of Bran the Blessed was revealed, and no more set its face against the foreign people. If King Arthur had not shunned a sharer in his glory, but had joined with his strength the strength of Bran, then surely the Island would have been a possession of the Britons to the end. But Arthur scorned the idea that Britain needed any defence but his; and he did not wish that the protection of the Marvellous Head should lessen the praise of his valour.

Indeed, as King and warrior Arthur was triumphant, though he also found the other fate Morgen foretold. There was never a woman faithful to him, but every path he trod was trodden by others. Although Gueneva his Queen was never matched for grace and beauty, it was not long he was happy at her side; and as for her, her eye and smile were readier for any man than for him: a cold bed he found with her. After he fetched her back from the City of Glass, where Melwas, King of the Summer Country, had taken her, Arthur never lay with her again. He had many mistresses, and these are the chief of them: Garwen, daughter of Henin the Old; Guil, daughter of Gendaut; and Indeg, by whom he was the father of Lachu, the glorious hero. Each was famed for beauty, but he did not find a steadfast love among them. Thus the curse of Morgen worked against Arthur all his life, nor was this the worst of the tragedy attending their union.

A youth came to Camalod, and asked a place among those who learned war there; and when his lineage was told, he was the son of Arthur that Morgen bore him, and his name was Amros. He was admired of all; not one of the youths or boys of Camalod surpassed him, not even Arthur's son Lachu of marvellous promise.

Arthur made the boy welcome and called him his son before the court; but when the youth declared his parentage the heart of the High King grew sick. For learning Amros was unequalled, also for eloquence; yet Arthur took no delight in him or his fine spirit, nor was he pleased by the lad's comeliness; the day he did not see Amros was a good day to him.

When the day came for the boy to be a warrior he proved himself his father's son in his deeds, yet still the King could not rejoice in it. And the end of it was bitter, the greatest sin of Arthur's life. He was riding alone with his son in the lands about Severn, and after their meal Amros sang to his father, and when the song was done looked at him laughing; and his eyes and smile were like another Arthur had seen, so that he was filled with love and horror, and rose up and killed Amros with his own hands.

When he saw the young man lifeless on the ground, all the love Arthur had never felt for him came upon him at once; he was overwhelmed with grief and shame. He cried aloud, "Alas, Amros, for my fault and not your own I blamed you! Woe that ever I saw your mother, or that ever she sent you to me. You were the flower of the young men of the Island, young hawk of battle; no foe could overcome you. If the loss of Caledvolc would give back your life, if my right hand would buy it, I would part with them!"

Then he made Amros a tomb by his own labour, and buried him where he fell. That tomb is called Licat Amros, and it has this peculiarity, that no one has ever been able to find the length of it, for it varies each time it is measured. And out of the grave of Amros grew a hazel; whoever ate of those nuts was gifted with marvellous knowledge. Such was the death of Arthur's son, and not until his last days did Arthur know grief like his grief for the killing of Amros.

There was a young man even dearer to Arthur than Amros, dearer even than Lachu. He was Modrat, eldest son of Cordav Chief Officer of Britain, whose task it was to watch over the Island whenever the King was absent. Modrat and his brothers, Kideboc and Idaug, were in fosterage with Arthur, and Arthur loved him above all save Gai and Bedvir. When Modrat became a man he was as great in judgment as in battle, and Arthur endowed him with the office of Cordav his father; and when he crossed with his companions into Ireland to hunt the Boar Troit, he left Modrat to rule Britain in his place.

Modrat protested, "I would rather go with you."

"No," said Arthur, "for there is no other to whom I would give the care of Britain."

Then he went in pursuit of Troit. That pig was a King who for his wickedness had been changed into the form of a boar, and his evil sons into his brood of piglings. It was a hard task to hunt him. He laid waste one of the five provinces of Ireland, and when the host of Britain came there and fought him he crossed into the Island of the Mighty and made havoc there. Arthur and his host pursued him the length and breadth of Britain, and many noble men died in that chase. At last they killed all his young, but Arthur held to the trail of Troit, and in Cambria they saw the boar going fast towards Severn.

The King said to Gai and Bedvir and the men with him, "Too many men of mine have died to this boar and his vicious brood. By the fame of their valour I swear, while I live he will not go into Cornwall, but I will close with him, life for life!"

He struck heels into Leaping Silver, and the matchless horse sprang forward, and Cabal too. If it had been hard to keep Troit in sight it was harder yet to overtake him, and would not have been possible for any but Arthur's mare of surpassing leap. From Penlimon they sighted the boar, and then Leaping Silver made a day's journey at a bound, for she leapt from the top of Penlimon and did not come to ground again until the Black Mountains, although near Buelt she struck one hoof upon a stone to lengthen her leap. The stone bears the print of her hoof to this day. They caught Troit beyond Wye, near the banks of Severn.

There Arthur held him at bay for a day, until Cabal reached him. Then Cabal rushed in on Troit, and Arthur too, and Troit fought them both. All three plunged into Severn, and savage was the fight that followed. The hound hung on Troit's throat, while the King thrust his spear again and again into the heaving body, and still the beast fought; at last he slashed Cabal with his tusks and gave the great hound his death wound.

Then Arthur seized the boar's feet and rolled him over in the water, and held him there. That was a struggle like Gogmagog's with Corineus. Arthur nearly lost his life, and he did lose the sheath of Caledvolc, for it was filled with water and carried away by the river. But Arthur held Troit until the monstrous boar was drowned. Then he dragged the creature to the shore, and Gai and Bedvir were waiting there. Arthur took Caledvolc and cut off Troit's head and Gai and Bedvir loosed the jaws of Cabal, in death still embedded in the torn body. Then the three of them leaned on their spears about the carcass, and looked at each other, spent and weary.

"Friends," said Arthur, "we grow old. From now on let us leave adventures to the young men."

Then he knelt by the body of the hound and stayed there for a space cradling the great head in his lap. And presently his companions had the grave ready. He laid Cabal in the earth and raised a cairn over him, and on top of the cairn he put the stone with Leaping Silver's hoofprint on it. It is called Cairn Cabal still. Then Arthur went over into Cornwall to rest at his court of Celliwic.

But in Camalod a great woe had begun for Britain, for love had sprung up between Gueneva the Queen and Modrat, Chief Officer, so strong that they did not know how to defend themselves against it. Gueneva's heart was broken with love of the young man, and she dreaded the return of Arthur; yet neither spoke any word to the other. For Modrat was a man of flawless honour, a great champion and steadfast in his love for Arthur, and from regard for that Gueneva too kept silent; until they had word that Troit was slain and the King would soon return. Then Gueneva was filled with despair.

She said to Modrat, "I never loved a man until now, but now love has destroyed me. By the truth that is in your tongue I bid you tell me, whether or not you love me!"

He answered sadly, "Alas for the day the King refused to take me into Ireland! This is an evil word you compel from me, that I do love you; and alas that I must speak it. Yet you have no need of my love, with the Dragon of the Island for your husband; nor may I betray him who is my King and my foster father besides. Therefore I will leave Camalod, and the company of heroes here, and King Arthur, and the sight of you."

Gueneva cried, "Then I put bonds on you, that wherever you go you take me with you! If I were given the choice of the Dragon and you, I would choose you. There is no love nor the dealings of man and wife between me and Arthur. By my two sisters I swear, I do not desire his return nor my place as Queen of the Island, only your voice in my ears and your arm under my head at night!"

Then Modrat kissed her; and after he had done so she said, "Your duty to Arthur you know best, but I have a claim also. Therefore I bid you to come to me tonight, and never again unless you wish it."

So Modrat went to her that night, and they lay together; and what had been once must be again. From that time they were lovers, as well when Arthur returned as before. Gueneva was joyful in those days, but the heart of Modrat burned him.

After the killing of Troit no more great adventures came to Arthur. There were no more monsters nor giants in the Island, and the Saxons were utterly subdued. The High King began to weary of board-games and feasting, of hunting and remembering old deeds; and then word came to Britain that the rule of Rome had fallen to unworthy men.

"By my head," said Arthur, "shame to me if I do not deliver the greatest city of the world from those men!" And he resolved that he would rule there himself.

So he gathered an army and entrusted the rule of the Island of the Mighty again to Modrat, Chief Officer of Britain; neither did Modrat protest at it. But the night before Arthur's departure Gueneva went secretly to his chamber; and she took Caledvolc, and left in its place a sword made in its likeness. And Caledvolc she hid.

Then Arthur departed with great splendour into Gaul. There the Gauls and the Britons of Armorica gathered to him, and they fought against the Franks and won many victories; and though it was not Caledvolc in Arthur's hand he did not know it, because there was still none who could withstand him.

Gueneva was left at Celliwic, and Modrat was at Camalod. He said to himself, "This deed I shall do now shall leave me no honour so long as my name lives; but the Queen will be preserved from blame by it."

He gathered his own warband and led them to Celliwic, and there he dragged Gueneva from her chair and struck her a blow, and carried her off. Then the people of the court rose up in a roar, and there was fierce fighting between them and the warriors with Modrat, and when Modrat left the place there was great ruin in Celliwic. That was the first of the Three Costly Ravagings of this Island; the second was the one Arthur made in return.

Modrat said to his love, "For that battle and the men who died in it, Arthur will not forgive me."

Gueneva answered him, "You need not seek his forgiveness while you have this at your side!" And she gave him Caledvolc that she had stolen.

Messengers left Britain, and came to Arthur with all speed. When he had heard all their tale it was hard to know if his grief or his rage was the greater. The host of Arthur returned swiftly to the Island of the Mighty, and Modrat sent a force to resist them. Then there was killing between the men of Britain, which had not been so since Vortigern died; bitter was the day. Arthur's nephew Gualcmai, his sister's son, was slain in that battle, and where the ninth wave breaks on the shore is his grave.

At his death Arthur's fury increased. He cried out, "The blow that Modrat gave my Queen was a harmful blow for Britain, as harmful as the blow Matholug the Irishman gave Branwen!"

Then he went to Modrat's house and utterly destroyed it; when he left there was nothing to show where it had stood, and neither man nor beast living there. And he killed Kideboc, who had defended the fortress, with his own hands, although the man was his foster son.

At news of his brother's death Modrat was roused to fierce enmity against Arthur; he did not make war with half a heart after that. He raised a host, and his warriors fought the warriors of Arthur in many places. The Kings and Princes and chieftains of Britain were divided, some for one and some for the other, and some only to be free of any High King. Britons killed Britons, law was forgotten, and when he saw it Arthur cried aloud in pain.

After that first battle he held aloof from the strife, and in a battle in the North his son Lachu begged for the leadership of the host. Arthur said, "I have lost Amros and Gualcmai and Modrat; I would keep you at my side." But he yielded to the young man at last, and gave him the sword from his own side to bear in the battle. Then Lachu rode before the battle-horsemen; renowned in war was he, the raven of a host. But that day he fell, and Arthur's son was slain before his eyes. His heart nearly broke with bewilderment.

When they fetched the young man's body to him Arthur said, "If Lachu could be slain, it could not be with Caledvolc in his hand!" He looked at the sword closely, and perceived that it was not his own; and he understood the treachery of Gueneva. So died Lachu, the best son of great Arthur, and they buried him on the hillside.

Arthur rode away mourning. "Cabal is dead, and the girl I won from the giant betrays me, and a sword not Caledvolc is in my hand without my knowledge; I grow old."

Nor was his grief at an end, for in the next battle Guidaug, son of Menester, slew Gai. Terrible was the grief of Arthur for his foster brother, and the grief of Bedvir also. Arthur pursued Guidaug and killed him, and he was roused to a deadly wrath; he gathered all his hosts, to seek Modrat himself and compel him to battle.

Twice they came up with Modrat's host, and twice the host gave way before Arthur and would not do battle. Relentlessly the Dragon of the Island pursued them, and the third time, in the west, he penned Modrat and his host in a crooked valley from which there was no escape except by battle. The name of the place was Camlann.

In the night before the battle Modrat did not sleep, oppressed with sorrow and shame. Nor did Arthur rest; he paced with Bedvir at his side, and gazed at the host encamped opposite his own. And weariness came on him, the rage and hatred in him burned low, and he remembered how he had taught Modrat, how he had watched his growing and loved him. He thought of Britain, her strength wasted, laid open to her foes, and he said to Bedvir, "Gai is dead, and Lachu, with other companions of ours, and countless men of the Island of the Mighty. If war was to end now, my life would not see this harm made good. And tomorrow worse will be done."

Bedvir said, "It is a great strife for a wanton woman; yet so did Troy fall."

"I have forgotten every woman I ever loved. What is Gueneva to me, or the place where she makes her pillow, if Britain can be spared?"

He called Idaug, the third of Cordav's sons, and said, "Of three brothers, one is faithful. Will you go to your brother Modrat and give him offers of peace from me?" Idaug consented, and Arthur gave him messages for Modrat. But as he went towards his brother's host Idaug remembered Kideboc: and his heart was roused against both the enemies. So he gave Modrat not Arthur's message, but one full of insults.

"I have deserved them all," said Modrat. Sadness filled him, and he gave Idaug a courteous reply to Arthur.

Yet Idaug returning thought, "It is easy for him to forget our brother's death; and why not, since he was the cause of it? But it is hard for me." And he changed the message again, pretending that Modrat had taunted Arthur with not daring to fight while another wielded Caledvolc.

Arthur's face darkened at that, and he turned away. But presently he said to Bedvir, "What is an insult to me, against such danger to Britain?" And he sent for Idaug again. A second time the agitator went between them, and from each received a gentle message, and to each delivered a harsh one.

"It is not for my honour to do more!" cried Arthur. Yet when the dawn wind stirred he said, "With day comes the death of Britain. Let Idaug try once more."

So again he sent a fair offer to Modrat, and again Idaug altered it. And this time he said to Modrat, "He taunts you, that you shrink from battle like a coward; and he marvels that you would make peace with the man who killed your brother. And so do I!" Then anger blazed up in Modrat, and he drew his sword. He cried, "Kideboc will be avenged before sunset!"

Idaug galloped back along the valley, and this time there was no need of a message, for the charge came behind him.

"There is no making peace with this man," said Arthur to Bedvir. "Therefore let us give thanks for all the times that are gone, and end like warriors!"

So began the battle of Camlann, the most grievous that ever befell the Island of the Mighty. All day it raged in that valley, and the din of it was heard far off, while the terror of it was felt throughout the land; in all Britain there was not a face that smiled that day. Terrible was the slaughter; ravens waded in blood there. Custenhin died that day, and Caranguen son of Gai, and many other gold-torqued lords of battle; a hundred thousand men of the Island fell there. Those who died before that day were fortunate; the last days of the world will show nothing more fearful than that battle, when the glory and the safety of Britain were cast away for the sake of a faithless woman, and by the wiles of a contentious man. Such was Camlann, where Arthur and Modrat fell.

Sunset came, and of Arthur's host eight men only were living; and of Modrat's, he alone remained, but he had Caledvolc in his hand. The King's companions gathered to him, and Modrat yelled defiance at him.

"Sheathe your swords," commanded Arthur, "for he is mine."

He took Rongomiad in his hand and ran at Modrat, and the keen spear pierced him through, giving him his death wound. But Modrat struck at the shaft and sheared it through, and with the spear in him he hurled himself on Arthur, and wounded him with Caledvolc. Arthur grappled with him, and wrested the sword from his hand; then Modrat fell dead, and Arthur slid down beside him.

Seven men were left alive, and Arthur; but Arthur had a mortal wound. His few comrades gathered about him weeping, and raised him up to carry him from the field, for Leaping Silver too was dead. Arthur said, "Not far away there is a lake with an island in the midst of it; carry me there."

So they did as he asked, though it cost them hard pains, for there was not a man without a wound. They found the lake, dark and broad, and far across it an island, and on the shore of it they set the High King down. He opened his eyes and smiled at them. These were the men who were with him at the end: Bedvir and his son Ambren, the bards Taliesin and Morvran, Petroc Splintered Spear who never took up arms again but became a saint, Idaug the provoker of battle who was distracted with grief and did penance for his deed all his life after, and Cador son of Custenhin.

Arthur said, "Such kingship as there is in Britain, let Cador have it."

Then in the twilight a boat came over the water, and in it sat a woman of surpassing beauty, and two maidens attending on her. The boat came to shore, and the woman came out of it to Arthur, and kissed his brow. She said, "Alas, my brother; why have you kept so long from me?" After that she examined his wound. "There may be help for this," she said, "but not in Britain."

She went back into the boat, and her maidens lifted Arthur lightly into it, and he laid his head in the lady's lap. His companions began to weep, but Arthur said, "Be comforted. I go to Avalon to be healed of my wound; but when my strength is restored, I will return. Let Britain watch for me!"

So Bedvir put Caledvolc in the King's hand, and the boat turned from shore and went away to the Place of Apples, while the seven men stood watching. All wept, save Bedvir; and his heart was broken beyond tears. Thus did King Arthur pass from mortal knowledge; nor since that day has any man seen him.

Some say he died in Avalon; others, that in the Holy Island none can die, and all wounds heal in time. No one has ever seen his grave. Who knows the truth? Maybe he sleeps, or rests in the Place of Apples. Maybe he feasts there, with his heroes about him, awaiting the hour of Britain's need, when the Dragon shall be roused from slumber, and Arthur again shall be King.

AND THEY TOLD THE STORIES OF ARTHUR IN ALL THE REALMS OF THE BRITONS, from Kernow to Manau Gododdin; to the exiles in Armorica, and to Princes of Cymru. Owain ap Urien heard them, sitting with his Ravens about the campfire, and the men of Catraeth before they rode to battle. They were sung by bards in Gwynedd and Dyfed, in Elfed and Rheged and Powys.

But not in the kingdom of Britain. For the tale of the Island of the Mighty was ended, and there was no such realm anymore.

ABOUT THE AUTHOR

JOY CHANT is best known as a writer of fantasy. Readers first encountered her imaginary world of Vandarei, peopled by the Khentorei, (wandering nomads whose gods include a magnificent equine divinity, along with many other races and tribes) in *Red Moon, Black Mountain*, and *Grey Mane of Morning*.

Miss Chant says of herself, "I was born in London right at the end of World War II of mixed Irish, Cornish, Somerset, and West Highland stock . . . I learned to read very early indeed . . . and folktale, myth, and legend, with the later addition of history, were my diet." It is not surprising, therefore, that Miss Chant's adult interests should include unravelling the mysteries that shroud the early Celts, a tribal people who surrounded themselves with myth and marvel and invested everyday events with a glamour that lighted their whole culture. She is thus able to indulge her passion for fantasy and realism at one and the same time—to the greater enjoyment of all her readers.